Halfpenny Field

Iris Gower

BANTAM PRESS

LONDON • TORONTO • SYDNEY • AUCKLAND • JOHANNESBURG

Dedicated to Dr Brinley Jones, who inspired me
to tell the magical story of the cattle drovers.

TRANSWORLD PUBLISHERS
61–63 Uxbridge Road, London W5 5SA
a division of The Random House Group Ltd

RANDOM HOUSE AUSTRALIA (PTY) LTD
20 Alfred Street, Milsons Point, Sydney,
New South Wales 2061, Australia

RANDOM HOUSE NEW ZEALAND LTD
18 Poland Road, Glenfield, Auckland 10, New Zealand

RANDOM HOUSE SOUTH AFRICA (PTY) LTD
Endulini, 5a Jubilee Road, Parktown 2193, South Africa

Published 2004 by Bantam Press
a division of Transworld Publishers

A catalogue record for this book is available from the British Library.
ISBN 0593 050835

Typeset in 11½/14pt Plantin by
Falcon Oast Graphic Art Ltd.

Printed in Great Britain by
Mackays of Chatham plc, Chatham, Kent

1 3 5 7 9 10 8 6 4 2

Papers used by Transworld Publishers are natural, recyclable products
made from wood grown in sustainable forests. The manufacturing
processes conform to the environmental regulations of the
country of origin.

CHAPTER ONE

Jessie Price pushed back her dark auburn hair and gazed at the wild, windblown landscape of Wales, the country she was leaving to travel to Smithfield market in London. It was 1833, nearly a year since she'd fled from London's cholera outbreak, and now she was taking the trail back again – but she had to make a living and cattle droving was all she knew.

She'd tried working in service for a time but the indoor life didn't suit her. Then she'd found work as a milkmaid and she was happy – until the aged farmer had tried to force his attentions on her. But now she wondered if taking to the road again had been a mistake.

Ahead, the long narrow lane wound uphill and she wished herself anywhere but on the drovers' roads with Jed Lambert, whose dark looks and blazing eyes frightened her.

Jessie glanced back and saw her friend Flora still knitting as she walked steadily along. Flora caught her eye and smiled. 'I'll have plenty of stockings made by the time we get to London. Good sales for hose in them London shops. Come now, cheer up, Jess. London's not so far.'

Jessie's heart was warmed: Flora could always be relied upon for a comforting word when anyone was downhearted. She hung back until she was shoulder to shoulder with her friend. 'I'm weary of this journey already,' she said. 'I've never been good at knitting, and for all Jed's nagging I know I'll never make any money on socks.' She glanced at Flora. 'Thank goodness you're here – you can help me when I drop my stitches.'

'So that's all I'm good for, is it?' Flora's words sounded cross but she was smiling. 'In any case, you're better than me at weeding – bending over in the fields all day makes my back ache.'

'I don't know why I came on this drove,' Jessie murmured, staring at Jed Lambert on his horse, like a king on his throne. 'I don't like Jed. He gives me the evil eye whenever he looks at me.'

'I feel the same, I'd rather be with Caradoc Jones's team any day,' Flora said. 'Fair man, he is, good with his people and the animals – but beggars can't be choosers, see. We needed work and Mr Jones's drove wasn't ready to travel. I've one bit of good news, mind. Morgan the smithy's joining us soon. I haven't seen him since last year's droves. He's a lovely man, and so handsome I wouldn't mind a tumble in the hay with him.'

'For shame on you, Flora!' Jessie said. 'Morgan's heart is somewhere else. He's still daft about Non Jenkins. We all thought they'd get together some day.'

'Ah, but Non was a cut above the rest of us, clever too. That's how she came to marry into the Jones family,' Flora said.

Jessie fell silent, thinking about the good old times. She'd made some real friends in those early days – look at her and Flora, as close as sisters. Jessie was suddenly startled by one of the men calling a warning, 'Look up there!' He was pointing to the top of the hill. 'There's a highwayman hiding behind the trees waiting to pounce on us. Can't he see who he's up against?'

Jessie smiled to herself. The highwayman, if there

was one, was a fool if he thought he could force Jed Lambert to part with his money. Jed was a hard man, used to striking out with his fists. The other men on the drove were afraid of him but they followed his lead, caring little about their cattle and less about the women who walked the drovers' roads behind them.

The roadway was opening out now and sloped up to the top of the hill. This was where the highwayman would attack. Jessie looked up a little nervously, but there was no sign of a rider on the hill. She took out her knitting and stared at the tangle of wool. She'd never been any good at it and, despite what Flora had said, she was little better at weeding, both tasks expected of a woman on a drove.

She heard a sharp cry, and then the sound of hoofs beating a tattoo against the land. 'He's coming,' Jed cried, 'but I'm ready for him.' He guided his horse to Jessie's side. 'Here, Jessie, take him the bag and leave the rest to us.'

'Why me?' The bag was heavy and Jessie clutched it in horror. 'Why can't one of the men go?'

'Just do as you're told,' Jed said harshly, 'and leave the rest to us. Keep him talking a bit.'

Jessie lifted her skirts and made her way unsteadily to the highwayman, who gazed down at her. He had wide shoulders and his face was half hidden by a scarf. His eyes, though, were kind as they rested on her. 'Sent a woman to do a man's job, eh? Shows what weaklings they are.'

'I don't mind.' Jessie searched frantically for a few words to keep him with her. She had no idea what Jed was planning but she knew it would be something horrible. 'Look, take the gold and get away,' she said urgently. 'Jed Lambert is a cruel man and he'll have no mercy on you.'

Then she saw that one of the drovers was behind the cattle with a catapult in his hand. He would have lead bullets in his pocket and he knew how to use them to kill man or animal. She opened her mouth to shout a warning but she was too late. The highwayman leaned over to take the bag and a bullet grazed his ear. The next came from a different direction and caught him in the neck.

Jessie screamed and dropped the bag, whose contents spilled out on the ground. It had contained not gold but bits of metallic ores.

The highwayman looked at her with blank eyes, then fell slowly from the saddle to land with a thud on the dry earth.

Jed came up beside her. 'That'll teach the bastard to rob an honest man,' he shouted. One of the drovers came out into the open and picked up the highwayman's pistol. Slowly, he began to undress him. Jessie watched him, sickened, as he put on the dead man's clothes.

Jed shrugged and took the highwayman's horse by the reins. 'Come on, men, let's get on with it,' he called. 'We've a long road to cover before nightfall. You.' He pointed to Jessie. 'Pick up the bag and the metal. We might need them again.'

Jessie did as she was told. It didn't do to provoke Jed into one of his rages. A few minutes later, she was back with the other women and cast a glance at the dead man lying on the ground with nothing to cover his nakedness. She took off her shawl and, averting her eyes, spread it over the body and said a prayer for the poor man's soul. Then she picked up her pace. Soon she would be in London, and Jed Lambert would be nothing but a bad memory.

CHAPTER TWO

Manon Jones sat in the plush drawing room of the big house and stared listlessly through the window. The garden was washed with sunshine and the light and shade through the trees threw soft patterns on the terrace. Beyond lay rolling fields and leafy trees. Broadoaks was one of the finest houses in the county but she was shut inside the walls feeling like a prisoner.

She heard her son's faint cry from upstairs and started to her feet, only to sink back into her chair again, knowing that the efficient nurse employed by George Jones would be tending to the baby's needs. Mr Jones managed everything as he managed his business, leaving little room for the wishes of others – especially the daughter-in-law he did not approve of.

Non had arrived at Broadoaks as an unmarried woman with a bastard child, the butt of crude humour among the servants. Her marriage to Caradoc Jones, favoured son and heir, had done nothing to improve her standing in the house. George had always resented her, only softening his attitude to her when she helped cure his son of cholera. Now the danger was over, her father-in-law openly showed his hostility to Non, especially when her husband wasn't there to protect her.

Caradoc's sister Georgina had never been Non's

friend. She showed her claws as often as she could. If Caradoc knew how badly Non was being treated he would never have left her behind at Broadoaks, however urgent the need for the journey.

The door opened and George Jones came into the room, his eyes narrowing as he saw her. 'You're not a prisoner, you know,' he said. 'If you'd rather be in Swansea that can soon be arranged. You could peddle those herbal remedies you're so fond of making. If that's what you want then you're free to go.'

'And my son?'

'Why, Rowan can stay at Broadoaks. He'll be well looked after. Here, the boy has everything – a fine home, a nurse to tend him day and night, and his grandfather to oversee his future.'

'His future is with me,' Non said quietly. 'Wherever I go, my son goes too. It's what Caradoc wants.'

'Caradoc was never in love with you.' George spoke coldly. 'He was infatuated at first, I agree, and the need to make his son his legitimate heir was important to him. But he will come to his senses and soon. You must have seen how often he is away from you – his work is more important than you are, Miss, and don't you ever forget it.'

'You keep sending him away,' Non protested, 'you play on his sense of duty, pretending that you are being kind to me while he's on the road.' She lifted her chin and looked levelly into his eyes. 'You never meant to make me welcome here, did you, Mr Jones?'

'Look, why don't you admit defeat,' George said. 'You would be well provided for, you can have enough money to set yourself up in a house and you can find a husband more suitable to your station – Morgan the smithy, perhaps.'

Non pressed her hand against her breast. 'You

10

forget,' she said breathlessly, 'I am already married.'

'What's done can be undone, make no mistake.' He turned as his daughter came into the room. 'Georgina, I've been trying to tell this foolish woman that she has no place in our lives.'

'Save your breath, Papa, she's out to be lady of the manor. She wants Caradoc and his fortune – she won't settle for less.'

Non turned wearily away. What was the use of arguing? The Jones family only had one point of view and that was their own. She turned back to the window. The sun dappling the lawn looked tempting, perhaps she would walk for a while in the fresh air. At least she'd have a rest from the nagging of her father-in-law and the sharp tongue of his daughter.

Non walked slowly across the room. She felt weak but she comforted herself with the thought that once Caradoc was home again she would talk to him, tell him the truth about her position in the Joneses' household. He would take her far away, out of reach of his family.

When she made to open the door Georgina spoke sharply to her. 'Where do you think you're going? No one gave you permission to leave the room. Have you no manners?'

Non sighed. 'I wasn't aware that I needed permission to walk in the garden.' She felt a little faint, and could do without a lecture on manners.

'Well, in polite society it's usual to make an excuse for leaving the room.'

'I didn't realize I was in "polite society". You have been anything but polite since I came here. Your behaviour gets worse every time Caradoc leaves for London. You need to learn some manners yourself, if you ask me.'

She left Georgina with her mouth open, and walked

11

out into the fresh air, sighing with relief. She made her way to the big gates at the end of the long drive and found them closed. She sank down in the shade of the trees and lay against a hillock. The grass was cool and soft beneath her cheek, and it was comforting, but how she longed for Caradoc to be home, to have his arms round her, to hold his hands, to touch his dear face. In spite of her efforts to be brave, bitter salt tears began to roll down her cheeks and as she leaned back she let the tears flow freely.

The darkness was intense for the moon was behind the clouds, and Jessie felt afraid. The countryside was so different from the town of Swansea where she'd been born. There, the candles in the houses were like welcoming beacons and the streets were always crowded. The constant flow of carts and carriages along the high street and into Oxford Street was like music to her ears. She wished she was at home now, wished she'd never joined Jed Lambert's drove.

Jessie was about to retrace her steps towards the barn where the other women were bedded down for the night when she heard the sound of a fiddle. Curiosity drew her towards the well-lit windows of the Lamb and Flag inn. She crept forward and peered inside. Candlelight flickered on the faces of the drovers, who were cheered by drink and looking forward to a good night's sleep. She longed to join them but it wasn't allowed: Jed Lambert was fond of the women but only as playthings – he would never put his hand in his pocket to provide them with a drink.

She jumped as she felt a hand rest on her shoulder. She spun round to see Flora standing behind her.

'*Duw*, Flora, I nearly jumped out of my skin! What are you doing creeping up on me like a thief in the night? I thought the highwayman Jed killed had come to have his vengeance on me.'

'Time you came to bed, my lady,' Flora said. 'No good ever came of snooping on the men.' In spite of her words, Flora stood on tiptoe and gazed through the window. 'Mind, they're having a good time, all right. There'll be a few sore heads in the morning, I bet a penny. Oh, look! Two of the men are scrapping – looks like there's going to be a fight. And there's Morgan. I knew he was joining the drove but he must have got here before us. Such a handsome man, he is. I'm glad he's come. He makes me feel safe somehow.'

The door burst open and Jed Lambert almost fell out. Then another man staggered after him and aimed a fist in Jed's direction. It grazed his chin and the roar Jed gave out was enough to make the cattle stampede.

'God have mercy on us!' Jessie said. 'It's poor old Sam Figgins. He don't stand a chance against Jed.'

Jed found his feet and hit the other man full in the face. Sam's nose seemed to split in two and the man screamed out in agony. Jed hit him again and again, until Sam lay on the ground, crying like a baby.

'Morgan's going to put a stop to it,' Flora whispered. 'He's so brave. Just as well he's stepping in or Jed would kill Sam.'

Jed swayed drunkenly towards Morgan. 'Who told you to stick your beak in?' He tried to push Morgan aside, but the other man was too strong to shift. Jed, knowing he was beaten, turned his anger back to Sam. 'As for you, Figgins, you're finished here. Get out of my sight before I kill you.'

'Come on,' Flora said. 'We'd better get back to the barn before Jed sees us or we'll be getting our marching orders too.' The two girls hurried across the rough ground arm in arm.

Back in the barn, Jessie felt the darkness press in on her – she'd never liked the dark. This drove was turning into a nightmare, what with highwaymen being killed and the men fighting each other. She never wanted to do it again – putting up with the mud and stench and looking at cows' backsides all day wasn't her idea of fun.

But soon they would be in London and she would leave the drove and Jed Lambert behind her for good. In London there was a boy, a bit younger than she was and thin as a stick, but he had the most lovely smile she'd ever seen. His name was Albie.

CHAPTER THREE

Non spent a great deal of time in the garden, keeping out of the way of her in-laws. One fine evening she was sitting on the grass, watching the moon sail behind the clouds. She wondered where Caradoc was, and tried to bring to mind the roads the drovers took from Carmarthen to London, the starlit skies – they should be etched on her mind for it had been under the stars that she'd given herself to him, heart, body and soul.

The air was growing cooler and soon she would have to go indoors. Reluctantly she got to her feet, brushing the grass from her skirts. In her old gown, she looked out of place in the grandeur of Broadoaks.

She retraced her steps and stopped for a moment outside the imposing, pillared front door that was closed to her now, another ploy to emphasize her lowly place in the household. She took a deep breath and rang the bell. Soon she heard footsteps cross the hall and a maid stood there. 'You're to go to the back, Miss,' she murmured. 'Mr Jones's orders, see. Sorry, Miss.'

The door was closed in Non's face and she bit her lip. George Jones was doing everything he could to humiliate her, to break her spirit. Well, he wouldn't succeed. She had fought hard battles before and this one was just another she had to win.

★ ★ ★

The next morning Non woke early as the maid drew the curtains. She tried to sit up but her head was aching and she felt hot and shivery. Her mouth was dry, too, and her throat sore. She tried to ask for water but her voice was little more than a croak.

The maid left the room, and she leaned back against the pillows, trying to muster the strength to get out of bed and fetch some of her herbal medicine. But the effort was too great and, with a sigh, she let the warm darkness take her.

'That girl has sulked in her room all day.' Georgina shook back her hair. 'I don't know what she hopes to gain by starving herself. She hasn't even sent an apology for not joining us at supper.'

Her father took a piece of salmon and slid it on to his plate. 'The maid told me she's sick. Seems she has some sort of fever. Perhaps I'd better send a message to the doctor.'

'Why bother, Papa? Let her heal herself. She claims she cured Caradoc of the cholera with her plant medicines.'

'I don't know about that, but she watched by his bedside day and night, and there's no doubt he recovered well.'

'Caradoc has a strong constitution, Papa. And lots of people who never set eyes on Manon Jenkins recovered from the sickness.'

'I suppose you're right.'

'In a day or two she'll be on her feet again, you'll see.' Georgina was bored with the conversation. She wished Non would disappear from her life for good. Just looking at the girl reminded her of the time she had gone on the drove with the girl as chaperone. That trip

16

had changed Georgina's life for ever: she had met Clive Langland and married him in foolish haste. She'd been punished for that: her husband had walked out on her before their marriage bed was cold. Afterwards her father had made her a small allowance, but she felt she deserved more – she couldn't help it if her husband had deserted her.

'Rowan is coming along nicely, don't you think?' Her father's words interrupted Georgina's thoughts. 'He recognizes me now. He's inherited his intelligence from our side of the family.'

Georgina didn't reply. She was sick of hearing about the baby, sick and tired of her life at home with her father. But what choice did she have? She was a married woman: she could never find another man to take care of her while Clive still lived and breathed.

'I hate that man!' she said aloud.

Her father looked at her in surprise. 'Who on earth are you talking about?'

'Clive Langland, my so-called husband, that's who I'm talking about.'

'You're well shot of him. That man was only after money, and once he learned you had nothing except the allowance I made you he vanished. Surely you're not pining for him?'

'No, Papa! Didn't you hear me say I hated him? Your time is so taken up with that child upstairs you can think of nothing else.'

'Don't take that tone with me!' George frowned. 'You're forgetting that I gave you a roof over your head. Count your blessings, my girl, or you might find your-self out on the street.'

Georgina subsided in her chair. She wanted to lash out at her father, at life itself for giving her such ill luck, and somehow it was all bound up in her hatred for that witch, the girl of lowly birth who now fancied herself as lady of the manor.

Non turned restlessly in the bed. She was in London, her baby still unborn, at the hospital, helping with the sick. Then she was in the mean rooms by the river where she'd built up her shop, where folk respected her herbs and their healing qualities. Then she was with Caradoc and he was holding her, kissing her, telling her he wanted her as his wife. Soon after he was gone and she was alone.

She dragged herself into consciousness. Someone had placed a glass of water at her bedside and she reached out and drank some. She knew she must get up, find one of her remedies to bring down the fever, but she was weary, so weary. She slipped out of bed on to her knees and crawled across the room. Her bag was in the cupboard. Somehow she managed to prise the door open. More by touch than anything, she found a bottle of Angelica elixir and poured a little into her mouth. She looked back across the room: the distance to the bed seemed too far to travel. She stretched out on the carpet and closed her eyes.

CHAPTER FOUR

Jessie looked doubtfully at the river swirling round her legs. She hated water and the Wye could be treacherous.

'Get a move on, Jessie.' Jed was on horseback and the water scarcely touched his boots. 'You're all so slow on this drove that we'll be overtaken by Caradoc Jones if we're not careful. He's a man who likes to travel fast and I don't want him getting into Smithfield before me, you hear?'

Jessie felt like shouting at him that the delays were his fault: every inn they stayed at was an excuse for Jed to get blind drunk. Instead, she modified her tone.

'Yes, Mr Lambert.' She felt the current take her skirts and swirl them. 'But you're up there on a horse and we women have to struggle as best we can on foot.'

'You've got it easy, you lot have. Some drove masters would expect more work out of you than I do. It's no hardship to cross a river. A bit of sun, and your petticoats will soon be dry. I don't know why I brought you along – you're not worth your pay.'

He rode away and Jessie looked to where Flora was lifting her skirts above her knees in a vain attempt to keep them dry. 'Full of charm, isn't he?' she said drily. 'It don't pay to cross a man like Jed, remember that, my girl.'

'I wish I was on the drove with Caradoc Jones,' Jessie

said. 'He thinks of his girls – takes the river crossing over the bridge when he can.'

'Aye, well, we'll know better than to travel with Jed Lambert again. I'd rather stay at home.'

'Me, too.'

Jessie fell silent, thinking of the happy days when she had enjoyed the travelling, enjoyed the sunny days and the star-filled nights. Now it was all hard work and no fun. Still, Jed Lambert was no Caradoc Jones, and it would pay her to remember that and keep a still tongue in her head.

Caradoc Jones looked doubtfully at the waters of the Wye. The crossing he'd planned would have to be delayed: the river was higher than he'd anticipated and was running swiftly over the rocky bed.

One of the innkeepers had told him Jed Lambert had crossed here a few days ago, and Caradoc planned to catch up with him so that both herds would reach Smithfield at about the same time. He looked with pride at the beasts gathered on the fields behind the river. His herd was quality, and Jed Lambert wasn't fussy about the animals he brought to market.

Caradoc wanted this trip over so that he could get home to his wife and child. But the drove had been a disaster ever since it began: the prize bull, the main reason for the trip, had broken free and capturing him had taken several precious days. The heifers, nervous at best, had turned stubborn and were reluctant to move on. There had been enough delays and Caradoc didn't want to waste time on another.

He sat on the grassy bank and stared at the fast-flowing water. He should be at Non's side, telling her how much he loved her and their son. He knew that his father was disappointed that he hadn't made a good marriage with someone from his own class, but George was delighted with the baby and had seemed to accept Non as one of the family. Still, Caradoc felt uneasy: there had been a pleading look in his wife's eyes when he'd left her. The sooner he delivered the cattle to Smithfield, the sooner he could go home. But for now the animals could rest and feed on the lush grass beside the river: he would make the crossing once it was safe to do so.

CHAPTER FIVE

A well-built young man made his way around the perimeter of Smithfield market, looking for likely pockets to dip into. The smell of the animals was overpowering and a 'London Particular', a thick fog, had come down, obscuring the buildings surrounding him. The slaughterhouses were busy, killing and preparing the meat for the butchers' stalls. Huge sides of beef hung on hooks, blood soaking into the sawdust that covered the floors. Newcomers to London usually shrank from the sights and smells but Albie had been born and bred to it: he loved everything about it, even the mean street where he lived.

For a moment he felt sad: a month ago he'd lost his grandfather, who had brought him up from birth. The house was empty without him – but he had his friend Ruby, and even though she was not quite old enough to be his mother, she treated him like a son.

A drover leaned over the pen and prodded a beast with his stick. 'Prime bit of beef, but not such good stock as my herd of Welsh Blacks,' he said, to no one in particular. Albie smiled at the easy dip he was about to make. He would have to be quick – the man looked mean and there was a nasty turn to his mouth. The heavy bag of money was in Albie's hand before the drover had finished his inspection of the animal. He slipped away into the crowd, glancing behind to make sure no one had noticed him, with a cheery grin on his face. He had enough in his hand now to keep himself and Ruby in comfort for a month of Sundays.

Then he caught sight of a woman in a shawl. She had her back to him but a big bag hung over her arm. She was clearly a newcomer to London or she would have been more careful with her possessions. He made his way towards her. She was young and upright with a faded bonnet on her head, a countrywoman by the look of her shabby dress, probably in London to buy a length of cloth or a new hat. Deftly, he slipped his hand into the bag and felt about for a purse. There was a snap and his fingers were caught in what he could only think was a mouse-trap. 'Bleedin' 'ell!' He tried to pull his hand free, but the drawstring of the bag trapped it.

'Try to steal my money, would you?'

The voice was familiar, with a distinctive Welsh lilt. When the girl turned he recognized her. 'Jessie Price! For Gawd's sake, let me go – me 'and's killing me.'

Jessie laughed. 'Albie! I might have known you'd be here pinching from decent folk.' She opened her bag and released him. '*Duw*, haven't you grown into a big boyo since I saw you last! Quite handsome too.'

Abashed at being caught, Albie sucked his fingers. 'Never mind that! You nearly took me 'and orf. What are you doing in London, anyway? I thought you'd gone running back to Wales when the cholera came.'

'I did, but then I got itchy feet so I joined the drove. I'm not with Mr Jones, though. I came up with a different master – there he is, a nasty piece of work. Travelling with Jed Lambert has been awful, there's not the fun on the trail there used to be.'

Albie recognized the man as the drover he'd just

robbed. Hurriedly, he took Jessie's arm. 'Come back to the house with me. Ruby will want to see you again.'

He guided her through the crowd with such speed that Jessie was soon out of breath. 'What's the hurry?' she gasped.

Albie laughed. 'I don't want to linger and get my pockets picked, do I?' He slowed his pace a little. 'How's Non getting on? Set up a shop for her herbs, has she?'

'Dunno. Last I heard she was living in the Joneses' house. Sitting pretty, is Manon Jenkins, and not before time. Married quick she was, to Caradoc Jones – at least, that's what the gossips say.'

Albie felt a pang of nostalgia for the days when he and Non had lived in the same house with his grand-father and Ruby. Non had become famous in the streets of London for her healing herbs. 'Well, I hope she'll be happy. Caradoc Jones is a good man, and she deserves a bit of luck.'

As they drew nearer to the riverside Jessie held her nose. 'It still smells bad here. Couldn't you have found your new home away from the Thames?'

'Me and Ruby are proud of our house in Treacle Lane. We've made it clean as a new pin and we have fresh ammonia cloths at the windows every day to keep out the smell.'

'I don't know about that – ammonia smells almost as bad as the river,' Jessie told him.

Albie hustled her along the narrow street, inhabited by thin cats and a stray pig, then pushed her into a doorway. 'Go into the kitchen. You'll find Ruby up to her arms in spuds or flour, one of the two.'

He watched as Jessie hugged Ruby. '*Duw*, it's good to see you, both of you,' she said.

'Sit down, Jessie, love, and have a cup of tea. You

look done in. Been traipsing around London all day, I'll reckon.'

'We came in this morning and I haven't had time to find myself somewhere to stay yet.'

'Well, you'll stay here with us. There's a room spare at the back.'

'I can't pay much,' Jessie pushed off her shawl, 'though I'd love to be with folk I know.'

'No need to talk of paying. Albie and me have been doing well for ourselves. I keep lodgers, like always, and he . . . well, he works.'

Jessie winked at him. 'Aye, saw him at work, I did, but he didn't get away with anything from me except a sore finger.'

Albie caught himself staring at Jessie. Her lips were full and luscious, and her eyes had a merry look in them. She met his gaze and winked again, whereupon he realized that she was an attractive young woman. Older than he was by a year or two, but what did that matter? He saw the swell of her breasts beneath her bodice, the slimness of her waist, and the slender thighs outlined beneath her skirts. He was becoming aroused. Embarrassed, he took off his cap and held it in front of his trews.

'What are you looking at, Albie?' Jessie's voice was teasing. She moved her knees to adjust her skirts, and revealed a slim pair of ankles.

'Don't know what I'm looking at, it hasn't got a bleedin' label on, has it?' He hoped his face wasn't as hot as it felt.

'Cheeky!' Jessie leaped to her feet, grasped him round the waist and tickled him. 'You'll take that back or I'll make you laugh so much you'll die.'

Albie tried to push her away, smiling in spite of himself. His hand accidentally brushed her breasts. She paused, looking up at him, her smile fading. 'Well, Albie, my boy, looks like you've become a man while I've been away.' She returned to her seat. 'I bet you're even shaving now.'

'I've been a man for a long time.' Albie was no longer in a playful mood. Somehow things had changed between him and Jess. Albie had a chaotic mixture of feelings about her. He didn't know if he wanted to walk out of the house and slam the door after him or sit down at the table and try to calm himself.

Ruby broke the uncomfortable silence. ''Ow about that cup of tea I mentioned? You going to put the kettle on the fire, Albie?'

He nodded. Bending over the fire would supply him with an excuse for the hot colour in his cheeks. He felt unsettled, as if he'd had a bad day at the pickings, and almost angry with Jessie: she had made him feel like a bumbling fool.

He prepared the tea, avoiding her eyes.

'Where's Granddad, then?' Jessie rested her elbows on the table and stared at Albie.

Again, Ruby intervened. 'We lost him. Old age. He's sorely missed.'

'Oh, Albie!' Jessie said. 'There's sorry I am for you, my love.'

For a moment it seemed that she meant to rise and hug him, but she remained in her chair. 'He was a fine man. We'll all miss him.'

Albie still couldn't speak when the old man was mentioned. He'd been to the cemetery a few times to put some flowers on the grave. He talked to his grandfather there, telling him about his problems, but he couldn't talk to anyone about what he felt for Jessie. He tried to lighten the mood: 'Jess caught me out good an' proper,' he said, but he knew his tone was far from

26

jocular. 'A trap she had in her bag – nearly took my finger off.'

'You thought I'd be easy, dressed in my shabby clothes and straight up from the country.'

'I suppose I did, but I soon learned different. You in London for a while or are you going home soon?'

Jessie laughed, her head thrown back to expose the white column of her throat. Albie looked away. Why did she make him feel so uncomfortable? She was just Jessie, a cattle woman who walked from Wales to London.

'See? He wants rid of me already. Well, bad luck, boy, I'm staying put, at least for a while. I've had enough of walking and the drovers' roads.' She sighed. 'It's not like when I travelled with Mr Jones and Non. Those days are gone for ever.'

Albie poured the tea, hot and strong as he liked it, and peered over the rim of his mug, trying to appear casual as he watched Jessie. She'd taken off her shoes and her small feet were red and rubbed from days on the trail. Something about her blistered toes caught at his heartstrings.

'Got any plans?' Ruby asked.

Jessie shrugged. 'Perhaps I'll sell strawberries when they're in season or get a job in trade, or maybe a place in one of the big houses. But all I know is cattle. Who would take me on?'

'You could be a milkmaid,' Ruby suggested, 'work for one of the cow-keepers, and in the hot weather you could sell strawberries in Covent Garden.'

Jessie laughed, and Albie noticed the dimple that appeared in her cheek. 'You've got it all sorted out for me,' she said, 'and it's not a bad idea. I know how to milk a cow – I've even helped deliver a calf on the trail.' She paused to sip her tea. When she put the mug down, Albie stared at her mouth. He would like to kiss those lips, he thought, part them and taste her sweetness.

'You know something, Ruby?' she said. 'I think I'd make a good milkmaid, and if you don't mind me staying here I could pay you for my keep.'

Ruby patted her arm. 'Don't worry about finding work. Just rest for now – you must be tired after weeks on the road.'

'I'm young and strong,' Jessie said, 'and I like the open-air life – but some of the women who walk the roads get old before their time, skin dried by the sun and wind.' She lowered her eyes. 'And look what happened to my friend Flora – got herself with a full belly and the man she thought loved her threw her over. She came up with Jed's drove, like me, but I lost sight of her at the market. I hope she's all right.'

'Well, girl,' Ruby said, 'you got your whole life in front of you. Look forward, is my advice. Think of the future and not of the past.' She turned to Albie. 'Go and get some blankets out of the big cupboard on the stairs. You can help me make up a bed for Jessie.'

'You sit down, Ruby,' Jessie said. 'If Albie shows me where to get the bedding I'll see to it myself.'

'Go on, then. I've been cooking and cleaning for the lodgers all day so it would be nice to put my feet up.'

Albie led the way upstairs and opened the cupboard door. 'How many blankets do you want?'

'That depends,' Jessie said. 'If I'm to bed down on my own I'll need three.' She pinched his cheek. 'But if I gets myself a big strong man to share with, well, I'll be warm enough.' She laughed.

Albie's heart sank. Jessie still saw him as a boy to be teased. He took three blankets out of the cupboard, then pushed open the door to the back bedroom.

28

'You're in 'ere. The stink of the river comes in when the wind's blowing hard, but as you're not paying you'll put up with it I dare say.' He dumped the blankets on the high, narrow bed. 'I'll leave you to it, then, will I?'

'No you will not! Go round the other side of the bed and help me. We have to make it tidy, mind.'

Albie tucked in the blankets with angry jabs, but Jessie smiled at him so warmly that his bad mood vanished. He wanted to take her in his arms, throw her down on the bed and prove that he was no longer a boy but a man with a man's needs. But he did no such thing. He walked to the door without a backward glance and hurried down the stairs.

Jessie followed at a more leisurely pace, giggling. Albie knew she was laughing at him. Didn't she realize he had feelings and didn't like to be mocked?

'For Gawd's sake, stop poking fun at me, Jess. I don't need you laughing behind my back.'

'Oh, love, there's sorry I am.' At the bottom of the stairs she stopped and put her arms round his neck. 'I'm only teasing, see, 'cos I think you're much too handsome for your own good. But you've grown up, Albie, and I don't know how to talk to you any more.'

She smelt of grass and the open air and Albie's head spun. He wanted to press her close, to taste the sweetness of her mouth. He held her away from him. 'Just treat me like a man, Jess. Is that too much to ask?' Jessie moved away from him. He forced a laugh. 'Come on, let's get back to Ruby or she'll think we've been up to something.'

Jess's eyes met his. 'No such luck!' she said, and then she held up her hand. 'No more teasing, I promise.' She slipped her arm through his as they made their way along the passageway and into the warmth of the kitchen.

CHAPTER SIX

The raucous voices of the men calling to the cattle echoed on the still morning air, and although Caradoc was familiar with the sounds of the drove getting under way, for some reason, the noise irritated him.

He had spent the night under the stars; the cattle were bedded down at a nearby farm, free to graze and sleep at will in the fields. It meant paying the owner of the land a halfpenny a head but that was better than forcing the animals into the cold water of the river Wye in darkness and risking a stampede. The animals would take more kindly to the crossing in daylight, and the early-morning signs heralded a fine day.

He thought of his dear Non and their boy, safely at home. His father George, when presented with a grandson, had mellowed and welcomed Non into the family. Caradoc wasn't so sure about his sister though, as Georgina could be sharp at times. Yet at heart she was a decent girl to whom life had been unkind and in consequence she'd become a little bitter. Who could blame her?

He walked the short distance to the ford of Cabin Twm Bach, as the locals called it, and gazed at the swiftly running water. Yesterday's wind had subsided and the sun was beginning to break through the clouds. It was a propitious sign: the animals were easier to control when the weather was fine.

He made up his mind: he would drive the herd into the river straight after breakfast, and by noon the drove would be well on its way to Radnorshire.

He heard footsteps and looked round to see Morgan approaching. He nodded to the man. 'Morning, Morgan. I'm glad I arranged to meet you here – some of the beasts need shoeing. How did your trip with Lambert go?'

'Not bad.' Morgan was a man to keep his thoughts to himself and Caradoc respected him for that, but he could see from the smithy's face that he had no time for Jed Lambert. 'If you can see to my animals early we should be able to cover about sixteen miles today,' he said.

'I dunno, still running fast is the Wye and the beasts are easily frightened by water. And there's the big bull. The creature's skittish and the fierce look in his eye could mean trouble,' Morgan said. 'I wouldn't chance a crossing – we could go by road instead or wait for the cattle ferry.'

'Who's the master of this drove?' Caradoc was piqued: no man could tell him how to run a drove.

'Well, you are,' Morgan ran his fingers through his thick hair, 'but I reckon the wind will get up again before long, and there's rain in the air.' With that, he shrugged his broad shoulders and turned away. As Caradoc watched him go, he felt somehow as though Morgan had bested him in the argument.

The animals were flighty: having eaten their fill of grass the night before, they refused to move from the lush fields and the crack of the whip rang out on the air.

At last, the herd was coaxed down the riverbank to the ford, the young heifers protesting at the strength of the flowing water. Caradoc looked up and saw the sun being elbowed aside by the clouds. It looked as though Morgan had been right, and there would be rain before long, but with luck the crossing would be over by then, the animals safe on the opposite bank.

He rose in his stirrups and blew his horn loudly. The dogs started to bark, and as Caradoc spurred his horse into the river, he felt the creature stumble on the shiny stones that lay beneath the surface. He felt a dart of misgiving – about a quarter of the herd was already in the water so there was no turning back. Had he made a bad decision? He'd know soon enough.

Jessie drew aside her skirts as she passed a mangy dog snuffling in the gutter. London could be such a fine place, with elegant houses where gentlemen and ladies lived in splendour, but the poorer people had to rent accommodation close to the stink of the river.

Ruby had told her where to find the house of the nearest cow-keeper. It was a good walk from Treacle Lane, but Jessie was used to walking and arrived in high spirits. The house looked small and insignificant, but there was a good patch of land at the rear.

She knocked on the open front door, but there were no sounds from inside. She looked about and saw a gate to one side of the fence, then heard the distinctive sound of cows impatient to be milked. As she pushed open the gate, she saw the broad shoulders of a man, his cheek against a cow's flank as he pulled on the teats to send a steady flow of milk into a pail. Jessie watched for a moment before approaching the man and her heart beat swiftly with hope. This was going to be easier than she'd thought. ''Scuse me,' she said quietly, 'but have you got a job for a milkmaid?'

The man looked round and she saw a pleasant smile

crease the corners of his mouth. He looked her over from head to toe and nodded. 'I might have.'

She could tell by his voice that he was Irish and she liked the Irish. They were good folk. 'Well, if you have a job, I'm here to offer my services,' she said. 'I'm used to beasts. I've walked the drovers' trail from Wales to England more than once and done a fair bit of milking on the way.'

He continued to milk the animal until the flow turned into a trickle. 'Well, to be sure I could do with some help.' He got to his feet and she saw that he was not much taller than she was, but he had a handsome face and good hands. 'I'm Frederick Dove.' He studied her. 'How am I to know that you're honest?'

'I can get a letter from the master of the drove,' she said. 'I'm clean and neat and used to hard work. Ruby says I could sell at Covent Garden maybe in the summer if cow-keeping gets slack.'

'Who's Ruby?' he asked. 'She sounds a sensible woman.'

'She's a friend. She lives in Treacle Lane near the river.'

'And you lodge with her?'

'I do.'

'Well, it's a long way for you to come every day, but if you're willing to work hard and have time off when I don't need you, I'll take you on.'

'Oh, that's lovely.'

'Don't you want to know how much I'll pay you?'

He was smiling again, and she noticed his teeth were pearly white. Folk who drank a lot of milk usually had good teeth. 'Well, yes, I suppose I do,' she said.

'Three shillings a week and your food while you're working. Will that do?' He rubbed his hand on his apron and held it out to her. She shook it, and he said,

'That's settled, then. You'd better tell me your name.'

'Jessie,' she said, enjoying the strong grip of his hand.

'Well, Jessie,' he said, 'you'd better come and meet Kathie, my wife.'

Jessie felt as if she swallowed something hard, and she coughed a little. She hadn't counted on there being a wife.

The cow-keeper's wife was thin and pale with red hair that made her skin look sallow. She held a wailing baby in her arms and nodded at Jessie without much interest. As soon as the introductions had been made, she sank into a chair and unbuttoned her bodice to reveal a painfully small breast. 'Make me a cup of tea, Fred, to be sure I could do with one. I'm parched and the baby keeps crying so I can't put him down for a minute. I'm longing for a bit of a sleep if the truth be told.' She sighed. 'I sometimes wish I was back home in Ireland with me mammy to help with the baby.'

The infant moved his mouth searching for succour but the woman began to cry. 'I haven't the milk to feed him.' Big tears rolled down her cheeks. 'He won't grow big and strong unless he gets some milk.'

Jessie knelt beside the chair. 'How old is he?' She touched the baby's little hand, and his fingers curled into hers.

'Sure I worry he'll die on me, and him only six months old.'

'Well, if he's six months he can have milk from the cows, see?' Jessie stood up and looked round the kitchen. 'We need a jug with a lip on it and you . . .' she hesitated, not knowing how to address Frederick '. . . you fetch some cow's milk for me.'

'You can't feed my son on milk from the cows!' Fred said.

'Why not? I've seen more than one baby thrive on it.

You just mix in a little boiled water and a touch of sugar to tempt the little one, and you just watch him drink!'

Soon, Jessie had the baby snuggled into her arms, sucking at the lip of the jug as if his little life depended on it. Jessie was sure it did. 'That's right, little one, you drink your fill and you'll grow up to be a fine healthy man like your daddy.' Her eyes met Fred's, and she looked away quickly.

'Is it all right if I go up to bed for a little rest?' Mrs Dove looked appealingly at Jessie. 'Can you manage the little one just for a while?'

'You can't ask a stranger to take care of our son.' Fred spoke quickly. 'You go on your way, Jessie. I'll see to the little one.'

'I'll stay for a bit. Mrs Dove looks fair washed out.'

'Well, then, that's kind of you.' He moved to his wife and put his arm around her thin shoulders. 'Go on, then, Kathie, my love. You try to rest. The baby will be all right, don't you worry.'

When his wife had left the room, Frederick looked at Jessie and smiled. 'If you're sure you're all right, I'll go and finish the milking.' He hesitated in the doorway. 'Just call if you need me.'

Jessie found herself in the silent kitchen; the baby in her arms seemed content with milk bubbling round his rosebud mouth. She had come looking for a job and found one but she could never have imagined that she would be sitting in a stranger's kitchen holding a baby in her arms. She'd have a great tale to tell Ruby when she got home.

Caradoc guided his horse back to the bank and watched as the cattle forded the narrow part of the river, bellowing and protesting every step of the way.

The heavy clouds had turned into rain and now the water ran ever more swiftly, frightening the animals so that they pushed and struggled to be first to the opposite bank. Then, there was only the bull, the great black beast pawing the ground uneasily, watching the rushing water with red-rimmed suspicion in his eyes.

Caradoc pulled on the rope that was attached to a ring through the animal's nose and urged the bull into the water. Towards the middle of the ford, where the river bed was ridged, the going should be easier but the bull resisted, pulling the rope from Caradoc's hands with a turn of its huge neck. With a great bellow, the beast attempted to reach the bank, surging forward and sending eddies of frothy water in Caradoc's direction.

'Damn it!' Caradoc held on to the reins of his horse, sensing the animal's panic as the water slapped against its flanks. He'd been a fool. He should have taken Morgan's advice and delayed the crossing. Another rush of water battered the horse's straining neck and the animal reared up in fear, pawing the air in a silent tattoo.

Caradoc felt the saddle begin to slip beneath him, twisting him sideways. He saw the bull head up the bank on the other side of the river and breathed a sigh of relief. At least his father's investment in the precious animal was not lost. Another wave swept towards him; he felt his feet slip from the stirrups. He hit the water, and it closed icy cold over his head. He surfaced and shook the water from his eyes, and saw his horse rear in terror. He tried to swim away but the current was too strong. He saw the huge hoofs above him crashing down on him and then there was only blackness.

CHAPTER SEVEN

Non opened her eyes and looked blearily at the maid who was standing at the end of the bed. Her face was pale and tears were spilling down her cheeks. Non sat up so quickly that her head spun. She was over the worst of her fever but she still felt weak and light-headed. 'What's wrong?' she said anxiously. 'Is my baby all right?'

The girl nodded. 'The little boy is well enough, but . . .' She started to cry fresh tears, dabbing at her eyes with the back of her hand.

Non slipped out of bed and stared at the maid, almost afraid to ask any more questions. She swallowed hard. 'Come along, girl, tell me what's wrong.'

'Morgan the smithy is here, Mrs Jones. He says he won't go until he tells you the bad news himself.'

Non pulled on her dressing-gown and made her way towards the door. Something had happened to Caradoc. Why else would Morgan leave the drove?

Morgan was standing in the hall and, through the open door of the sitting room, Non could see her father-in-law slumped in a chair, his head in his hands.

'Morgan, tell me quickly, what's happened?'

He took her hands. 'I'm sorry to be the bearer of such upsetting news, Non, but it's bad, very bad.'

Non sat down on the stairs, her legs no longer strong

enough to support her. 'Don't tell me, there's been an accident. It's Caradoc, isn't it? Is he hurt?'

She remembered her old friend Mary, gored to death by an angry bull, and her heart missed a beat. 'Just tell me,' she said, as Morgan hesitated, unsure how to go on.

At last he spoke. 'We were taking the beasts through the ford at Cabin Twm Bach. I tried to warn him the weather was turning bad but . . .' He swallowed hard. Non could see the distress in his face and tried to steel herself against the awful news that surely must come. 'The rain was fierce and the animals got stubborn. The bull was wicked and Caradoc had to let go of the rope.' He looked at Non with pain naked in his eyes. 'I'm so sorry to tell you, Non, but Caradoc's horse reared and kicked, he wouldn't be quieted. Caradoc fell off in the river and the terrified animal trampled him badly. Last I saw of him he was taken downstream into deep water.'

An iciness settled over Non. 'He's dead, isn't he?'

'I don't know, Non. Me and a couple of men followed the current hoping to find him but there was no sign. What I did see was a scrap of material from the boss's coat caught on the branches of a fallen tree.'

He paused, trying to choose his words well. 'I'm sorry. The currents are strong just beyond the ford.' He touched Non's shoulder. 'I waited until morning but there was no sign of him and I knew I had to come back to tell you what happened.'

Non felt her throat constrict. She pictured Caradoc, pounded by the horse's hoofs, spun by the water, pulled helplessly to his death. But no, she wouldn't believe he was dead – not unless she saw his body. She forced herself to speak. 'Are the men still searching?'

Morgan nodded. 'They'll search all day and all

night, but the river is long and wide. I'm sorry, but the chances of finding Caradoc are not good at all.'

Non's head began to swim. Caradoc was gone. She would never again feel his arms round her, never touch his mouth with her own. A heavy blackness swept over her, and she gave herself up to it thankfully.

As Morgan walked away from the big house he was frowning. Non was ill, pale and weak, and the shock of her husband's accident had been too much for her. He had carried her back to her room and, with the maid's help, had tucked her into the bed. He had even taken it upon himself to have a word with George Jones.

'Manon needs care and attention,' he'd said flatly, but the old man had waved him away.

'Go and see to the cattle,' he said curtly. 'We can't lose an entire herd. Bring them back home or deliver the beasts to Smithfield, I don't care which. In the meantime I'll send men to search every part of the river Wye. Caradoc must be found.'

Morgan unhitched his tired horse and led the beast back down the hill to the town. He'd need a fresh mount to ride back to where the drovers were waiting for him and it looked as if he was expected to make a decision about the next move.

He was torn: he longed to stay at Non's side – he could see she would have no sympathy from old Mr Jones – but it was his duty to return to the drove. No one else was capable of taking the herd on the road.

At the stables in Singleton Street, he exchanged horses. 'Send the bill to Mr George Jones,' he told the groom.

His back and legs ached from the long distance he'd travelled overnight but he needed to press on. The sooner he delivered the herd to Smithfield, and that was what he had decided to do, the sooner he could come back home and make sure Non was being treated properly. He made one overnight stop at Brecon, and without bothering to eat a meal he fell into bed and was asleep instantly. He woke to the unfamiliar sensation of silence. He was used to the noise of the cattle, the sound of the horn, the stamping of hundreds of hoofs against the dry ground. Now there was only the occasional bird's song to disturb the morning stillness.

It was late afternoon when he caught up with the herd. He saw that the men were sitting listlessly by the riverbank, unable to believe the fate that had overtaken their boss and unable to make a decision to move on. To his surprise Flora was with them, her face pale with fatigue.

'I heard what happened,' she said. 'Me and Jessie split up when we got to London and I stopped for a meal at the Old Drovers' Arms with some of the other women. One of the other drovers had passed the Joneses' drove on the trail and he told us about the accident. I was so shocked. I knew you'd have to stop here for a few days so I caught a ride back. I wanted to be with you.'

'You're an experienced hand, I'm glad to have you with us.' He looked over her head at the waiting herdsmen. 'I've spoken to old Mr Jones,' he said, more loudly, 'and he's left the decisions to me.' He slipped from the saddle. 'Tomorrow we make for Smithfield. We collect the money and make sure you men and women are paid your wages.'

No one spoke, and Morgan took a deep breath. 'Old Mr Jones is sending men to search the river,' he said. 'We can do no more here.' He spoke with authority, knowing that any sign of weakness from him would lead to complete chaos. 'Tomorrow we take to the road to Smithfield market as planned.'

Non sat in the elegant drawing room facing her father-in-law. 'Has there been any news?' Her voice shook with the pain of it all.

George looked at her almost kindly. 'The men I've hired haven't come back yet, but if my son is in that river they'll find him.'

Georgina came into the room, her face puffy with weeping. For a moment, as her eyes met Non's, there was almost a kinship between the two women.

'I can't believe we've lost him,' she said. 'He'll be found, won't he, Papa?'

'Of course he will. He must have been carried well down the river before he found his way to the bank. But he's alive, I just can't believe we've lost him.'

Non felt as though she was in a nightmare. None of this was real, it was all a part of the fever that had left her weak and vulnerable. Her only comfort was holding her child close to her. But since her sickness that pleasure had been denied her. George had decided that Rowan be kept apart from his mother until she was fully recovered. It was sensible, she supposed, but all the same it hurt to be parted from her son.

She looked up at the sound of hoofbeats on the hard ground of the courtyard and the neighing of a horse made her tremble. The men were back from their search for Caradoc.

George moved quickly and flung open the front door. Non followed him and stood in the doorway as the first rider dismounted and came to stand in front of George Jones, his hat twisted in his hands.

'Found the rest of his shirt, sir,' he said, 'with blood

on it, caught among the branches of a tree but there's no sign of a body.'

'That means he must have got out of the river,' Non said. 'Doesn't it?'

'Don't mean anything, Mrs Jones. The river is deep in parts and the currents strong. Young Mr Jones might have been washed out to sea.'

'Go back and search again,' George said heavily. 'And don't come back without him, whether he's alive or dead.'

Non felt tears well up in her eyes and she cried silently. It was all too awful to bear; she needed Caradoc like she needed air to breathe. How could she face life without him?

He sat up in bed, wincing as pain shot through his head, and raised his hand to find a bandage around his brow. His left arm was in a sling and it hurt when he tried to move it. He looked round the unfamiliar room, the pale curtains fluttering in the breeze, a bowl of flowers on the deep window sill, and wondered where he was – *who* he was.

The door opened and an elderly woman came in. 'So, you're back in the land of the living, are you?' She was tall, upright, with iron grey hair tied back in a knot. He noticed all this even as he wondered who she was.

'I'm Mrs Martha Lyons, and now perhaps you'll be able to tell me who you are and what you were doing lying on the bank of the Wye with a crack to your skull that would have killed a weaker man. You have a broken leg and damaged arm and you must be in a great deal of pain – you've been moaning in your sleep like a cow birthing a calf.' She smiled to soften her words and sat on a chair beside the bed.

He slumped against the pillows and studied the

cracks in the whitewashed ceiling. 'I don't know,' he said, and his voice was thin as though it was a long time since he'd used his vocal cords. 'Where have I come from?'

'We were out driving when we found you. You were lucky because our cottage is well away from the river, hidden up here on the hill behind the trees. No one visits us and we don't visit anyone.'

'Who is "we"?' he asked.

'My granddaughter Gwenllyn and I. We'd been staying in Hereford for a couple of days doing some shopping.' She paused. 'The Good Lord must have been on your side that day, mind.'

'I'm very grateful to you and to the Good Lord,' he replied with a wry smile.

'Try to think. Are you a traveller, perhaps? Your trews were tattered and torn and you had no shirt to cover you so we couldn't tell what trade you were in. Though, by the way you talk, it's clear you're a gentleman.'

'I can't remember anything,' he said.

'You had no papers, but it was clear you'd had an accident. You must have fallen into the water and been washed downstream.' She shrugged. 'That's all we know, but I'd say you were lucky to be alive.'

'So you don't know anything about me?'

'That's right.' She eased her back against the creaking chair and her shrewd bright eyes regarded him steadily. 'There's a few things come to mind. You could be a traveller set upon by footpads and tossed into the river. Or you could be a visiting preacher, come to tell us all that we're sinners.' She smiled. 'If you weren't so genteel you could be one of those travelling quacks who come to sell us medicine claiming it will cure anything from gout to a sore head.'

43

Something stirred in his mind, the word 'medicine' struck a chord but the thought was too tenuous to hold on to.

'How long have I been here?'

'Only a few days. My granddaughter has been nursing you – taken to you, she has, and who can blame her? You're a fine figure of a man, or you will be once you are healed.'

He rubbed his head. 'I don't even know my name. How can a man lose his memory like that?'

'The knock on your head is to blame for that – you must have been washed against the rocks, I reckon. Don't worry, once you've rested, had a few good meals, your head will right itself.' She rubbed at her leg. '*Duw*, the arthritis is bad today, comes of being out in the damp.'

Rocks. That word also rang a bell. He closed his eyes. 'Rocks,' he said. 'Rocks. My name is something that sounds like rocks.'

'There, see, you're starting to get better already.' She twisted the long beads at her neck, a thoughtful expression on her face. 'Your name could be Craig. That's Welsh for "rock".'

He shook his head. 'No, it's not Craig, I think it's a longer name than that.' He felt like punching his skull. 'If only I could remember.'

The old lady patted him with a blue-veined hand. 'Don't worry about it now. I'll tell Gwenllyn to bring you some bread and milk. That'll be all you can stomach for now.' She rose awkwardly from the chair and straightened her back. 'You just be easy. Fretting will only make everything worse.'

As she left him he wondered how anything could be worse than the state he was in now. He was in a stranger's house, with no money, no means of knowing

44

who he was or where he was from. He rested his aching head against the pillows, closed his eyes and tried to pull his mind together.

The door was pushed open and a young girl came in with a tray on her arm. 'Hello.' There was a brightness to her eyes and a lift to the corners of her mouth that made him like her on sight. 'Hello. You must be Gwenllyn, I feel as if I know you already.'

'Well, I've nursed you since you were brought here, and now you're awake I want to talk to you.' She placed the tray on the table beside the bed. 'Here, let me help you to sit up a bit. You don't want to have milk all over Granddad's nightshirt, do you?'

With a docility that surprised him, he allowed the young girl to spoon-feed him. The milk was warm and the bread slipped easily down his throat.

'You don't even remember your name?' she asked, holding the spoon carefully to his lips. 'Nanna tells me you think it's something to do with rocks.'

He nodded and pushed her hand away. 'I don't want any more to eat just now, thank you.'

'Come on, *cariad*, just a little bit more. It will bring your strength back and perhaps your memory will come back too.'

'*Cariad*,' he said softly. 'That sounds familiar.'

'It means "sweetheart".' She blushed. 'I'm not being forward, just trying to coax you to eat a little more . . . please.'

Obediently, he finished off the meal. 'I feel better for that,' he said. 'You're probably right. Once my strength returns I'll be all right.' He watched as she placed the dish on the tray. She was a pretty girl, with the bloom of the young. Her face was softly contoured, and her honey-coloured hair was taken off her face in a becoming knot. 'Have you a sweetheart, Gwenllyn?'

he asked, and she looked at him from long golden lashes.

'My nanna doesn't like me to mix with the villagers.' She glanced at the door as if the mention of her grandmother's pet name would bring her into the room. 'I suppose I'd better leave you to rest,' she sighed softly. 'I'll try to come back later on and read to you. That would help pass the time, wouldn't it?'

'That's kind of you, Gwenllyn,' he said. 'Both you and your grandmother have been very good to me.'

When she'd gone, he lay back against the pillows feeling sore and weary. Surely tomorrow, or the day after, he would come to his senses and remember who he was. A great weariness swept over him. For now, all he needed was sleep.

CHAPTER EIGHT

Albie put his hands to his head. He was sick and tired of hearing about Jessie's marvellous new job. He looked out of the kitchen window, staring at nothing, hoping she would take the hint, but she kept on talking excitedly, not even noticing his patience was running out.

'So what about this cow-keeper? Ain't he got a wife, then?' He interrupted her flow. All he'd heard since she returned home was how clever this geezer Fred was, and how beautiful was his baby son. How she'd helped Fred out by feeding the child cow's milk and how grateful Fred was.

'Course he's got a wife, silly,' Jessie said impatiently. 'A lovely Irish lady, I told you. She's not very well. She didn't talk much, too tired I suppose.'

'You made up for her, by the sound of it.'

'Why are you being nasty, Albie? Could you be a bit jealous of Fred?'

'Why should I be jealous of a cow-keeper?' Albie said hastily, aware that Jess had hit the right spot.

Ruby came into the room. 'It's boiling in here. Could it be all that hot air you're favouring us with, Jess?'

'Oh, so you're having a go at me now. Well, all I want to do is tell you I got a job just as you suggested, Ruby. You should be pleased.'

'Well, I am pleased but I think we've all got the message now. Jess's got a job with a handsome milk seller whose wife and baby are sickly and who needs her help very badly. That sums it up – how about giving it a rest now and putting the kettle on for a cup of tea? Supper's in the oven, won't be long now.'

Albie sighed. Ruby had spoken – now perhaps they'd have a rest from Jess's ready tongue.

'You haven't heard *my* news. I got a good day's pickings today,' he said. 'Managed to get at the purse of a drover.' He took it out of his pocket and weighed it in his hand. 'Must be 'bout twenty shillings in here.' He grinned, well pleased. 'That'll keep us in comfort for a long time.'

'Albie!' Jessie said sharply. 'You shouldn't rob the drovers. They work hard for the money.'

'Well, who should I rob, then? The doctor? The baker? The pieman? They all work hard for a living but if they can't take care of their money, I got to do it for them.'

'Anyway,' Jessie said, 'twenty shillings isn't much to take from a drover. They deal in hundreds of sovereigns.'

'That's funny.' Albie was stung. 'I thought they didn't carry gold but used George Jones's Bank of the Black Cow. That's what you told us.'

'The Black Ox, stupid,' Jessie said. 'Some drovers are old-fashioned and won't trade with anything but cash.'

'I might as well make the tea myself,' Ruby said. 'You two are like cat and dog. I never saw such a pair for quarrelling – anybody would think you two was married.'

Albie felt his heart plummet in his chest. The thought of being married to Jessie made the blood rush through him. Albie turned away, angry with Jess and with himself.

Ruby made the tea and pushed the mugs to the centre of the table. Albie watched the golden liquid being poured like sweet honey into the mugs as though it was the most important thing in his life. He tried to ignore Jessie's giggles and Ruby's raised eyebrows. The itch was in him to have a woman and not just any woman: his own sweet Jessie.

He drank his tea in silence and tried to sort out his feelings: was this love he felt for Jess or just the lust of a boy growing to manhood? Whatever it was, it was giving him an awful lot of trouble. Perhaps he should visit one of the whores he met on the streets – he had plenty of money and could pay well. But even as the thought came into his head he dismissed it. When he made love to any woman, it would be sweet and honourable, and he would be faithful to her for life.

He looked at Jessie's face, pensive now. He tried to guess what she was thinking, and then she looked up. Her eyes locked with his for a long moment, and his heart leaped. She smiled her slow smile and he sank back in his chair well pleased. One day he would make Jess his wife, nothing was more sure than that.

Morgan raised himself from the saddle, his feet firmly in the stirrups, and surveyed the herd moving slowly but surely to their next stop. He needed to ride ahead and find a place to settle for the night.

He turned to the head drover. 'Harold, once I've settled our night-time expenses I'll be back. Try to keep the men moving and the cattle under control. I won't be long.'

'Aye, don't you worry about us, Morgan, man.'

'I don't want any more mishaps. Losing the boss's son is catastrophe enough for a lifetime, let alone one trip.'

It was good to get away from the stink and dust of

the herd and ride along the trail into the fresh summer air. It was a golden day, a day for joyous thoughts, but Morgan had lost all his joy once he knew Manon Jenkins had married Caradoc Jones. True, he was missing, he might well be dead, making Non a widow, but she was far out of Morgan's reach now, as the mother of George Jones's grandson.

He wondered what his future held: he couldn't imagine falling in love with any other woman. Non was the wife of his heart, and any other would always be second best.

When he arrived at the Full Moon inn, he paused for a moment looking up at the sky. The clouds were light and fluffy, and he was reassured by the sight of them. The drovers were without a leader and there would be chaos if there was an unexpected storm while he was away.

He saw the landlord and made arrangements for the night. The man was a typical landlord with a jolly red face and a big beer belly protruding over a canvas apron.

'Animals bedding down in the fields, are they?' He smiled broadly. 'That'll be a ha'penny a head as usual.'

'That's all right.' Morgan knew where the store of cash was kept, which was just as well. He was in charge now and the thought gave him a sense of satisfaction. Then, on the heels of that thought, came guilt that Caradoc was probably lying on the bed of the Wye.

Flora stopped at the back of the herd and stuffed her knitting into the large pocket of her apron. One of the cows was lying in the grass beside a stream, bellowing. Flora walked round the cow and the animal stared back with wide frightened eyes.

Harold rode up on his horse. He slipped from the

saddle and stared at the distressed creature. 'What's wrong, not some sickness, is it?' said Flora.

'The poor beast is going to have a calf,' said Harold.

'Will we have to call a halt here for a while?' she asked.

'No, you can stay behind but the rest of the herd and I are going on towards the next stop. Morgan will have arranged for our night's sleep.' He shrugged. 'The herd needs to rest and graze in the halfpenny field. You understand that we can't waste Mr Jones's money on looking after one cow.'

'But I don't know much about calving,' Flora protested. 'What if she dies?'

'You'll leave her here and catch up with us later.' He swung into the saddle and looked down at her with spiteful eyes. 'You've whelped a pup yourself so you must know a bit about birthing. A cow can't be much different to a woman.'

Flora felt the colour suffuse her face. 'Harold!' She looked up at him with tears in her eyes. 'That was a long time ago. I was young and foolish then and didn't know any better. Now I've learned not to trust any man.'

Harold laughed and turned his horse. 'See you later – if you're lucky.' He rode off in a cloud of dust, and Flora sank down into the cool grass. She fondled the cow's ear, remembering her own pain when she lost her child. And yet it was a relief: where would she be now if she was saddled with a baby?

She walked around the cow and lifted the animal's tail. It looked as if the birth was imminent, and what she would do when the calf was born, she didn't know. She sighed and took out her knitting. It was going to be a difficult night out here alone. Harold was a fool: a cow and a calf were worth good money, and he had left a girl in charge. Morgan would never do such a thing; he would be furious when he found out.

A little later she realized she must have fallen asleep because the sound of the cow bellowing echoed through her head and brought her fully awake again. She went to the rear of the animal and saw the thin legs of the calf protruding. The cow's belly was contracting and Flora knew the beast was in trouble. What should she do?

She heard hoofbeats against the ground and crouched near the animal, frightened.

As the rider drew near, she saw, with relief, that he was Morgan.

He dismounted and tied his horse to a tree. 'Flora, are you all right?' He knelt beside her. 'Harold told me a cow was calving – that man hasn't the brains of a sheep.'

'Oh Morgan, thank God it's you, I was so worried here on my own.'

'He should have left a man with you.'

'This poor thing is going to need some help.' Flora twisted her skirts into a bunch at the waist and knelt on the ground. 'We'll have to get the calf out somehow or both animals will die. Give me a hand, Morgan.' She took a deep breath and caught the calf's hoofs firmly. 'No, you're much stronger than me – you pull it out.'

Morgan rolled up his sleeves, took the hoofs and gave a mighty heave. Slowly but surely, the calf slid from its mother and lay pulsating on the ground.

'Good girl!' Morgan said and Flora looked at him wondering if he was praising her or the cow. She smiled up at him.

'After a bit of a rest, they'll be strong enough to go on to the next stop, won't they?' she asked.

She saw Morgan look round at the deepening gloom. 'I think we'd be better off here. I'll light a fire and there's some food in my saddlebags.'

Flora stood up and saw Morgan's quick glance at her bare legs. Hurriedly, she pulled her skirt free and it fell in crumpled folds to her ankles.

'Me, I'm going to have a wash.' She moved purposefully to where the stream was bright in the moonlight and soaked her hands to the elbows in the running water. What a strange thing to happen, here she was alone with Morgan on a summer's night – how the other women would envy her.

She dashed some water on to her face and breathed deeply. She was attracted to Morgan, she couldn't deny it. 'Behave yourself, girl!' she said sternly and Morgan looked up at her.

'What's that, Flora?'

She returned to his side and sat down, her legs crossed and her bare feet covered with her skirt. 'You and me, on our own all night – the others are going to talk.'

'Let them.' Morgan shrugged his big shoulders. 'If they're gossiping about us, they will be giving some other poor soul a rest.'

Soon the fire was blazing, and Morgan put his can on top of the flames. 'I'll have tea ready in a minute, Flora. You deserve it after what you've done tonight.'

'Aye, it was very good of me, wasn't it? I've brought a calf into the world, and me not a nurse or even a wise woman like Non Jenkins.'

He flinched at the name and impulsively Flora caught his big hand in hers. 'There's sorry I am, love. I didn't mean to remind you of Non. Why can't I keep my mouth shut?'

He put his arms around her. 'You're a kind girl, Flora, and I know you wouldn't mean to say anything to hurt me.'

She put her arms around his neck and felt the strong

53

muscles beneath his shirt. Suddenly her heart began to beat faster. It was a long time, such a long time since she'd been in a man's arms. She pressed her lips to his and taking his hand, placed it over her breast.

Morgan's breathing became ragged; he gently tried to pull away, but she clung on, unwilling to let him go. She lay down, pulling him with her.

'No, Flora,' he said. 'You're too good to give yourself to just any man.'

'But you're not any man, Morgan. You're handsome and kind and I want to be loved.' She reached down and touched him. 'Come on, Morgan, love. Who's to know what we've done tonight?'

He leaned over her, no longer resisting, and she sighed happily as he pushed her skirts aside, then took her with the fierce desire of a man too long without loving. She thrilled to his touch, moving with him, the stars making crazy patterns above her head. Small moans escaped through her parted lips as she relished the moment that she had dreamed about for so long.

Later, he lay holding her in his arms securely, as though she was dear to him. He did not turn his back on her as Thomas used to do. Flora's heart warmed with love for him.

When she woke it was morning. Morgan was already up, the fire was alight and the can of water bedded in the flames. She touched her face and tried to think clearly about what she'd done. She had practically forced Morgan to make love to her last night. Now she had to face the consequences.

'Good morning.' He smiled, and her heart lifted. He wasn't going to blame her for what happened, but then Morgan was a decent man. Last night he had been hers – and today? Well, who knew what a new morning would bring?

CHAPTER NINE

Non held her son close to her heart, kissing his downy head, while her tears ran unchecked. Two weeks had passed since Caradoc had gone missing.

She stared out at the garden, not really seeing the bright flowers and the neatly trimmed hedges. At first, when the men were out searching the riverside for him, her hopes had been high, but this morning they had returned to Broadoaks downcast, having found nothing to explain Caradoc's disappearance.

George Jones came into the room, his expression bleak. Georgina came directly after him and seated herself at his feet crying copious tears. Non didn't doubt that Caradoc's father and sister felt the loss of him deeply but they had no idea of how deep the cut went into her soul. Caradoc, her love, her life, had been snatched away from her and she didn't think she could bear it.

'There's nothing for it but to accept Caradoc is dead.' George spoke thickly, his throat constricted by tears and Non looked at him with compassion.

'There's still hope. He might have been washed downstream. He might be lying somewhere injured and unable to let us know,' Non protested.

George sighed heavily. 'Don't allow false hope to cloud your judgement,' he said. 'My men were offered a reward if they found anything – even the smallest clue as to what happened to my son. If there had been the slightest hope they would have told me.'

'Can't you send the men back again?' Non felt as if her heart was being squeezed by a heavy weight. The pain in her chest made her gasp. Was this what people meant by a broken heart? she wondered.

The baby, as though sensing her distress, began to cry. She looked into his face, saw Caradoc's image, and fresh tears burned her eyes.

'I suppose I can offer a bigger reward.' George seemed to take heart from her suggestion. 'I'll send them at once. You're right, Non, we have to keep trying.'

The baby's crying was reaching a crescendo. 'Best send Rowan to the nursery,' George said in his usual authoritative tone. 'Let the nurse soothe him.'

Non got to her feet reluctantly and Georgina, seeing her hesitation, rang the bell.

'The woman can come and fetch him,' she said. She rarely referred to the baby by name. 'That's what she's paid for, after all.'

Within a few minutes, the nurse was taking Rowan into her arms as though he belonged there. And, in truth, he seemed to be more comfortable with the nurse than with his own mother. Non bit her lip. It was no wonder – George insisted that the baby be brought up properly and that meant being with his nurse most of the time.

She stood quite still. She felt so alone in the world, so isolated from all she knew and loved. Perhaps she should go back to London, live with Ruby and Albie and work at her medicines.

She glanced at her father-in-law. He had little tolerance for what he called 'her hobby' so she'd almost given up thinking about her herbal remedies. She swallowed hard. Perhaps a new life away from Broadoaks was what she needed. Without Caradoc, the idea of living with George and his petulant daughter in this house was intolerable.

But she would wait. It was just possible that Caradoc would still come home. Another thought lit a flame of hope within her: she knew the drovers' roads well – perhaps she should follow them and find Caradoc herself. 'I think I'll go to my room,' she said, and when there was no response from either George or Georgina she left the room. Non walked with heavy tread up the broad staircase, tears of misery rolling down her cheeks.

They had decided to call him Craig, which was something like his true name, which hovered on the edges of his memory but would not be drawn into his conscious mind.

Gwenllyn came into the airy parlour and smiled at him. 'You're getting better by the day, mind.'

'Am I? Then why hasn't my memory returned?'

'All in good time, just be patient.'

He put his fingertips to his brow, as though to clear away the clouds within. He was restless – he needed exercise. Perhaps he would go out into the fresh air, walk down to the river.

'I'm going for a walk,' he said. 'Would you like to come with me, Gwenllyn?'

'*Duw*, there's kind of you, but I've got to help Nanna with the vegetables for dinner.'

She was staring at him with an expression on her face that he couldn't quite understand. 'Why are you looking at me like that? You haven't found out anything about me, have you?'

She shook her head. 'Though I did find a piece of a

leather saddle this morning, it was in the river just where it curves round the village.'

A saddle, well that was little help. Many people kept a horse or two. Yet a fleeting memory told him he used to ride, over long distances. If only he could remember something about his past.

'Don't mean nothing to you, does it?' Her voice rose and he shook his head. She seemed to breathe a sigh of relief. 'Well, try not to worry. There's plenty of time for you to get better. I doubt your leg's strong enough for walking, though. I'll take you down in the pony and trap, leave you there and call back in about an hour's time, is that all right?'

'That will be just fine, Gwen, thank you for your kindness. I just might remember something if I stare at the river for long enough.'

'Aye, I suppose so but don't go doing too much now.' She helped him to the door and he resisted the temptation to shake off her guiding hand. She only meant to be kind, and he should count his blessings that he was found by two women who had been prepared to look after him.

It was a fine day with a few wisps of cloud floating against an azure sky. He breathed deeply, trying to ignore the pain in his body as the trap bounced over the hilly terrain. As she'd promised, Gwenllyn took him to the riverbank and helped him from the cart. She seemed reluctant to leave him.

'Go home now. You've better things to do than nursemaid me,' he told her.

'All right, but I won't be long.'

He watched her drive away and walked with difficulty down the bank that sloped away from the hills to where the waters of the Wye ran swiftly away from him, leading heaven knew where.

He looked into the water. What strange quirk of fate had brought him here? He couldn't have lived close by, otherwise someone would have recognized him. So where was he from?

The pain in his leg was intense – it had been foolish of him to try to walk on it. He sat on the bank and tried to clear his mind. The breeze was warming, lifting the hair from his brow. It had grown long and was almost touching the collar of the shabby shirt he was wearing. It had been passed on from Gwenllyn's late grandfather, and he should be grateful for it: according to old Martha, he had drifted to the bank wearing little but the threads of his own clothes.

He lay back against the bank, the sun comfortably warm on his skin. Soon he slept, unaware that only half a mile away his father's men were searching for him.

'I'd like to search for Caradoc myself.' Non sat at the dining-table, her gaze fixed on the phalanx of candles that shimmered and wavered in the draught from the open door. 'I know the roads, and the moods of the rivers and I think I might be successful where others have failed.'

George straightened in his chair and glanced at his daughter before answering. 'Well, you are free to leave Broadoaks whenever you wish. I've told you before, you're not a prisoner here.'

'I will take my son with me,' she said, forcing herself to be strong.

'That you will not!' George said indignantly. 'Rowan stays where he belongs, here in Broadoaks. Even you must see it would be impossible to take a child on such a hazardous journey.'

Non had to concede that he was right. She listened patiently as he continued to protest.

'In any case, what could you give him? Nothing, except poverty and hardship. Even if you did manage to make some sort of living for yourself, how could you deprive your son of the education that I can provide for him? No, I won't have it. If you're planning to walk through the rough countryside, you can't possibly take Rowan with you.'

Non rubbed her eyes wearily. Her husband or her child – how could she choose between them? But Rowan was safe here at Broadoaks, while Caradoc might be lying sick and injured and all alone. She made up her mind and looked her father-in-law in the eye. 'Will you give me a horse and enough supplies to last me a few weeks?' she asked.

George returned her gaze steadily. 'If you leave Rowan in my care I will give you all you need. I'll send a man with you to take care of you,' he added.

Non shook her head. 'Thank you for the thought, but I want to go on my own. I'll be all right – I know the drovers' roads well enough.'

George hesitated, then nodded. 'All right. You know the risks too, but if you want to go on your own it's up to you.'

The matter was decided then. 'You take care of Rowan and I'll go and search for my husband.'

'Craig.' He spoke the name aloud, but it was meaningless. He heaved himself to his feet and stood on the bank, staring into the river, as if somehow the swiftly flowing water could offer him answers to his questions.

He heard the pony and trap. He felt helpless, Gwenllyn had come to fetch him all too soon. He was disappointed by his fruitless attempt to recover details of his past.

'What are you standing by here for?' Gwenllyn came up behind him and rested her hand on his arm. 'You don't want to catch a chill now or slip on the wet bank, do you?'

He looked down at her and smiled. 'I couldn't inflict all that on you again. Once is enough. He took her hand. 'But this idleness can't go on. I must find some work, earn my living. I can't expect you and your grandmother to support me any longer.'

Gwenllyn frowned. 'But what work could you do? You're a gentleman, mind, not used to labour.'

'There, you have me.' He smiled.

'There's nothing to do about here but farming,' she said, 'heavy work, mind, pulling up rows and rows of potatoes, and putting the horse to the plough. You got to be bred to farming.' She turned his hand and studied his nails. 'Never done much of either by the look.' She laughed. Her teeth were small and white, like those of a baby. 'Come on home. Nanna's got our dinner ready and after that you must have a rest. This walking is too much for you.'

He sighed heavily and Gwenllyn looked up at him with eyes that were liquid pools of tenderness. He realized she was growing to care for him, she was a pretty girl and he felt a great warmth towards her. He drew himself up sharply. 'Do you realize, Gwenllyn, I might be a married man with a brood of children?'

'We may never know that,' Gwenllyn said quietly. 'You look pale. Not feeling sick again, are you?'

'I'm fine, thanks to you and your grandmother.' He smiled down at her. 'I've never really thanked you, have I? But I am grateful. I would not be here now, if it wasn't for your kindness.'

Gwenllyn stood on tiptoe and kissed him. It was intended to be the chaste kiss of a friend but he turned his head towards her and their lips met. She was soft in his arms, so young and inexperienced.

'That was lovely.' She was blushing deeply. 'I've never been kissed like that before.'

'I'm sorry, I'm taking advantage of you. As I said, I could be married.'

'Well, there's no ring on your finger, see?' She picked up his hand and kissed the palm. 'I don't think you're married. You're still young and your kind don't marry until they're good and ready.'

'Why do you say that?'

'Well, you're rich, anyone can see that. Men from good families have their marriages arranged, don't they?'

'I don't know.' He pinched her cheek. 'How is it you know all this about rich men?'

'Well, I worked up at the manor house for a while, but then I fell sick and Nanna kept me at home,' Gwenllyn said. 'She still thinks of me as a child, see?'

'How do you make a living?' He was suddenly concerned.

'Well, we sell eggs and we've a few cows for milking. We do all right for ourselves, don't you worry.' She released his hand.

'But a few chickens won't bring in enough money to feed us all. I should find work.'

She spoke reluctantly. 'Nanna was left some money so we've a tidy sum put by. Don't you go worrying that you'll be a burden on us because you won't.'

'Who left her money?' He was curious.

'She had a friend, they were very close.' She glanced up at him. 'He was the old Lord of Wyeford but he died about five years ago now.'

He knew then what she was talking about; her nanna, the proud old lady who had nursed him back to health, had been a mistress in her younger days. It was difficult to imagine her as she must have been then, as beautiful as her granddaughter.

He wondered if the present Lord Wyeford had fancied a dalliance with Gwenllyn – perhaps that was the reason for her leaving her work and returning home to live with her grandmother. He could imagine the old lady being very protective of the young girl.

'So you see,' Gwenllyn pressed his arm, 'it's no hardship for us. We've got more money than we'll ever need, so no more talking about finding work. You just rest and get well.'

He looked round him at the fields and then at the beautiful girl by his side and wondered why he wasn't happy. As she said, he was probably free from matrimonial ties – but he still must have relatives, a father and mother, perhaps brothers and sisters?

She helped him up the steps into the trap and her eyes were soft as they looked into his. He was playing with fire and yet how could he stop Gwenllyn caring for him?

When they came in sight of the cottage he looked at it in a new light. It was a large building with many windows that winked and gleamed in the sunlight. There were high chimneys and the thatched roofs were well kept. Roses climbed around the door. Lord Wyeford must have been very much in love with his mistress to leave her so well cared-for.

As he ducked his head to enter the house he sniffed appreciatively. 'Your grandmother must have made us a game pie, judging by the smell coming from the kitchen.'

He looked down at Gwenllyn; her face was rosy from the sunshine and her eyes shone. It was so tempting to bend down and kiss her lips again. He moved away from her quickly. 'Why haven't you got servants, Gwenllyn?'

'We don't want servants. We manage very well on our own. In any case, the villagers don't bother much with us and we don't bother with them. Jealous, some of them are, that Nanna got this lovely house.'

He could well imagine a small village gossiping, judging. Oh yes, if Gwenllyn's grandmother had taken a well-to-do lover she would have become an outcast. He rested his hand on Gwenllyn's shoulder. 'I'll go and wash and then I'll help in the kitchen. It's the least I can do.'

'Go on with you. You'll be more hindrance than help.'

He didn't see Gwenllyn run upstairs to her room, didn't see the pouch torn from a saddle hidden in her closet, or the paperwork inside. Gwenllyn took it out and read the name Caradoc Jones before ripping the paper into tiny pieces and throwing them into the small fire burning in the grate.

CHAPTER TEN

Jessie felt the weight of the yoke on her shoulders as she walked towards the large, elegant square ahead of her. The job was proving more difficult than she had thought. She rested for a moment, bending so that the weight of the buckets rested on the cobbles. She looked round and her heart lifted as she saw that already some of the maids from the big houses were waiting on the steps with jugs in hand to take the milk.

They crowded around her, speaking all at once, clamouring to be served. They were all beautifully dressed in crisp mob caps and pristine aprons over long dark skirts.

'Morning to you,' Jessie said happily, as she proudly scooped milk into the jugs. She had milked the cows on her own this morning, leaving Fred to get on with his other work.

His wife was looking more poorly each day and it fell to him to feed the baby, a task which took up a great deal of his time. But it was worth it. The boy was flourishing, sleeping contentedly now that his belly was being filled.

'Where are you from, then?' The last maid had hung back on purpose. 'Wales by the sound of it.'

'That's right,' Jessie said. 'Are you Welsh too?'

'Aye, I am, though I've been here some years now.'

She held the jug with both hands as it was being filled. 'My mistress is related to one of the droving families, something to do with people from a bank called the Black Ox. One of the drovers has had an accident, died sudden like.'

Jessie almost spilled the milk as her hand shook. 'Not Mr Jones, is it?'

'Yes, that's right, Mr Jones.'

'But the old man doesn't ride the roads any more. It's his son Caradoc who leads the drove these days.'

'That's him, then.'

'What happened?' Jessie couldn't believe what the girl was saying.

'Seems he drowned, poor soul, and him with a wife and baby. Searched for days, the drovers did, and then the father sent other men to search but it was no use. He'd gone into the river and been dragged down – at least, that's what my mistress Miss Prudence thinks. I hear her talking about it often. Anybody would think it was something to be proud of, losing a nephew like that.'

Jessie shook her head. 'Poor Non. She must be out of her mind with grief. What a terrible thing to happen.'

'Who's that, then?'

'Manon Jenkins, as she was when she was last in London. Cured folk of the cholera. A real saint is Non – you must know about her.'

'Aye, course I do, I remember now, I heard a lot about her from the other maids. Fancy! She's married into riches – who'd have thought it?'

'But from what you say she's a widow now. Poor Non.'

There was a sharp call from a house across the road and the maid pulled a face. 'I'm being scolded for talking so long. Better get back before I'm kicked out of my job.'

Jessie watched her cross the broad square, pondering

on the awful things that happened in the world, Non a widow before she had time to get used to being married. It was tragic.

Jessie worked all the streets around the affluent area of Bloomsbury until her buckets were empty. Then she turned for home – but where was her home now? Her time was spent running between Ruby's lodging house and Fred's yard where the cows were kept.

At the thought of Fred, her heart lifted, he was a fine man, a good man, loyal and faithful to his wife. What a pity she hadn't met him when he was single.

The night was dark, the moon was sulking behind the clouds, and in the trees soft wind rustled the leaves. Non left through the back door of Broadoaks, fearing even now that George Jones would change his mind and prevent her leaving.

She clutched her bag of provisions to her side to prevent her medicine bottles from clanging together; she would need her remedies if she was to make some sort of living while she was on the drovers' roads. And if Caradoc was out there she'd find him, however long it took.

She walked for the best part of the night, wanting to put as much distance between herself and her in-laws as possible. Her legs were trembling by the time she reached the half-way point between Carmarthen and Swansea. She knew she must rest: she was scarcely over her illness and no longer used to walking great distances. The thought of walking all the way to London was daunting, yet she had made the journey before and she would do it again.

As the morning turned from blue to soft pink, she sank down on the grass and ate a little of the bread the maid had packed for her. It tasted like sawdust in her mouth. She knew she must keep up her strength. She drank a little water – she would need more before too long but when she reached the fresh springs in Swansea she would drink her fill.

She thought of her son and her arms ached to hold him. Tears filled her eyes and yet her heart told her she was doing the right thing. Rowan would be treated like a prince while she was away, and once she had found Caradoc and taken him back home, everything would be resolved.

She knew in her heart that Caradoc was alive. She could taste his kiss on her mouth, feel his body close to hers urgent with need. They couldn't be parted: they were one being.

The day was going to be warm. She packed her bag and started once more on her way to find the man she loved more than life itself.

'The little witch has gone.' There was a note of triumph in Georgina's voice, as she faced her father across the breakfast table. 'The maids went into her room and found it empty. Her bed's not been slept in. She must have crept out in the night.'

'But Rowan is safe,' her father said with satisfaction. 'At least she had the sense to leave the boy with us where he belongs.' He dabbed his eyes self-consciously. 'I know he can't replace Caradoc, no one ever could, but it's a comfort to have my grandson with me.'

Georgina felt a familiar sense of irritation with her father. It always came back to Rowan, the bastard child who had brought shame on the family. Why couldn't her father see that? Instead he drooled over the boy as though he was the most precious thing in all the world. 'We all feel the loss of Caradoc deeply, Papa. There's no need to fret about the child. For goodness' sake, sit down and enjoy your breakfast.'

'Georgina, don't take that tone with me. You are here at my behest. You made a foolish marriage and I will bear the burden of your upkeep for the rest of my life. The least you could do is try to curb that vile temper of yours.'

Georgina saw she'd gone too far. 'I'm sorry, Papa. It's just that you give the boy more attention than you ever gave me.'

'I've always given you the best of everything.' He sounded contrite and Georgina pressed home her advantage.

'Let me go to Aunt Prudence for a while. I could do some shopping, make new friends. In the eyes of the society ladies here I'm branded as a deserted woman. No one wants to know me and I'm the focus of their gossip. I know what they say: "Georgina Langland deserted by her husband." The less charitable ones say I deserve all I got. I've got to get away, Papa. Please let me go.'

He sighed heavily. 'I'll send someone to book the mail coach for you. Perhaps a few weeks away would do you good.'

Georgina smiled. 'And give you a rest from my sharp tongue, Papa?'

George held his hands up. 'Whatever you say, my dear, now leave me to my breakfast.'

Georgina spent the rest of the day sorting out her clothes for the journey to London. She wouldn't take too many dresses because she would buy new ones, the latest fashions. She'd show the women of Five Saints that she didn't care about them. Perhaps she would stay with Aunt Prudence for ever – at least it would get her away from the horrid child Non had foisted on them.

She stood for a while at her bedroom window,

looking out at the gardens, the flowers a riot of colour against green – and then she saw him. One of the gardeners was crouched beside a flower-bed, his sleeves rolled above muscular arms. He turned as if feeling her scrutiny and looked up at her. He smiled then and Georgina felt her stomach turn over. He was so handsome, so masculine, and it was such a long time since she'd been in a man's arms.

Her thoughts of new clothes vanished as she hurried downstairs and outside. Slowly now she made her way to where he was standing. He glanced her way, then held her gaze. Although she thought him rude and forward, there was a charm about him that was undeniable.

'Good day to you, Miss Jones.' He bowed his head but his proud stance didn't change. 'Fine summer weather we're having.'

'It's fine enough,' she said haughtily.

'Sorry to hear about young Mr Jones.' He bent to pull some weeds and she saw how strong his thighs were beneath the blue material of his trousers.

'We're all so sad about it,' she said. 'Caradoc was a wonderful man.'

'He was well thought of by all the staff at Broadoaks, so they tell me. I never met him – I only started here this week, Miss.'

Georgina pretended to examine the flowers. 'It looks as if you're doing a good job. What's your name?'

'Matthew Robinson, Miss, but most folks call me Matt.'

Georgina hugged the knowledge to her. She looked at his hands. He had long fingers and she watched as he picked a dead head from one of the plants.

'Do you like gardening . . . Matt?' It thrilled her just to say his name. She felt like an innocent young girl again. Her heart was beating fast and she had difficulty breathing.

'I do, Miss. I spend my time outdoors and it gives me great joy to see something I've touched grow into a beautiful bloom.' His eyes met hers and Georgina tried to read his expression. Was he flirting with her or was he merely being polite?

'Show me the greenhouses, Matt,' she said.

He led the way across the lawn, walking easily beside her, as though he was used to the company of the mistress of the house.

As they approached the secluded part of the garden where the greenhouses stood, she paused, seeing how the glass glinted like jewels in the sunshine. It felt good to walk and talk with a man again. Of course they were not equals, they could never be that, but . . . She let her improper thoughts drift away.

As Matt opened the greenhouse door, the heat hit Georgina. She drew a deep breath, moved inside and his arm brushed hers.

'Explain to me how you keep the plants so glossy and green in all this heat,' she said, though she had no interest in the plants at all. 'Is this an orchid?'

Slowly, with resonance in his voice, Matt began to talk to her about the flowers and shrubs. She took the opportunity to look closely at him. He was more hand-some than any man she'd ever met. He was tall and he bent a little towards her as he talked. He smelled sweet like the grass and Georgina had the silliest impulse to put her arms round his neck and pull his mouth down on hers.

Matt interrupted his explanations and looked at her in concern. 'Is it too hot in here for you, Miss? You look a little flushed.'

She nodded. 'It is hot. In any case I'd better go back

to the house.' She smiled up at him. Her body pulsed with energy and she felt more alive than she had done for months. It had taken her a long time to recover from her husband's unspeakable behaviour in abandoning her, and then her dear brother was taken from her as well. It was all too much.

Suddenly tears sprang to her eyes. She took a square of lace from her sleeve and dabbed at her cheeks. How she had suffered and no one seemed to care, not even her father.

'You're crying, Miss. Is it anything I've said?'

She shook her head and swayed a little towards him. 'It's just I feel fate has dealt me some hard blows.' Her sobs became audible and, after a moment, Matt touched her arm. She laid her head against the broadness of his chest and slowly, satisfyingly, she felt his arms embrace her.

She drank it in, the feel of him; his sheer masculinity was enough to overcome her inhibitions. He held her closer, his hand pressing warmly against her back. She felt triumphant, he would be easy prey. But she must not allow him liberties – at least, not yet. Reluctantly, she drew away from him. 'I'm sorry, Matt. What must you think of me?'

'I think you're a beautiful lady, with a kind heart and tender feelings. There is no need for you to be sorry – tears are natural in a woman.'

'I shall go indoors and rest now – but, Matt,' she allowed her hand to lie on his arm, 'I hope I might talk to you again some time.'

She lifted the hem of her skirts and when she made her way out of the greenhouse and across the lawns she was smiling. Her plans to visit London must be delayed. There was much to keep her here at Broadoaks.

CHAPTER ELEVEN

It was hot in the kitchen and Albie was at a loose end, watching Ruby make bread. After kneading the dough she placed it in the hearth to prove, her deft hands covering the dough with a pristine white cloth. He realized the fire needed to be roaring up the chimney but outside the day was hazy and heavy, hot enough without all the cooking. The stink from the Thames was all-pervading, and contributed to Albie's sense of gloom.

But if he could have put a finger on it he would have realized that he was missing Jess, that was the real source of his bad mood. He wondered how she was getting on at work. She seemed to love her job and Albie had the unpleasant feeling that she was more than half in love with Fred. He was a married man but who could resist Jessie if she decided to turn on the charm?

Restlessly, he walked to the open door and looked out at the rubbish-strewn street. There was scarcely any breeze and the clouds hung thinly just above the bristling chimney tops. He heard the slap of oars against the water before he saw a boat appearing through the mists. He lifted his hand in greeting to the oarsman and the oarsman called back, his voice low, blunted by the noise of the river.

'Why don't you go out and do some work?' Ruby's

voice penetrated his thoughts. 'You're like a rat trapped in a sewer.'

'I don't feel like working.' Albie knew he sounded like a petulant child, and realized that was how he felt. 'Sorry, Ruby, it's just that I'm wondering if Jess is all right, working all hours with the cow-keeper.'

'Jessie's got a good head on her shoulders,' Ruby said. She stared at him closely. 'You're falling in love with her, ain't you?'

He was about to protest, but changed his mind. He pulled up a chair and sat astride it, facing Ruby as she wiped the table clean of flour and bits of dough.

'I like Jess. I wouldn't want her to make a fool of herself over a married man.'

'She's too sensible to do that,' Ruby said reasonably. 'You're worrying over nothing.' She looked at him shrewdly. 'You want her for yourself and there's nothing wrong with that, so don't be ashamed of your feelings, right?'

Albie shook his head. 'She thinks I'm still a child to be teased and tormented. Why can't she see I'm a man now?'

Ruby touched his cheek. 'Why don't you get yourself a proper job? Jessie likes this Fred Dove because he's making an honest living. She worries about you getting caught by the law – and so do I, come to that.'

Albie blinked. 'Go straight? Me? After all this time learning my trade? You can't mean it, Ruby.'

'Oh, I mean it. Picking pockets might be all right for a boy but if you want to take a wife, you've got to grow up, make something of yourself.'

'Like that Fred Dove, you mean?'

'Why not? You've got some money in your pocket, buy yourself a few cows and be a milkman like Fred. Then Jessie might take notice of you.'

Albie nodded slowly. 'I could give it a go, I suppose – but I don't know nothin' about cows, do I?'

Ruby tapped the side of her nose. 'That's where Jessie comes into it. Tell her you need her. Tell her you'll go straight if she'll help you. Use a bit of that cunning. Remember, there's more than one way to skin a rabbit.'

Suddenly Albie felt full of hope. 'I'll start now,' he said. 'I'll get over to Smithfield, take a look at those cows and find out how much a pair would cost me.'

'Right, then, get off with you. I've got lodgers to feed and rooms to clean.' She winked at him. 'I might even be working for you some day.'

Outside, the air was heavy, and beyond the clouds the sun was struggling to shine through, casting an eerie glow over the river. Albie gazed into its depths, trying to imagine being the head of his own business. The thought pleased him, he could become someone to be reckoned with.

He thought of the money he'd lifted from the drovers' pockets. It was ironic that now he would be asking one of them for advice about the cows they brought to London.

Smithfield was crowded: there was a new drove in town and the animals were packed tightly together while butchers and farmers moved among them, prodding and poking, deciding which animal would be good for breeding and which would be best for meat.

Voices seemed loud on the stagnant air as men haggled good-naturedly – with the exception of one. Jed Lambert stood with hands on hips and chin raised, barking out his objections when one eager buyer made him an offer for a fine bull.

Albie realized he was the drover whose pocket he'd picked so successfully a few weeks earlier. Jed Lambert was a nasty man, a man Jess had travelled the roads with. She'd told Albie about the time when Jed killed a footpad, then watched the man being stripped naked, not even allowing him dignity in death.

Albie edged up behind Lambert. Perhaps he could work the market one more time? The man had his hand over his pocket. Albie guessed that was where his money was kept. He was wary, the man was on his guard. Still, it was a challenge for Albie and worth a try. With more money he could rent a piece of land, perhaps even buy a house with a reasonable yard where he could start up his business.

Excitement ran through his veins. He felt strong and indomitable, ready to lift any profit Jed had made from his trip to London. Albie bided his time as, one by one, deals were concluded. Money changed hands and Jed's pocket began to bulge. Then Albie saw his chance as Jed was struggling with a recalcitrant bull. The huge creature refused to be moved out of its pen and Lambert cursed, striking the creature several times and bringing bellows of protest from the animal.

Albie dipped into the man's pocket and his fingers fastened on the bag containing the money. It was heavy – not easy to lift without being detected. He'd have to be quick and make a sharp getaway.

As he moved the purse, Jed spun round and grasped his wrist, almost breaking bones in his anger. 'You little bastard!' His eyes bulged and spittle formed on his beard. 'Thief! I'll break your filthy little neck.'

He punched Albie hard on the side of his head and raised his fist to strike again. Albie threw the purse on to the ground and the money began to sink into the mud of the market floor. Jed took his eyes off him, and Albie seized his chance. He twisted away from the man and began to run. He heard Jed shouting orders to his men, heard the pounding of feet, and ran until his lungs were almost bursting. He knew the back-streets of London better than anyone and he would get away – he'd have to escape or else he'd be killed for sure.

The sound of hoofs behind him made his blood run cold. He glanced behind him and saw Jed Lambert astride a horse swiftly gaining on him. Albie turned a corner and darted into a doorway. Jed rode past and Albie held his breath as the sound of hoofbeats diminished.

After a few moments, he glanced around the doorway. There was no sign of anyone, except a thin grey cat scratching itself in the road. Albie slipped out into the street and ran towards home. He'd lost his dip but at least he was alive.

He passed a mean lodging-house and slowed his pace. Perhaps Ruby was right and it was time he found a decent job. He had a nice stash of money, more than enough to give him a start. Stealing for a living was harder now: his hands were big, the hands of a man, and he was not as adept as he used to be.

Suddenly an arm went around his neck from behind, pressing against his windpipe. He smelt the fetid breath of his assailant and the odour of cattle. With a sinking heart he realized Jed Lambert had him at his mercy.

'I'll kill you!' Jed ground the words into Albie's ear. 'You're the same pickpocket who stole my money a few weeks ago.' He pressed more tightly on his throat. 'If you want to live you'll give me my money back, do you understand?'

Albie made a strangled sound. He could hardly drag enough air into his lungs to breathe properly. He tried to nod. Jed spun him round. 'I want my money and I want it now.'

Albie tried to speak but his throat was swollen and

sore. He pointed in the direction of the house in Treacle Lane.

'Right, go on ahead of me and don't try any tricks.' Jed pushed Albie roughly. 'Get going, I haven't got all day.'

Albie led Jed reluctantly towards home. He had spent some of the money he'd stolen buying a good cut of meat and some other luxuries to share with Ruby and her lodgers, but most of it was there and he could only hope Jed would be satisfied to have most of his purse back.

When he entered the kitchen with Jed Lambert pushing him roughly through the door, Ruby was startled. 'What's going on?' She sniffed as she caught the smell of cattle that hung over the drover like a tangible cloud. 'And why are you bringing your filth into my clean kitchen?'

She inserted herself between Albie and the drover, and stared up at him with a fierce expression on her face.

Jed Lambert pushed her aside and glared at Albie. 'Just go and get my money.'

Albie ran upstairs to his room and slid his hand under the loose floorboard. He picked up the purse and looked at it for a long moment, wondering if he could get away with keeping just a little of the money. He weighed it in his hand and sighed. It was better not to take the chance.

He clattered down the stairs and into the kitchen, where Jed had made himself comfortable. He had cut some slices of bread and a hunk of cheese, and had no doubt forced Ruby into making tea. Albie felt anger rise in him, but he offered the purse to Jed Lambert who took it and weighed it, glaring at him. 'There's money missing. You'll have to work that off, my lad. I won't let any man do Jed Lambert down.' He stretched out his long legs and bit into his bread and cheese, chewing slowly as though he had all the time in the world.

'What work? What do you mean?'

'You'll come on the trail with me. I've a few heifers left over from the sale and I'll be selling them on the way up country. Until I get rid of them, you'll look after them.' He glared at Albie. 'And if there's any nonsense, I'll kill you without a second thought.'

'You can't take Albie on the trail,' Ruby said quickly. 'The boy isn't used to looking after cattle. Look, you got your money back and Albie's sorry for stealing it. Can't you let it go at that?'

Jed looked her over, then glanced round the kitchen. 'If there's anything I can take in exchange for the money then we could have a deal.' He was silent for a long moment and then he shook his head. 'Nothing here I want so looks like I got a new cowhand.'

As he got to his feet the kitchen door opened and Jessie came into the room. Her smile quickly turned into a look of dismay as she recognized Jed. Albie cursed silently: why couldn't she have been late home for once? He glanced uneasily at Jed, fearing he'd take his anger out on her.

'Mr Lambert, what are you doing here?' She clung to the doorhandle. 'Are you looking for a room?'

'What? And have my pocket picked again by this little piece of dirt?' He pointed angrily at Albie. 'No one takes advantage of Jed Lambert twice, my girl. Now, some of my money is missing and I want to be repaid. What can you put into the pot?'

Jessie looked at him in bewilderment. 'I don't know what you mean.'

'I want repaying, if not in hard cash then in goods to the value. You got any money, Jessie?'

'Me?' Jessie laughed. 'Where would I have money from, Mr Lambert? What little I earned on the drove is all gone. I've got to pay my way like everyone else.'

Jed grabbed Albie by the collar. 'Looks like you're coming with me, then, boy.'

Jessie took a deep breath and Albie shook his head at her. She took no notice.

'Please, Mr Lambert, leave Albie alone. I've some savings you can have, and welcome.'

'No, Jess!' Albie said quickly. 'You don't want to do that. I'll work for Mr Lambert. It's not fair you should pay for what I've done.'

Jed nodded towards Jessie. 'Get the money, girl.' He shook Albie like a rat. 'Go on – and make haste about it or it'll be worse for the boy. Get moving before I get really angry.'

Albie heard her light footsteps on the stairs and closed his eyes in anguish. All the hard work Jessie had done was going to be thrown away and his dream for the two of them to work side by side as cow-keepers was vanishing into thin air.

Jessie brought her bag and handed it to Jed. Without releasing Albie, he opened it. 'It's not enough.' He looked her over meaningfully and leered at her. 'You could pay me in kind, I suppose.'

Albie knew what he meant and, with a great effort, twisted away from Jed's stranglehold. 'Run, Jess!' he shouted and, after a hasty look at Ruby, she obeyed. Albie sighed with relief: Jessie had learned her way around London, and on the streets she would be out of Jed Lambert's clutches.

Angrily, Jed smacked Albie across the head and he reeled from the blow. Jed kicked his legs from under him and he fell heavily to the kitchen floor. Ruby stood over Albie and glared at Jed Lambert, her rolling pin in her hand. 'That's enough! The boy will be no good to anyone if you beat him half to death.'

Jed's high colour receded a little. 'Get up!' He aimed a kick at Albie's back. 'I've finished talking. You'll repay me if I have to skin you alive.'

Albie struggled to his feet and held his hand up to Ruby as she moved towards him. 'I'll be all right, I'll soon be back,' he whispered to her, and managed a smile. 'And look what I'll learn about the animals while I'm on the trail.'

Tears welled in Ruby's eyes and he would have hugged her if Jed hadn't booted him upstairs, with instructions to pack his clothes and meet him at Smithfield in an hour's time.

CHAPTER TWELVE

It was a golden day. The sun was shining, the trees and the grass were lush and verdant. Caradoc was standing outside the cottage and the beauty of the garden brought him near to tears. Perhaps he had a garden like this somewhere. If only he could remember something, his name at least, even that would be a start.

'Hello, Craig.' He heard her voice and turned to see Gwenllyn approaching. Her hair was escaping from beneath her hat and shining in the sun. She was a vision of wholesome beauty. Why didn't he feel free to fall in love with her?

'You're looking better every day.' She slipped her arm easily through his. 'You're so tanned and handsome. Why can't you be happy?'

'I've lost my past, Gwenllyn. I might be married, have children and parents.'

'Can't you be content to stay here with me?' She sounded wistful. 'I would take care of you, cook good food and sew fine clothes – I know I could make you happy if you'd give me the chance.' She wound her arms round his neck and he felt her soft breasts as she leaned towards him. His body stirred with ancient needs, yet he held back.

He loosened her arms and turned away from the hurt in her eyes. 'I don't know why but I know I'm not free to love you, Gwenllyn.' He spoke with such assurance that she glanced up at him in surprise.

'Have you remembered something?' There was a hint of fear in her voice. He shook his head.

'No, nothing at all. I'm a man without a past and without a future. How can I live off you and your grandmother? I should be supporting myself, yet what would I do?' He held out his hands. 'I'm not a manual worker, yet my hands are tanned. I must be an out-doors man – a gentleman farmer, perhaps.' He rubbed his head in frustration. 'How did I come to be in the river?'

'Don't fret, Craig. Have patience and it will all come back to you.'

He touched her shoulder. 'You're a lovely girl, Gwenllyn, but you mustn't pin your hopes on me.'

'Hush, now, let me be. I'm a grown woman and I'll make up my own mind who I shall pin my hopes on.' She smiled up at him with such affection that he was suddenly afraid for her: one day, when his memory returned, she would be hurt because he would return to his old life.

They heard Martha calling out to Gwenllyn and she turned at once. 'Something's wrong,' she said. 'I can tell by my nanna's voice.' She lifted her skirts and ran back along the grass to the cottage. He followed her into the house and saw Martha leaning against the door, her face white with pain.

'Nanna!' Gwenllyn took the old woman's arm and led her to a chair. 'Sit there, and don't move. I'll run and fetch the doctor to see you.'

Martha shook her head. 'No need of doctors. I know what the trouble is, it's my heart's grown too old, like the rest of me.'

'I'll fetch the doctor,' Caradoc said.

'No. You stay with her. It'll be quicker if I go. It would take too long to explain which direction you should take.'

He nodded. 'You're right. Go on, then, and don't worry, I'll be here.' He heard the clatter of hoofs across the yard at the back of the cottage. 'She won't be long. Is there anything I can get you?'

Martha shook her head. 'No, just sit quiet while I talk to you.' She clutched his hand and stared up at him. 'I don't know anything about your past but my instinct tells me you're a good man, good enough to look after my granddaughter for me.'

'Don't talk like that, Martha. You'll be all right once the doctor brings you some medicine.' The word medicine played tantalizingly with his mind.

'She'll have all this after I'm gone,' Martha said, 'the cottage, the land, everything. Tell me you'll take care of her. That's all I want to hear from you. Call it my dying wish.'

'You're not dying,' he said softly, but he knew she spoke the truth. 'Just keep your spirits up till the doctor gets here.'

'I'll wait to see my sweet girl again, don't you worry,' Martha said, with a return of her old spirit. 'But soon I'll go to my God. It's time, Craig, and there's nothing anyone can do to alter it. Now, promise me you'll take care of Gwenllyn.'

He knew it was useless to argue. 'I will.' He brought a cloth soaked in cold water and put it on her brow. Sweat beaded her face and it was clear she was in pain.

She lapsed into silence, her eyes closing, and yet she would live till Gwenllyn returned. Her will was indomitable and he felt a great wash of admiration for the old woman.

By the time Gwenllyn returned with the doctor

Martha's face was ashen. Gwenllyn waited while the doctor examined Martha and looked at him anxiously when at last he was done.

'Heart,' the man said. 'I've some digitalis in my bag. Fetch it for me, Gwenllyn.' When she'd gone outside the doctor shook his head. 'Nothing I can do. I'm sorry, Mr . . . ?'

'Craig, just Craig.'

'Are you a relative?' The doctor was frowning. 'I'd heard a young man was living here with the ladies but no one knows anything about you.'

Caradoc was tempted to confide in the doctor, ask for his help, but with Martha lying on her deathbed now was not the time, so he remained silent.

Gwenllyn returned and handed the bag to the doctor. 'Nanna will be all right, won't she, Dr Howells?'

Martha opened her eyes and lifted her hand to her granddaughter. 'It's time I went to my Maker. I'm old and I'm tired, and you've got Craig to look after you now.'

Gwenllyn fell on to her knees beside her grand-mother's chair. 'Don't die and leave me, Nanna, I can't bear it.'

Her grandmother touched her face gently. 'There's no easy way to leave you, my dear girl, but Craig's given me his promise he'll take care of you.'

Caradoc felt uneasy: he might not have the right to give such a promise, and yet what else could he do?

'Craig?' Martha looked up at him. 'You won't go back on your word, will you? I shall haunt you from my grave if you leave my little girl alone without protection.'

'I won't, Martha,' he said. 'You've taken care of me, nursed me back to health and I owe you my life.'

Martha sighed. 'I'm tired,' she said. 'I'll wait until

the cock crows in the morning and then I'll go. Stay with me till then, both of you.'

They sat with her through the long hours of the night, scarcely talking, afraid to move even for a moment. And then, as the hoot of the owls faded and the light of dawn crept across the sky, the cock crowed in the barn and Martha slipped away.

Georgina stood by the window, her eyes fixed on the gardener weeding the borders. She wanted him so badly, it was like a sickness inside her. And yet she knew it might be catastrophic to begin a liaison with a man from the lower orders. What if there was a child? She could hardly claim it was her husband's because he'd gone out of her life some time ago.

The door opened and Georgina whirled round. 'Good morning, Papa. It's so quiet and peaceful without that troublesome woman.'

'The girl is foolish, travelling all the way to London alone. Anything could happen to her.'

'Then why didn't you stop her, instead of encouraging her to go on the trail?'

Her father shrugged. 'I don't know. I suppose I wanted to remove her from any contact with Rowan. The boy is better off without her.'

'I do agree with you, Papa, but what if Caradoc comes home? How will we explain Non's absence?'

'I'll tell him that she left my house in the night determined to get to London to ply her trade as a herbalist.' He sank into a chair. 'But will we ever see Caradoc again? He's been gone for nearly two months. If he was still alive he would have contacted us by now.'

Georgina brushed a tear from her eye. She cared about her brother, and wanted him back safe and well.

Yet she felt Papa had given up hope of finding him.

'He might be sick – he might have been taken in by strangers and cared for – anything could have happened on the road from here to London.'

'Aye,' her father said darkly. 'Footpads and villains hide around every tree and rock. I've travelled the trail enough times to know the dangers. We have to accept that Caradoc may never come home.' He looked up at her with hope in his eyes. 'But we have Rowan, and now she's gone we have him all to ourselves.'

Georgina hid her irritation. 'Yes, we have Rowan.'

Her father detected a hint of weariness in her tone and took a deep breath. 'Look, my dear, why not make the most of the boy? Rowan might be the only child you'll ever have.'

'What do you mean, Papa?'

'Well, you're a married woman, but without a husband and with no hope of having children of your own.'

Georgina frowned. 'Come, Papa. Clive Langland might divorce me, he might be dead. Surely you can't expect me to be tied to him for life?'

'I can't see anything else for you, Georgina. You married in haste and now you have all the time in the world to regret it.'

Georgina looked closely at him. Was there a hint of satisfaction in her father's voice?

'I thought I was in love, I believed Clive to be a gentleman, and remember, Papa, it was Aunt Prudence who introduced us. She was taken in by him too.'

George waved his hand dismissively. 'Well, what's done can't be undone, so settle to it, girl.'

'I don't agree with you, Papa. I could divorce Clive.'

'I wouldn't want the scandal damaging the

reputation of our family even more. In any case, you don't know where Langland is so put that thought out of your mind.'

'I won't!' Georgina stamped her feet in anger. 'I don't mean to live like a dried-up spinster. I want a home of my own, children and a decent husband to take care of me.'

'It's no good getting into a temper, girl. You made the biggest mistake of your life because you're head-strong. Now you must learn to live with the consequences.'

Georgina subsided into a chair. He was right. And, anyway, even if she could find Clive he might not grant her a divorce. Well, she would not go too long without a pair of strong arms around her. She thought of Matt the gardener. He had taken to her, she knew it, and one day she would submit herself to his desires and her father could go to the devil.

Gwenllyn stood at the graveside by the old village church and watched her beloved Nanna being lowered into her last resting place. She moved a little closer to Caradoc and he took her hand. She was glad he was there to give her support in her hour of pain.

She felt too numb to cry, her hurt went too deep for tears to be a relief. She looked up at him. 'You will stay with me and look after me, as Nanna wanted?'

She saw fleeting expressions cross his face and she knew he was fighting an inner battle. 'Please.'

'I'll stay for now, Gwenllyn,' he said slowly, 'but we must both remember I may have responsibilities else-where.' He caressed her cheek. 'I'll stay until my memory returns, until I know my own name.'

She swallowed the lump in her throat, and recalled the shred of paper from his saddlebag. She remembered the name written there, Caradoc Jones. She realized it might unlock his memories and lead him back to a life that didn't involve her.

At last the fresh earth was placed over the grave and Gwenllyn sighed. 'Goodbye, Nanna. You know I'll always love you.'

She allowed Caradoc to lead her away, through the cemetery gates and out of the shade of the trees into the sunshine. Gwenllyn hated the sun that day: there should be rain and thunder storms – the heavens should grieve with her.

In the cottage, she changed out of her best clothes and hung them carefully in the cupboard. There was no need to be frugal: Nanna had left her ample money, enough to last for the rest of her life, but old habits were difficult to shake. Now she must feed the hens and collect the eggs, and the cow needed to be milked. That used to be Nanna's job.

When she returned to the kitchen he was there, pouring tea for them both. Her heart lightened: he'd promised to stay with her and she felt he was a man who would honour his word.

'Sit down, Gwenllyn.' He spoke gently as though she was ill. 'You look worn out.'

'I have to work,' she said. 'The livestock have to be fed and—' She stopped as he held up his hand.

'I can do that, I'm used to animals.'

How did he know that? Was his memory coming back?

'I'd rather have something to do,' she said quickly. 'When I've drunk my tea, I'll feed the chickens. Perhaps you will milk the cow for me.'

As soon as she'd spoken the words she wanted to take them back. If he remembered he was good with animals perhaps tending the beasts, being close to them, would bring back his past like a flood tide.

'No,' she said. 'I've changed my mind. You see to the chickens and I'll milk old Sally.'

'Don't worry, I'll see to everything, you just rest.' He smiled. 'I want to be helpful, Gwenllyn. Please let me.'

'Thank you.' She wanted to call him her darling, her *cariad*, but he wasn't hers – not really. There might be a woman somewhere, crying for him, a child perhaps. She put the thought out of her head. All she knew was that she loved him and wanted him near her. Always.

CHAPTER THIRTEEN

Albie stood at the door and looked out at the dingy fog hanging over the houses. The mist and stink from the river was even worse than usual but, to him, London had never looked so beautiful.

Jessie came up to him and slid her arm round his waist. 'Don't worry, Albie. Once Jed Lambert's got his money's worth out of you, he'll let you go.'

'I can't bear it, Jess.' Albie heard his voice crack with emotion. 'I don't want to leave London or you. My life is here in Treacle Lane. I don't want to be in the countryside, looking after a few cows.'

Jessie leaned against his shoulder. 'I don't think you've got much choice, Albie. Just don't you go putting your foot in it with Jed Lambert: keep your mouth shut and do your work.'

Albie frowned. 'But my work is picking folk's pockets. I don't know nothing else.'

'Time you learnt, then, isn't it?' She smiled at him, and his heart missed a beat. 'Learn all you can about cows, Albie, because I've decided that one day we're going to have a business of our own. We'll be well off like Fred Dove and his wife.'

'Are you saying you'll wait for me, Jess?'

She hesitated and he saw a strange look come into her eyes. 'I don't know what I'm saying, Albie, except that we'll work together and make ourselves rich.'

'I'd better be grateful for that.' He hugged Jessie to him, closing his eyes as he breathed her fresh womanly scent. He released her abruptly. 'Ruby, I'm going,' he called.

Ruby came to the door, wiping her hands on her apron. 'You'll be back soon.' She kissed him soundly on both cheeks. 'Now you look after yourself or you'll have me to answer to.' She brushed away a tear and Albie felt a lump rise in his own throat. How could he be leaving all he loved and cared about?

'Go on.' Jessie gave him a push. 'Sooner you go, the sooner you'll be back. In any case it don't do to keep a man like Jed Lambert waiting.'

Albie slung his bag over his shoulder and stepped out into the street. The buildings seemed to lean towards him, the narrow courts were old friends – how would he bear the open road with the sky huge above him? He walked quickly, without looking back. He'd been caught thieving and now he had to pay for it. That was the greatest sin of all, getting caught, and he was ashamed. He strode along the familiar streets and into the huge arena of the market. He saw Jed at once and, as though sensing his presence, the man looked up at him.

''Bout time you put in an appearance, my lad. I wasn't going to wait much longer, I was coming to fetch you by the scruff of your neck,' he said. 'Come on, let's get started or we'll never get these beasts home.'

Albie began to walk, afraid to look around him, worried that he might cry and shame himself. The cows seemed docile enough, plodding on before him, but Albie was not used to animals and he kept well back from them, wondering at their size and the tracks the cloven hoofs made on the dusty track.

Jed was riding ahead; seated on his horse he was safe. Well out of range of the animals, should they turn nasty. He glanced back at Albie and a sly smile crossed his face. 'Scared of the cows, are you?' he called. 'Just wait till we get home! I'll be picking up about seven hundred animals and you'll be helping me bring them back to Smithfield.'

Albie shuddered. 'How long will that take us?'

'Well, we'll drop these unsold heifers at one of the farms on the way in exchange for a few pounds and a night's board, and then we'll have to walk the rest of the way to Wales, past Swansea to Carmarthen. I wouldn't count on being back in London for a month or so if I was you.'

Albie's heart sank. A whole month without Jessie – a whole month under the command of Jed Lambert: how would he survive?

'Don't look so downhearted, lad. There's a lot of fun to be had on the road. The wenches like to be in the company of any passing drovers because we tell them what's going on in the big towns. They don't know that most of the time we walk along narrow tracks with nothing to look at but the backsides of the animals we're selling.' He paused. 'Do you the world of good, this drove will. Soon your legs will be strong, and you'll have some colour in your pasty face. It'll make a man of you. But if you cross me, you'll feel the sting of my whip on your back. So don't pull any clever strokes, right?'

'I'll pay my dues,' Albie said. 'I won't let you down.'

Jed's gaze hardened. 'If you try to run I'll kill you, understand?'

He meant it and Albie nodded.

Soon the site of Barnet Fair came into view, but now it was silent, the fields empty of barkers and fairground folk. Albie remembered it was there that he had met Non Jenkins. He'd bought a ribbon for her – she was such a pretty girl. Since then so much had happened to her.

'Do you think we might find Mr Jones?' he asked Jed.

'Shouldn't think so, and I have no pity for him. Rich man's son, lording it over the rest of us drovers. Anyway, I don't want to find him – I've more than enough competition on the droves as it is.'

One of the cows bellowed and Albie started in alarm. Jed saw him and laughed out loud. 'Afraid of a docile cow? God help you when you see a whole herd, some of them bulls with sharp horns.'

'What's wrong with it? Does it need milking?' Albie brightened. If Jed could show him how to milk a cow he'd be well prepared for owning his own milking business.

'You poor ignorant fool. Heifers haven't been mated or dropped a calf. You'll get no milk from these beasts but you could try.' He slapped his thigh in delight. 'Wait until I tell the farmers about you. Lord above, I didn't know townsfolk were so ignorant.'

Albie felt foolish. 'Well, I don't suppose you know how to dip into a man's pocket and set yourself up for months on the proceedings.'

'Oh, got some spirit, after all, have you?'

Albie saw a mean look come into Jed's eyes. 'I meant I could teach you how to dip and you could teach me about cows.'

Jed leaned back in his saddle. 'You can't be that good because I caught you the second time, didn't I?' he sneered. 'You got a lesson coming, my boy. On the trail with me you'll learn to be tough, to handle yourself so that no man will put the screws on you.'

Albie was aggrieved now. Jed was judging him too harshly. He was a good pickpocket – well, he had been. 'The odds was against me when I tried to lift your purse,' he said. 'It was bleedin' heavy, and you moved at the wrong time. Otherwise I'd have got clean away with it. But forget that for now. I'm willing to learn all about the cows and the milking, if you want to show me.'

'Well, I'll think about it, though you're never likely to put the knowledge to any use,' Jed said lazily. 'And now get those cows moving. I want to be at Maysfield inn before nightfall, get a couple of beers down my gullet and perhaps find a wench who's willing.'

Albie fell silent. The prospect of staying at an inn instead of sleeping under the vast open sky pleased him. Perhaps the trip wasn't going to be too bad after all.

'I didn't realize how much I'd miss him.' Jessie sat in the chair in Ruby's kitchen and kicked off her shoes. 'Poor Albie. I expect he's finding it hard walking the drovers' road. I can tell you, it's not easy.'

For once Ruby was sitting down. The cooking was done, the lodgers fed, and now she was able to rest for a while.

'Jed's a bad man.' Jessie tried to smooth the creases in her skirt without much effect. 'I wouldn't trust him.'

'Albie's young but he's not dull-witted,' Ruby said. 'He'll work off his debt and then he'll be back.'

'What if he likes the drover's life?' Jessie felt her heart miss a beat at the thought. 'Perhaps he'll never come back to us.'

Ruby looked at her shrewdly. 'So you're really missing him? Perhaps now you'll stop giving me earache about Fred Dove.'

'Oh, I don't go on that much about Fred . . . do I?'

'All the time. And, talking about time, hadn't you better get off to work now?'

Jessie glanced at the clock on the mantelpiece. 'I suppose so, but I don't like leaving you alone without Albie to help you.'

'Stuff and nonsense! I've got me lodgers in the house. I've got too much company, if you ask me.'

'All right, then. I'll be off.' Jessie fetched her shawl from the hook at the back door and stood for a moment looking into the fire, thinking about Albie. Still, it did no good to worry about things she couldn't change.

'I'll see you later tonight,' she said. 'I expect I'll have to feed the baby for Fred – he's still not good at handling the jug right, he lets the milk dribble down the baby's chin.'

'When I go to the market I'll get the baby a proper feeding bottle with a rubber teat so he can suck from it easily,' Ruby said.

Jessie looked at her in astonishment. 'Do they make bottles for babies, then? Well, I never knew that. There's me trying to give the poor little mite a drink from a jug. Why didn't you tell me before?'

'Well, I didn't know about the jug till just now. Where's your common sense, Jessie?'

'I've never been around a baby before, so how was I to know anything about feeding one? All I've ever seen is cows giving milk to their calves, the natural way. I'd better go, and don't forget about the bottle, will you?'

Ruby waved her hand. 'Just go about your business, my girl.'

Once out in the street, Jessie hurried along. She was late and Fred would be waiting for her. The thought made her heart race. So many times when they'd been close, seeing to the baby or doing the milking, she'd longed to kiss his warm, generous lips. But Fred was a married man. He would never do anything to betray his wife.

Fred smiled when he saw her and his eyes were bright as they rested on her face. She was flushed from hurrying and he laughed as she shrugged off her shawl and collapsed into a chair. 'I've got to rest a minute,' she said breathlessly. 'I'm sorry I was late but I had to see Albie off.'

'Sure it don't matter. I'm just glad you're here now. The baby has done nothing but cry. I don't know what's wrong with him.'

'Leave him to me, you do the milking,' she said, resisting the urge to press her fingers against his brow and ease out the worry lines. 'By the way, Ruby is going to get us a proper feeding bottle and we should manage better then. Perhaps Mrs Dove could feed him herself.'

'Aye, perhaps so.' Fred rubbed his eyes wearily. 'Right, I won't be long. Put the kettle on for a cup of tea, and will you take one upstairs to Mrs Dove?'

Jessie watched Fred walk into the yard, a pail swinging from his hand. She felt a great tenderness rise up inside her. He was so patient, so good, that all she wanted to do was wrap him in her arms and comfort him.

Later, she sat in the kitchen and waited for him to return, her head against the smooth wooden back of the chair. She closed her eyes, and in her mind's eye she could see Albie, shoulders tense with the pain of leaving London and all it meant to him. He would find life on the road different. How would he manage to walk all the way to Carmarthen?

She was worried about him because she was very fond of him, she loved him like a brother. He was only a boy and she needed a man, like Fred Dove.

Even as she thought about him, the door opened and Fred came in. He looked so worn that Jessie rose instinctively and put her arm round his shoulders. 'Come and sit down,' she said. 'You look all in.'

Suddenly he turned and pressed his mouth gently to hers. She drew away in surprise. 'Fred!'

'I'm sorry, I didn't mean to do that.' He sank into a chair and covered his eyes with his big hands. 'I need affection, Jessie. My life seems to be all work and worry with no pleasure.'

'I'll make some fresh tea.' Jessie busied herself with cups and saucers and tried to sort out her feelings. She had been surprised when Fred kissed her but nothing more, no warm flurry of excitement. She was almost disappointed, but relieved too.

She gave him the tea and sat opposite him, her skirts neatly covering her ankles.

'I've something to tell you, Jessie.' He didn't look at her. 'I've fallen in love with you.'

'No!' she said sharply. 'You're a married man with a good, honest wife, Fred. You can't fall in love with me.'

'It's too late.'

She swallowed nervously. 'But, Fred, you're sad and lonely because your wife is sick. Once she's better you'll see that nothing has changed between you.'

'Things have already changed, Jessie. My wife has decided to go home to Ireland. She'll take the baby, of course, and I must decide if I want to go too.'

'Leave the business, you mean?'

He half smiled. 'There'll be enough in Ireland to keep me in work, I dare say.'

'But what about me?' Jessie knew she was being self-ish but she couldn't imagine her life without the milk round, without Fred and his family to care for.

'Well,' he hesitated, 'if you felt you could return my

feelings even a little bit I could stay here and run the business with you as before.'

Faced with the decision, Jessie knew that life with Fred was not what she wanted. 'I couldn't do that, Fred. I'm sorry.'

'Well, thank you for being honest.' He hesitated. 'Look, why don't you keep up the milk round on your own?'

'Could I manage it?' Jessie asked. 'And what about the house? Then there's the cows – how would I pay you for them?'

'You wouldn't have my family and me to worry about so it would only be seeing to the beasts and taking the milk around. It wouldn't be easy but you could do it, Jessie. You're young and strong enough.'

'And the cost?'

'Well, I own the house. I'd let it to you cheap, and as for the cows, I'd wait until you were making a fair living before I asked you for any money.'

It was a tempting proposition. Could she really manage the milk round alone? She stood up and walked slowly to the door.

'How long do I have to make up my mind?'

'The end of the month, Jessie.' He came to stand beside her and slipped his arm round her waist. 'Are you sure you couldn't love me even a little?'

'Fred, you have a wife and that's an end to it.'

'All right. Even if you don't take on the business, you'll at least help me until I go to Ireland?'

Jessie looked into his honest eyes and then at his mouth. She felt nothing but pity for him. Her 'romance' with Fred had been nothing but a foolish dream. She drew her shawl round her shoulders and opened the door. 'Of course I'll stay and help you, but I will be sorry to see you go.' She stepped out into the road with tears in her eyes. 'Goodbye, Fred. I'll see you in the morning.' She walked away feeling empty and hopeless, as if her secure little world had been torn into a million pieces.

CHAPTER FOURTEEN

Non was running out of water. The last clear stream she'd stopped at was at least five miles back. She stared at the narrow track between the trees. She felt lost and alone. She wasn't sure she was keeping to the right road – she didn't remember coming this way when she'd travelled with Caradoc. So far there had been no news of him. At every inn, she'd come across someone who remembered the drove going so far as the Wye, and then the trail was lost. Was he really dead, drowned in the wide river? It was getting more difficult to keep alive her hope that she would find him.

At the last stopping-place, Non had bought a horse. The animal was old and slow but good-natured and easy to manage. George Jones's promise of a good animal for her to ride the trail had come to nothing. She'd soon realized he never had any intention of helping her.

She'd left the house with only the few pounds George had given her when she first arrived at Broadoaks, when his mood had been more generous.

She urged her horse towards the brow of the hill and sighed with relief. Below her, in the far distance, she could see the gleam of the river, a silver ribbon against the rugged landscape. Before her the road split into two, with one fork winding uphill and the other down towards the valley. In the distance, she heard the tinkling of water over rocks and she guided her horse towards the sound.

The stream was fast and clean. Thankfully, Non filled her bottle. She missed her son badly, and she was so very tired. Had she been foolish to attempt the journey to London alone?

The Wye was further away than she'd thought and by the time she reached the broad river, Non and her horse were exhausted. There were a few cottages in sight, spread haphazardly along the bank as if they had been thrown down by a giant hand. It was getting dark, and some candles were lit inside the houses. Non wondered if anyone would put her up for the night.

A girl was walking briskly down the hill with a bag over her arm and Non slipped off her horse. 'Excuse me,' she called, and the girl looked at her. She was pretty, with lovely hair and eyes. But there was a guarded look on her face.

'I'm sorry if I startled you. I'm Non Jones, and I'm trying to find out what's happened to my husband. He came on the drovers' roads this far but then he disappeared.'

The girl shook her head. 'Your husband?' She emphasized the word as though it had special meaning for her.

'Yes. Caradoc Jones, cattle drover. He was riding to London with the herd when he was swept into the river. No one knows what happened to him then.'

'I'm sorry but I keep myself to myself. I don't listen to idle gossip.'

Non was taken aback at the sharpness of the girl's tone. 'I was wondering if there's anywhere I could stay for the night. I need a fresh horse too.'

'Why don't you cross the ford? There's an inn about a mile further on – you'll find a bed there for the night with no trouble.'

'Thank you.' Non felt as though she couldn't go another mile without a rest. In any case, there was something puzzling about the girl's manner. 'Could you offer me a bite to eat?'

'I'm sorry but no, I live a good few miles from here. I've only come down to fetch some things from the village shop.'

'There's a shop? Perhaps they'll know something about my husband.'

'I don't think so. The villagers don't like strangers poking their noses in where they're not wanted.'

Non swallowed hard. 'I don't want to poke my nose into anyone's business except my own. My husband seems to have vanished. Is there anyone around here who could have taken him in?'

'The Wye is long and broad. If your husband fell into it, what makes you think we'd know anything about him on this side of the river?'

'You're right, of course. Caradoc might have been swept ashore on the other bank. I didn't think of that.'

'I must go now. I don't know about anyone being found in the river so it's pointless asking me about him.'

Non felt baffled by the girl. She had turned her back on Non, and she simply wasn't interested in Non's problems.

She led her horse towards one of the cottages and knocked on the door. After what seemed a long time an elderly man opened it. 'I'm sorry to disturb you,' Non said, 'but do you know anything about the cattle drover who was lost in the river?'

The old man shook his head. 'Drowned, wasn't he? River runs strong around here and the day the poor man vanished it was raining so hard you couldn't see your hand in front of your face.'

A large woman appeared behind him. 'Come in, you old fool.' She stared suspiciously at Non. 'A woman travelling on her own? That's not a sight we see often round here.'

'I'm just trying to find out what happened to my husband.' Non was growing desperate. 'I feel sure he didn't drown – I just can't believe it.'

'Well, I wouldn't listen to anything this old fool tells you. He's not right in the head.' She dragged the man away from the door.

Wearily, Non mounted her horse. She would take the young girl's advice and go to the inn on the other side of the ford. The water was low now so she'd be able to cross without difficulty.

As she guided the tired horse into the river, its hoofs slipped against the rocks and she saw how easy it would be to fall in and drown. She held the reins more tightly and steadied the animal with soothing words. She would have to exchange mounts at the inn if she could or it would mean a delay for several days before the animal was rested enough to go on.

Once she reached the other side of the river she looked back. The cottage windows glowed in the growing darkness and Non felt alone and friendless. She leaned into the horse's neck for comfort. Then she took a deep breath. She needed to go on just one more mile that night. After a good night's rest, she would begin her search again.

Gwenllyn sighed with relief as she watched the woman ride away into the evening. She felt sick at the narrow escape she'd had. If the man she called Craig had come to the shop with her everything would have been lost. It was a nasty shock to learn that he had a wife, and one who was searching for him, but he didn't

104

remember anything about his past life. He was safe and well with her to look after him. What had happened to him before he was pulled out of the river, half drowned, wasn't important. He was with her now and she would make sure she never let him go.

CHAPTER FIFTEEN

Morgan looked at Flora, searching for words that would help her understand his feelings. He hadn't touched her since the night they'd made love after delivering the calf together. 'Flora, I've something to say to you.'

She glanced up at him. It was almost as though she knew what he had on his mind.

'I shouldn't have taken advantage of you that night, Flora. I can't tell you how sorry I am. Can we forget it?'

'Morgan, I'm a grown woman and you didn't take advantage of me. All that happened was my fault, and I'm not going to tie you down. Don't you go thinking of me like that.'

'I should have shown more self-control,' he said heavily.

'We have to work together, Morgan, so let's put it out of our minds.'

She was right, and Morgan knew it. He rested his hand on her shoulder. 'I'm sorry, Flora, it won't happen again.'

Flora smiled. 'Don't say that! We never know what tomorrow will bring, do we? Now, come on, we've fallen behind the herd. Let's get on or we'll never catch up with the drove – they'll be in London before us.'

He mounted his animal and gestured for her to climb

up behind him. 'I can't expect you to catch up with them if you walk.'

Morgan wished with all his heart that he could fall in love with her. Flora had learned some hard lessons in life but now she was calm and beautiful, in the full flush of womanhood. But Non was in his heart, in his blood. He could love no other woman, and Flora knew that as well as he did.

She clung to him. 'As far as the rest of the drove knows, nothing happened between us. We're the good friends we always were.'

'All right,' he said, but his heart was heavy with guilt.

Non slowed her new horse, which she had found at the last inn. He was fresh and eager to gallop. She reined him in and patted his neck. 'There, boy, take it slow.' She was becoming disheartened – perhaps she was fooling herself that Caradoc was still alive. And yet, inside her there was a thread of hope that somehow, somewhere she would find him.

She heard them before she reached the rise in the road: the bellow of cattle, dogs barking, the cries of the drovers and the occasional trumpeting of the horn. The sounds were so familiar to her that tears came to her eyes. It was on the drove that she had fallen in love with her darling Caradoc.

As she drew nearer the herd, she saw the dust rising on the dry road, smelt the cattle and moved her horse forward carefully, threading her way through to the head of the drove.

'Morgan!' He was sitting high in the saddle, his whip in his hand, ready to control the animals if they became unruly. 'Why are you leading the drove? I thought you were at home in Wales.'

'Non.' His face lit up, then the smile disappeared.

'Mr Jones made me lead drover. What are you doing, riding the trail alone?'

'Need you ask?' she said, fear drying her throat. 'Have you seen or heard of him?'

'No, Manon, I'm sorry. There's been no news at all. I've been up and down this trail for weeks and if there was anything to find out I would have known about it.'

Her shoulders sagged as hope drained away. She'd stopped at farms, at inns, and Caradoc hadn't been seen at any of them. He seemed to have disappeared from the face of the earth. Perhaps she was crazy to ride through the country alone, a mad woman who wouldn't accept the truth.

'Anyway,' Morgan's voice broke into her thoughts, 'ride along with us now and, once we get to London and I've dealt with the sale of the cattle, I'll see you safely home.'

'No, thank you.' Non guided her horse away from the herd. 'I'm going to search along the riverbank again. I feel in my heart that Caradoc would have stayed near the water. Someone has taken him in, that's what's happened, and he's been too sick to send me a message.'

'Don't pin your hopes on that, Manon,' Morgan said gently. 'The Wye is cruel when it rains and I did try to warn Caradoc about the danger of going into the ford before the weather improved. I was there when he fell – I saw the river take him and toss him like a rag doll. He didn't stand a chance, not with his horse trampling him.'

Non put her hands to her ears. 'Don't say any more, Morgan. I *know* he's alive.'

'I'm sorry.' Morgan shook his head. 'I'm only trying to warn you how slim the chances are that you'll find him. Please come with us to London. I can help you search on the way.'

Non caught up her reins. 'No, I have to search here first, then I'll follow the road to London. You have a job to do, and I'll let you get on with it.' She rode away, driving her horse hard as if speed could eradicate Morgan's words. Caradoc couldn't be dead, he couldn't be gone from her life for all time.

She stopped at the Farmer's Arms because her horse needed to be fed, but tomorrow, at first light, she would retrace her steps on the journey back to the ford. She felt with her whole being that the key to Caradoc's mysterious disappearance would be found there.

The landlord recognized her when he saw her standing in the doorway of his taproom. 'Good evening, Manon Jenkins. I remember you from when you came up with the Jones drove. Cured my boy of his sickness, you did. He was crying something pitiful and me and the wife were grateful, I can tell you.' He looked at her more closely. 'Didn't I hear that you saved folk from the cholera when you was in London?'

'I tried to help,' Non said quietly. 'I'm Mrs Jones now, and I'm searching for my husband. He failed to return from one of the droves. You must know him – Caradoc Jones, son of George Jones, owner of the Bank of the Black Ox.'

'Look,' the landlord took her arm, 'come and sit down. The boy will stable your horse.' He led her to a corner seat and beckoned to the woman serving the beer. 'Bring some brandy. This lady could do with it.' He sat beside her. 'Well known round these parts are the Joneses, I met young Mr Jones on several occasions.' He lowered his voice. 'I heard about the accident and I'm so sorry.' He took the glass the barmaid handed him and put it on the table. 'You shouldn't be riding the trail alone, a lady like yourself.'

'I have to look for my husband.' Non leaned back in

her seat. 'I know folk think he was drowned but I don't believe it.'

'Well, all I know is that Caradoc Jones was taken by the river. No one's seen hide nor hair of him since the accident.'

Non bent her head so the landlord wouldn't see her tears.

'Mind,' the landlord went on, 'I did hear there was a stranger living up in the hills a mile or two away from the river. Staying with old Martha's granddaughter. No doubt he's a relative come to help Gwenllyn after the old lady died.'

Non looked up quickly. 'Where is he staying?'

'Don't know the exact place – never been to the cottage myself – but perhaps one of the folk from the village could help.'

'I tried to talk to a pretty young girl there but she just hurried off up the hill leading away from the village.'

'That must have been young Gwenllyn. It seems that when Martha was young . . . Well, it don't do to speak ill of the dead, but there was an awful lot of talk about her flighty ways. No one round the village bothers much with Gwenllyn and she don't bother with them. She keeps herself to herself, though it must be lonely for her living in that big cottage on her own.'

'Perhaps I should talk to her again.' Non forced a smile. 'If you've a room I'll stay for the night and then I can find her in the morning.'

'Course we have a room. You're most welcome to stay here as long as you like, Mrs Jones.'

Later, as Non lay on the bed in the clean warm room, she stared at the moon through the window, wondering if her husband was lying injured somewhere nearby, waiting for her to come to his rescue. The thought brought fresh tears to her eyes. 'Oh, Caradoc, my love, please be safe. I need you so much.' She turned her face into the pillow stifling her sobs. She knew she would sleep little that night.

In the morning Non took her horse and went the short distance to the village. The cottages were small with tiny windows in thick walls, and all the doors were closed, as if to repel visitors. She knocked at the door of the nearest one and a thin, bird-like woman opened it to her. 'What do you want? Selling things, are you?'

'No. I would just like to know what direction I must take to the house where old Martha used to live.'

'Oh, her! She's dead and in her grave – the best place for her.'

'I need to talk to her granddaughter Gwenllyn.'

The woman sniffed. 'Just follow the track uphill. It's a place on its own among the trees, you can't miss it.' She closed the door with a bang, and Non stepped back, a little surprised by the hostile attitude of the villager.

She rode up the track for about two miles and then, turning a bend in the road, she came upon an imposing cottage with high chimneys and windows that shone like diamonds. From behind it she heard the muted sound of wood being chopped but she scarcely noticed it, she was so anxious to talk to Gwenllyn again.

The girl answered the door. 'Not you again,' she said, with an edge to her voice. 'I've told you once, I haven't seen any strangers in the village.'

'I'm sorry, I didn't mean to bother you, but the land-lord of the inn told me a young man had been seen around here.'

'Well, the only young man who's been round here is

my cousin.' Gwenllyn tugged her apron into place. 'He helps out sometimes.'

'I'm sorry,' Non said again. 'I shouldn't have come, but I can't believe my husband is dead and I had a glimmer of hope that you might have taken him in.'

'Look,' Gwenllyn said, 'I'm a young woman on my own. I've just lost my grandmother and I don't want to be pestered by you or anyone else. Is that clear?' She closed the door.

Non rode her horse down to the river with a heavy heart. She sat on the bank, her eyes blurred with tears.

Eventually she returned to the inn, tired and dispirited. It appeared her instincts were wrong: no one had news of a man saved from the river. She would continue on her way to London, and when she arrived she would go to Ruby and Albie. They would understand how she felt. As she left the village, she turned for one last look at the cottages, but there was no one in sight and all the doors were closed against her.

Gwenllyn sank on to a chair in the kitchen and watched through the open back door as Caradoc chopped wood for the fire. His health was improving, his face tanned by the sun. He met her gaze and smiled.

'Want a cup of tea?' she called, fanning her face with her hands.

'I'd rather have a glass of cold lemon water.' He straightened to ease his back. 'It's hotter out here than in your kitchen.'

He came in and sat at the table, pushing his sleeves above his elbows. His arms were strong and powerful and Gwenllyn imagined them holding her close.

'Did I hear someone at the door just now?' He leaned forward and he smelled sweetly of wood shavings.

'Oh, just one of the gypsy women from the camp over the fields. She was selling pegs.'

'I didn't know there was a gypsy camp near here.' He smiled but there was a shadow in his eyes. 'Perhaps I could get one of them to tell my fortune. Then I might learn who I am and where I came from.'

'Oh, you can't do that. They're moving on later today,' Gwenllyn improvised quickly. 'She told me I wouldn't have the chance to buy pegs for some time.'

'Anyway,' he said, 'what are you cooking? It smells good.'

'A piece of ham. We'll have parsley sauce with it and some boiled potatoes.' She was unable to resist touching his hand. 'I'm not the cook that Nanna was but I get by.'

'You get by very well.' He caught her fingers. 'I've been thinking, Gwenllyn,' he said. 'Perhaps I should move on. Now that you've lost your grandmother it isn't proper that we should live in the cottage, just the two of us.'

'Why ever not?' Gwenllyn's heart began to race. 'If you're worried about folk gossiping, then don't – they've talked about me and Nanna for as long as I can remember.'

'It's your reputation I'm worried about. I wouldn't like people to get the wrong impression.'

'You can't leave.' She was panicking now. 'You promised Nanna on her deathbed that you'd look after me.'

'I know I did, and I will look after you. I'll get work somewhere and stay at the inn. I can't go on living here at your expense.'

'Look, Craig,' she touched his cheek, 'why don't we get married?' She held up her hand as he made to protest. 'You can't have a wife already, can you? She'd have found you by now – you know that.'

He sighed. 'You're probably right, Gwenllyn, and I'd be honoured to have you as my wife, believe me, but . . .'

She touched his lips with the tip of a finger. 'Why don't we give it a little more time, wait and see what happens over the next few weeks? If no-one has come for you we'll talk about marriage then.'

He took her hand and pressed his lips to her palm. She felt a thrill run through her and, to her delight, he nodded. 'I expect you're right. No-one has come looking for me, have they?'

He released her hand and sat back in his chair. 'You are the most beautiful girl I've ever met and I'd be honoured to have you as my wife but, as you say, we'll give it a little time.'

Gwenllyn got up. 'I must see to the ham otherwise it will be spoiled. You won't think me much of a wife then.' She leaned over the fire, a smile curving her lips. One day, and soon, he would be hers. They would raise a family together and he would stop worrying about his past.

She glanced at him as he sat at the table and her heart melted with love. Then, in her mind's eye, she saw the pale face of his wife as she asked for him – but Gwenllyn couldn't be sorry for her: the woman was rich, you could tell that by the way she dressed. She would never want for anything and, one day, she would forget Caradoc and marry some other man.

She lifted the pot from the fire and stood it on the hob. 'Not long now.'

He got up and stood behind her. She felt his breath on the back of her neck. 'Something smells good,' he said, 'and I don't mean the ham.'

Gwenllyn blushed. She was winning him over at last. She felt happiness rise inside her and she started singing as she prepared the meal for the man she loved. It was almost as good as being married to him.

CHAPTER SIXTEEN

Jessie watched Fred as he washed out the milking pails. Soon he would be on his way to Ireland. He put the last one to drain and rubbed his hands dry on his apron.

'Are you sure, Jessie?'

She didn't pretend to misunderstand him. 'I'm sure, my lovely. If only I'd met you years ago it would be different but now . . . well, the best way to look at it is there's nothing to be done.' She gave him a mischievous smile, determined to lighten the mood between them. 'You've made your bed and there's nothing to do but lie on it.'

He returned her smile but there was a look of longing in his eyes. 'I don't want to go, Jessie. I want to stay here with you. You're so strong, so sweet and funny – our life together would be full of love and laughter.'

'Fred, your place is with your family. You'll soon forget me when you have your new life in Ireland.'

'I doubt it—' Fred broke off when his wife came into the yard, her face alight. She looked better than she had for weeks.

'I've had a letter from Cousin Patrick. He's got the house ready for us to rent and he's even bought us some furniture. I'm so excited, Fred. We'll all get on well in Ireland, so we will, the boy, you and me. Everything will sort itself out, you'll see.'

She smiled, and Jessie flushed. Did Fred's wife have an inkling of what her husband was feeling?

'Sure everything is turning out for the best. And, Jessie, I've you to thank for the way my son has grown strong and well. If you hadn't told me to feed him cow's milk the little lad would be with the angels now.'

Jessie returned her smile. 'They tell me Ireland is a lovely place with fresh air, sweet streams and mountains. Like my own home in Wales.'

'You going back there, then, Jessie?'

'I'm settled in London now. All my friends are here, and Ruby and Albie are all the family I have. Anyway,' she turned away, 'I'd better be off home. If I'm late for supper Ruby will give me a good telling off.'

Fred saw her to the gate at the side of the yard. 'I'm sorry, Jessie,' he said, 'that things couldn't have been different between us. I do love you, but you were right. My place is with my wife and child.'

They were alone now, in the shadow of the house, and Fred took her in his arms and hugged her. He smelt of milk, and Jessie knew she would think of him every time she milked a cow or did her round with the pails. He tipped her face up and, briefly, his lips touched hers. 'You're always going to be in my heart, Jessie.'

Back in Treacle Lane, Jessie went into the kitchen of the tall, narrow house. Ruby had the oven door open and her face was flushed with the heat as she slid a crusty brown pie out and on to a tray. 'We're having chicken pie tonight,' she said. 'What a pity our Albie isn't here to enjoy it with us.'

Ruby's attempt at joviality touched Jessie and she put her arms around her. 'Look, the road to Wales is hard, I can't deny that, and driving stubborn cattle is a job for a man. Albie's only young but he's got his wits about him and he'll get through it.'

Ruby rested her head briefly on Jessie's shoulder. 'It's not the trip I'm worried about, it's the way that man Jed treats him. Why, he might murder him on the trail and we'd never see him again.' She sank on to a chair and put her apron over her eyes. 'Oh, Jessie, I can't bear to think of it.'

Jessie sat opposite her and took her hands. 'Ruby, Jed wants his money's worth out of Albie and he won't get that by killing him, will he? No, Jed Lambert will want to keep him fit.'

'Are you sure?' Ruby rubbed her eyes impatiently.

'I'm sure. Albie will learn about animals while he's on the drove, and when he comes home to us, we'll set up a business together. You'll see, everything will work out fine.'

'Are you going to take Mr Dove's offer, then?'

Jessie swallowed hard and tried to sound positive, even though she was frightened by the responsibilities she would be taking on. 'I'm going to become a businesswoman and, one day, I'll have the finest milk round in the whole of London.'

Albie stood on the headland above the inn where he and Jed had stayed the night and stared down at the narrow road leading to the next valley. In the early morning light it all looked the same to him, wild and frightening, with great hills rearing menacingly into the distance. And yet, standing on the higher land, he could see what Jessie loved about the countryside of her birth: it was the clean air and the sparkling streams – from which you could drink without fear of falling sick. It was lovely – but give him the heart of London, with its stink and bustle, any time.

'What you standing there for, boy?' Jed snapped a twig from one of the trees and switched Albie's back with it. 'Now we're rid of the cows we can put on a spurt, get back to Carmarthen and gather a new herd. Then, my boy, if you're lucky, we'll be heading back to London Town.'

'And I'll be free?'

'That depends.' Jed smiled unpleasantly. 'See if you've worked enough to repay your debt first. There's a lot of work and danger in driving a full herd and you've had it easy so far. It'll be harder when you have hundreds of cattle to control.'

'But there'll be other men to help, won't there?' Albie asked anxiously.

Jed threw back his head and bellowed with laughter. He thumped Albie on the shoulder, almost dislodging him from his position on the rocks. 'You don't think I could drive a herd with just you to help me, do you?'

Albie was relieved. The journey with Jed, who goaded him all the time, was becoming unbearable. At least with other men on the road things should be easier.

'Right, let's get on with it then. Saddle up the horses and we'll be on our way.' Jed went to the hedge, un-buttoned his trousers and urinated. 'Hurry up, we haven't got all day.'

Albie was used to the horses now and clucked sooth-ingly as he tightened the girth beneath the great belly of Jed's horse. He was tempted to leave the saddle loose so that Jed would fall off but, much as he loathed the man, he couldn't stoop to murder.

Jed was silent as they rode the narrow roads. He seemed to have the strength to ride for hours but Albie's legs were soon aching with his effort to keep them round his animal's broad back.

'We'll stop near the river Wye,' Jed called back. 'I'm starving and there's a good inn a few miles on.'

Albie thought of the Thames, dark water running between muddy banks, and wondered what the Wye looked like. It was there that Non Jones's husband had been lost.

'The Wye is wide and rough.' Jed seemed to have picked up his thoughts. 'It takes animals and men into its belly, sucking them down to the stony bed. You'll see plenty of ghosts of drowned drovers there so you'd better take care.'

Albie shivered but kept his lips tightly shut. It wouldn't do to show Jed how frightened he was of riding a horse near the river. Once he showed fear, Jed would plague him with harrowing stories, laughing at him for being a townie.

'Not scared, are you, boy?' Jed reined in his horse. 'You've gone white as a sickly lamb, and you've good cause to be frightened. The river is like a woman – you never know which way she's going to turn.'

'Well, it's going to be an adventure for me. It makes a change from picking pockets.'

Jed leaned over and cuffed him. 'If I catch you touching anything of mine I'll kill you. I could drown you in the river and no one would know where you'd disappeared to, just like Caradoc Jones.'

'I've given up stealing,' Albie said. 'I want to start my own business once I'm home.'

Jed threw back his head and laughed. 'You? Start a business? What with?'

'I'll have to get a job, earn some money, and I know it's going to be difficult but I've had enough of stalking the streets, lifting a purse here and there.' He didn't mention that Jess had set alight in him a passion to work hard, settle down with a good woman and be

120

respectable for the first time in his life. He would show Jed Lambert and the whole world that he had more guts in his little finger than most men had in their entire body.

Jed stood up in the saddle as he approached the hill leading down to the river. The grass on the banks would be drying now that the summer was ending. He might be able to fit in another couple of droves, but then he'd have winter to contend with. Money would be tight – it always was when the dark months came upon the land. If only he could find another way to earn some, something to lighten the long winter nights.

Suddenly he saw the tall figure of a man leaning on the gate that led to a picturesque cottage. He recognized him – he'd only seen him a few times but there was no mistake: he was Caradoc Jones, son of the owner of the Bank of the Black Ox.

He reined in his horse meaning to talk to the man, but just then a young woman came out of the house and took Caradoc by the arm, cooing over him as though he was an invalid. He looked healthy enough to Jed. Although he was limping, he had a good colour in his cheeks.

'You,' he jabbed a finger at Albie, who hadn't noticed the man, 'go down to the river, look for a likely spot to rest the horses and stay there till I come.' He slid off his horse and made his way across the grass towards the cottage. It was an imposing place with high chimneys and a thatched roof. It looked as if Caradoc Jones had fallen on his feet. But, then, rich men always did.

He skirted the garden and walked round to the back of the house. He saw Caradoc in the doorway and lifted his hand in a tentative greeting. The man stared at him blankly and returned indoors.

The young woman came into the back garden and stared at him over the hedge.

'Can I help you, sir? Have you missed your way?'

'No.' He smiled. 'I'm about to rest by the river, then head home to Carmarthen, but when I saw Mr Jones I thought I'd come to shake his hand.' He caught the fear in the girl's eyes.

'He's not called Caradoc, his name is Craig.'

'Who said anything about him being Caradoc? I didn't. I'd just like to have a word with him.'

'He hasn't been well and he's happy here. Please don't say anything to him about his past – it will only upset him.'

'I only want to share happy times with him, tell him how his father misses him and how his poor wife walks the drovers' roads looking for him like a demented creature.'

'No! He's supposed to look after me – he promised my grandmother on her deathbed that he'd stay with me. Please, go away and leave us alone.'

'How much is it worth?' Jed thought of the winter nights that weren't going to be so dark after all. He smiled unpleasantly. 'Perhaps you and I should have a good talk.'

She swallowed hard. 'What do you want?'

She was going to take the bait!

'Money, of course, then I won't cause trouble for you.'

Caradoc chose that moment to come into the garden. He stared at Jed with suspicion written all over his face. 'Are you troubling this young lady?' He put his arm round the girl's shoulder and hugged her to him. He's made a cosy nest here, Jed thought, left his wife behind and found pastures new.

Jed frowned. Why was Caradoc looking at him as

122

though he'd never seen him before? They were never friends but they knew each other by sight, they'd attended enough markets together.

'Do I know you?' Jed asked cagily. 'You look familiar.'

Caradoc's face lit up. 'Do you recognize me? Do you know who I am?'

Jed saw the young woman shake her head and watched her lips form the word 'No.' He thrust his hands into his pockets. Something strange was going on. He looked at Caradoc carefully. The man's eyes held no alarm, only hope. And then the truth dawned on Jed. The man had gone into the river and lost his memory in the accident. Jed smiled slowly at the young lady. It was obvious to him now: Caradoc Jones, the poor fool, had no idea who he was and clearly this young woman wanted to keep it that way.

'Sorry,' he said. 'Now I've had a closer look I realize I don't know you at all.' He lifted his hat. 'I'll bid you good day.'

As he rode down the hill towards where the river cut a swathe through the land he was smiling: there was money to be made out of this situation, and he'd be the one to profit.

CHAPTER SEVENTEEN

Early the next morning, Non left the inn. She had done all she could to find Caradoc at the ford of Cabin Twm Bach but there was no sign of him. Yet she kept returning, drawn by some irresistible urge to the place where her husband had disappeared. She felt in her heart that the young girl in the big cottage was hiding something from her – but why would she? It didn't make sense.

She urged her horse on slowly past the deep waters of the river, and gazed at the ford one last time, willing it to yield its secrets. When she heard horses, she swivelled in the saddle – and started when she saw a tall man heading towards her. The light was behind him and, for a moment, she thought he was her husband. Then she recognized him – it was Jed Lambert. The disappointment was crushing.

Jed raised his hand to her and at that moment, she felt as though her heart would break. She noticed a smaller figure walking behind him, driving several cows. 'Albie! What are you doing here?' she exclaimed.

He rushed towards her. 'Non! Thank Gawd for a friendly face. But what are you doing here on your own?'

Non slid off her horse and hugged him. 'I'm looking for Caradoc – you know that he is lost?' Albie nodded. 'Morgan told me he went into the water here at the ford. I've searched and searched but . . .' Tears slid down her face. 'Oh, Albie, I just can't believe he's dead. I've ridden over every inch of the riverbank, and I've tried talking to the villagers but they're unable or unwilling to tell me anything.' She took a deep breath. 'But I'm being selfish talking about myself. It's you I should be concerned with – why are you on the drovers' road with Jed Lambert?'

'I owe him a debt,' Albie said awkwardly. 'This time I picked the wrong pocket.' He brightened. 'But I'm working off the debt and one day soon I'll be back in London.'

Jed reined in his horse and stared down at Non, with a strange look on his face. 'What would you pay to get your husband back?' he said.

Non looked at him anxiously. 'All the money in the world – if I had it,' she said. 'Why? Have you heard anything about him?'

He ignored the question. 'You must own a fortune – you've married into one of the richest families in Wales.'

'I haven't any money, though,' she said, 'only a little purse my father-in-law gave me, and that's nearly all gone.'

Jed took off his hat and scratched his head. 'Poor Mrs Jones,' he said, but there was no sympathy in his voice.

'Have you seen or heard anything about my husband?' Non asked. 'I'm desperate to find him – I can't tell you how much it would mean to me to hear even the smallest piece of news about him.'

'What if he's tired of his old life and made a new start?' Jed grinned. 'Perhaps his family wanted to get rid of you.'

'You know something, don't you?' Non said. 'Tell

me, please! I'll give you what's left in my purse if you can tell me anything at all.'

Jed took it from her, looked inside and sneered, then threw it back. 'I can see you're telling me the truth that you haven't any money, but I did hear something that might interest you.'

'What? Please tell me!'

'It seems he was swept right away from here, down-river. You've been searching in the wrong spot, Mrs Jones. Face it – your man's gone. He's dead. If I was you I'd go home and thank your father-in-law for giving you bed and board.' His tone was cruel and Non flinched. 'Come on, lad, we've got to get on or we'll be stuck in this God-forsaken place for another night,' he barked.

Albie looked appealingly at Non. 'When you get to London, stay with Ruby in Treacle Lane. I'll be back there as soon as I can. Are you goin' to be all right, Non?' He looked at Jed over his shoulder. 'Couldn't we just stay with her for a little—'

Before he could finish his sentence Jed was pointing his horsewhip at him. 'Shift. We've wasted enough time.'

'You go.' Non tried to sound reassuring. 'I've been travelling on my own for days and come to no harm. I'll see you in London – I should be there in a week or so.'

Non watched as Albie disappeared from sight. Suddenly she was weary. She would never find Caradoc – she must accept that he was lost to her for ever. She let the tears fall freely.

Albie was so angry with Jed he wanted to kill him. 'Why did you taunt Non about her husband like that?' he said. 'You don't know any more about him than she does, so why taunt her?'

'Shut your mouth! I know what I know, and I don't answer to you or anyone else.'

Albie was no match for Jed and he knew it. For a time they travelled in silence and Albie wished, once again, that he was back in London. He even missed the familiar stink of the Thames.

Now the river Wye was behind him and open green fields were at his side and before him. He felt small, lost. He hated the space, hated the silence, and he wanted to get back to where he belonged.

That night, Jed booked them a bed in an inn. The place was smoky and smelt of candle grease and stale beer. 'You'll take the mattress on the floor,' he said to Albie, 'or sleep outdoors with the animals.'

Albie nodded his thanks. 'I'd sleep on a bleedin' bed of nails if I 'ad to.'

Jed sank on to the bed and stuck out his foot. 'Boots,' he ordered. Albie swallowed his pride and tugged them off. Jed grunted, fell back against the pillows and, almost immediately, began to snore.

Albie sank on to the pallet and stared up at the roof timbers, then at the cracked and dirty windows. He closed his eyes and thought of Jessie, her clear skin and the long hair with red lights in it, those eyes – at one minute they could warm a man's heart, and at the next, freeze it. At least she was safe in London, not wandering the drovers' road like a lost soul as Non was doing.

He looked across at Jed, whose arms were splayed out, his snores louder. He wondered if the man knew anything about Caradoc Jones. It was strange that he'd asked Non for money. If Jed had any information about Caradoc, it would be in his saddlebags.

He got up, slid cautiously across the room and deftly opened them. A quick search revealed nothing unusual. There were only a few papers he couldn't read but he knew figures and there were mostly bills for the animals to stay in the halfpenny fields. Jed knew nothing, he was just playing on Non's grief.

Albie slid back on to his lumpy mattress and closed his eyes. He felt weary, his legs ached, and he needed to sleep. Perhaps in the morning Jed would release him and let him go home.

London was as busy and crowded as it had always been and the fog was thick over the rooftops as Non tried to get her bearings. She was cold and miserable – soaked to the skin by a sudden shower of rain.

She discovered she was in Monmouth Street, and could smell the rank odour of old clothes for sale in the area. A few ragged children played in the gutter and she realized she had taken a wrong turning. She was far away from Treacle Lane. She was muddled and confused, tired after her days of riding, tired of the disappointment that dogged her search for Caradoc.

Perhaps if she turned the horse and followed the snaking line of the river she would have a better idea of where she was going. But London was a maze of streets, broad squares and tiny courts, and it took her almost two hours to find Treacle Lane. At last she reined in her animal and slipped off the saddle. She saw the open doors in the dingy court, the skinny cats on the cobbles, and felt suddenly as though she had come home.

Jessie stood in the yard watching Fred milk the cows for the last time, his broad shoulder leaning comfortably into the animal's flank, the milk drumming into the bucket. 'When are you leaving?' she asked.

'At the end of the week, Jessie. I know you'll make a go of things round here. Sure you'll have to get a boy in to help you lift and carry, but other than that you'll be all right. You're an intelligent young lady and . . . soon you'll meet a handsome young man who is free to love you.'

'Well,' Jessie said slowly, 'I'd better get home. Ruby will be wondering what's keeping me, you know how she fusses.' She walked slowly towards Fred. 'Give me a kiss to remember you by,' she said softly.

Fred took her into his arms. 'Jess . . .'

'I'll come in on Monday morning and take over. When Albie comes home he'll help me run things here.' Her voice cracked. 'Don't you go worrying about me.'

He held her very carefully as though she might break, bent his head and kissed her lingeringly. Then stepped away. 'Goodbye, Jessie, and God be with you.' He stumbled across the yard into one of the cowsheds. She knew he was crying but she took a deep breath and turned away. She must be strong.

She walked across the city in a daze, thinking of Fred, his gentleness, his goodness, and tears came. By the time she reached Treacle Lane, she knew that this was for the best.

She let herself into the house. She heard Ruby's voice, and went into the kitchen to find Non sipping some horrible smelling drink.

'Non! What are you doing in London?' Her friend's face was thin and pale, her eyes heavily shadowed.

'I've been searching for Caradoc,' Non said slowly. She sipped more of her own home-made remedy. 'I can't find him, Jessie, but I can't believe he's dead.' Tears trembled on her lashes and Jessie hugged her.

'Life can play some hard tricks on us, Non,' Jessie said softly, 'but I know you'll fight through it all and you'll make a good life for yourself and your son.'

She turned to kiss Ruby on the cheek, who had taken charge by the look of it. Jessie sat down at the table. 'I've got a bit of gossip for you. When I was on my round I was talking to a Welsh maid from one of the big houses. She told me that old Mr Jones has come up to London with his sister Miss Prudence. He brought the baby with him.'

Non looked up quickly. 'Rowan is in London?'

'That's what I heard – and Miss Georgina stayed at home with the housekeeper to watch over her.'

Non brightened with excitement. 'You couldn't have brought me better news! I'll go and fetch him at once – I miss my baby so much.'

'No, you won't,' Ruby said firmly. 'You're far too tired to go anywhere tonight.' Non looked as if she might cry.

Jessie changed the subject. 'You've heard about Albie, how he's gone on the trail with that awful man Jed Lambert, I suppose?'

'I met up with them,' Non replied, 'by the ford in the river Wye. I kept going back there, feeling somehow that Caradoc was near.'

'And Albie,' Jessie asked, 'was he well?'

'He's getting used to walking the trail instead of the streets of London, but I know he'll be glad to come home.'

Jessie took the cup of tea Ruby handed her and watched as Ruby put her hand on Non's shoulder. 'It's time you went to your bed,' she said. 'You'll never ride that awful trail on your own again – I won't let you. I don't know what Mr Jones was thinking of to allow it, he's a wicked man. Now, come on, let me settle you down for the night.'

Jessie watched as Ruby helped Non to her feet. The medicine she'd drunk was taking effect. Jessie let her thoughts drift back to her own problems. Could she cope without Fred? Could she make a success of the milk round on her own? Suddenly it all seemed too much for her. She laid her arm on the table, buried her head in her sleeve and wept.

CHAPTER EIGHTEEN

It was quiet in the house without her father and the baby, and Georgina had never known such freedom. Today she walked in the garden, watching Matt at work, plotting for the day when she'd take him for her own. It was fine and sunny, a day made for love, but now was not the time. She would tease him just a little longer, enjoy the thrill of the chase and wait for the perfect moment.

She turned her attention to the letter that had arrived that morning. She knew before she opened it that it was from Aunt Prudence. The paper crackled between her fingers and the bold handwriting was sprawled across the page. Aunt Prudence had finally taken up dancing and claimed she had danced with the pick of London's young men. She wrote of the latest fashions, the stiffening of the hemline, the pretty row of ribbons that adorned the front of one's gown, the sheltering brim of bonnets that ensured the pallor of one's complexion. However, she ended with a word of warning: 'Do not come to London just now. Your husband Clive Langland is in Town and threatening to come to see you.'

Georgina folded the letter. How dare he try to see her after the way he'd deserted her? For a moment she almost wanted to catch the next coach to London and vent her anger on him, but then Matt came into view, his bronzed arms gleaming in the sunshine.

Her heartbeat quickened and she felt like a girl, in love for the first time. She resisted the urge to run across the garden to him, and waited for him to approach her.

'Morning, Miss Georgina.' Matt smiled as though he knew exactly how she felt about him. 'You're very beautiful today, Miss, if I may say so.' His eyes met hers and she read desire in them. 'Would you like me to cut a few roses for you?'

He was sure of himself and his effect on women, Georgina thought. She wondered how many he'd bedded and the thought made her breathless. 'I don't want any flowers but I'd like you to walk with me. I'm lonely now that Papa has gone to London.'

She moved past the flower-beds and he fell into step beside her. She glanced up at him, wondering if she could resist the urge to fall into his arms. She thought of his mouth on hers, his hands caressing her. He would make her feel loved and desirable, something her husband had never managed to do. She shivered.

'Are you getting a chill, Miss Georgina?'

'Someone just walked over my grave,' she replied. 'Let's go into the conservatory and sit for a moment.'

'As you please, Miss.' Matthew's words were respectful, but his eyes were bold.

They sat together, not too close but Matt was within easy reach: all she had to do was stretch out her hand, take his, and he would respond with passion, she knew it.

'Are you married, Matt?'

'Not me, Miss, I'm too busy to find a wife. In any case, I mean to get on in the world, perhaps work at Covent Garden selling fruit and flowers to the folk in

London.' His eyes crinkled at the corners. 'But for now I'm happy to be here with you.'

'I expect you say that to charm every young lady you meet,' Georgina retorted. Her husband had proved that fine words meant nothing. Then she wondered if she'd been too harsh. 'It's nice to have a compliment, though.'

'It's sincerely meant,' Matt said, in a low voice. 'You're undoubtedly the most beautiful lady it's been my good fortune to meet.'

She preened, seeing that sincerity gleamed from him like a bright light. Still, she had to be cautious. Clive had seemed sincere until he realized she had no money of her own. 'I'm not a lady of fortune, you know,' she said.

'And I'm not a fortune-hunter,' he responded quickly. 'I mean what I say, Miss Georgina. I don't use words idly.'

Georgina got up. 'I must go indoors now.' The sun was slanting into the conservatory.

'I think I'm falling in love with you,' Matt said. 'I'm not a fool, I know you're far above me, so far that I can't ever reach you, but I want you to know how I feel.'

'Matt,' she said softly, 'do you know what you're saying?'

'I do, and I apologize for the impertinence but not for the words. They come directly from the heart.'

'Oh, Matt.' She swayed towards him but as his lips met hers, another gardener came into view.

'Look,' she said, 'we must be sensible. We cannot allow anyone else to know how we feel.'

'Then can I dare to hope you feel something for me?'

'Oh, yes! But we must be careful.' She stepped towards the door. 'I'll see you later. Come to the front of the house and I'll open the large window in the drawing room.'

'I'll be there after nine, just as dusk is falling.' He left the conservatory without another word and stopped outside to talk to the other gardener. Georgina wondered what he was saying, but she knew he would be discreet. At last she'd met a man she could trust.

Jessie's shoulders ached from carrying the yoke all day, and now that she was back at the yard, she could allow herself to feel tired. She washed the milk pails carefully: any residue would turn sour and spoil the fresh milk the cows would yield in the morning.

Inside the house, which she now rented from Fred, she sat on an upturned box and looked around her: the room was bare of furniture because Fred had needed it for his new home in Ireland. One day, though, she would own a fine table and elegant chairs. Indeed, she would furnish the whole house . . . but none of it would come without a great deal of hard work.

The silence seemed to creep round her worse than fog. One of the cows bellowed – they were hungry and needed to be turned out on to the grass but Jessie sat still and wondered if she'd taken on too much of a job for a woman alone. 'Never mind,' she said, her voice echoing in the silent kitchen. 'Albie will be home soon. He'll help me.' But those fine words meant nothing: she needed help now. She couldn't go on milking, fetching and carrying, and hope to make a success of her business.

Suddenly she had an idea: why not get a cart she could push around instead of carrying the outdated yoke on her sore shoulders? One of Ruby's lodgers was a carpenter: she would ask him to build one for her.

She looked around the empty, silent room and felt lonely. Though she was tired, she made up her mind that she would feed the animals, then walk over to

Ruby's house and tell her the plans she had for the business.

She wished Albie was there: he would be so proud of her, and he would support her. But he was on the trail with Jed Lambert. Sometimes Jessie feared he would never come back. The drovers' roads were hazardous at the best of times, and if Albie got into any difficulty Jed would be the last person to help him.

She splashed water over her face and arms, then pulled on a fresh skirt, enthusiasm lending her energy. All at once she felt happy again. She was a lady of property, and she would make a success of her business if it killed her.

Matt came to Georgina that night, just as they'd planned. He stood framed in the open window, a big man who smelt of fresh grass and the open air. Georgina drew back for a moment, wanting him, yet afraid of the step she was about to take.

The two of them stood in silence for a long moment, until Matt took her hands and drew her close. His lips were warm as they came down on hers, and then she was in his arms clinging to him. It had been so long since she'd been held like this, and with her husband she'd never felt as she did now, hot, eager and head over heels in love. What she'd felt for Clive had been as nothing in comparison, she could see that now.

'Come upstairs,' she said softly, and together they crept up the broad stairway. Once in her room, illuminated only by firelight, he led her towards the bed and lay with her, kissing her neck, her shoulders, the swell of her breasts.

She sat up. 'Let me be free of my gown so that I can hold you close to me.'

When she was undressed, he kissed her shoulders,

then his mouth closed around one of her nipples. She gasped in delight. His touch was sure, as if he'd had many women. He caressed her thighs, and waves of desire sent a shudder through her. She felt she would die if she didn't have him now. 'Please, Matt,' she whispered, 'please come to me. I need you – I want you . . . oh, my love . . .'

He stayed with her until the dawn sent trembling fingers of light through the curtains. He went to get up from the bed, but she held him. 'Stay a little longer, please, Matt.'

He made love to her again, and then came a torrent of sensations she'd never experienced before, so intense she could hardly breathe. The dazzling moments were all-consuming and then, satiated, she fell back against the pillows.

He lay beside her and cupped her breast with his hand. 'My lovely Georgina,' he said softly. 'My lovely, lovely Georgina.'

She put her face against his shoulder and felt like weeping for joy. 'Matt,' she said, her lips against his skin, 'I've fallen in love with you.' She couldn't believe she'd said it aloud. She was a high-born lady, her father a rich man – and, worst of all, she was married. Yet none of it mattered as long as she could keep Matt with her.

'You've drifted away from me,' he said, turning her chin so that she was looking into his eyes. 'Are you sorry for what we've done?'

'Never!' she said at once. 'I don't know what I'm going to do, but I mean to be with you, Matt, and nobody is going to stand in our way.'

She propped herself on her elbow and traced the outline of his strong mouth with her fingers. 'I love you, Matt. I will have you, whatever anybody says.'

137

The door opened abruptly and Georgina looked up, ready to remonstrate with the maid for coming into her room without knocking. Then she shrank against Matt. A man was standing in the doorway, a leer on his self-satisfied face.

'Clive! What are you doing here?'

He rubbed his hands with delight. 'What a tale I'll have to tell! Your father will have to pay me well if I'm to keep this little secret.'

Matt leaped out of bed, fists bunched. 'Who are you?' he said in a hard voice.

'Oh, didn't she tell you?' Clive Langland said. 'Georgina, how remiss of you!' He smiled. 'The woman you've just bedded, my friend, is my wife.'

CHAPTER NINETEEN

'So you'll be able to make me a cart, then, Mr Rogers?'
Jessie stood in Treacle Lane and looked hopefully into
the face of the lodger.

'I'll make you two, if you like.' He grinned toothlessly. 'Tell me, what size do you want it?'

Jessie pondered. 'Well, it has to carry at least six
buckets of milk. Now I have to walk to and from the
dairy, carrying two buckets at a time on my shoulders.'

'You should have asked before,' Mr Rogers said. His
mouth closed around his gums like a purse pulled tight
with string.

'I never thought of it when I was working for Mr
Dove, but now I'm in charge and it's time to smarten
up the business.'

'Well, I 'opes you 'ave the money for the timber not
to mention the wheels.' Mr Rogers chomped on his
gums. 'Nothing comes cheap, see, Miss Jessie.'

'I'll be able to pay, of course I will.' Jessie thought of
her small supply of money but, on balance, she was
making a wise move: the business needed improve-
ments and this was only the first of many.

'So, you're not going to live with us any more?' Mr
Rogers had taken a stub of a pencil from one of his
pockets and, from another, produced a scrap of paper.

'I'll have to be on the premises of my business, see?

I didn't want to leave you all, especially Ruby, but times change, don't they?'

Mr Rogers didn't reply: he was busy scrawling on the piece of paper. 'Wheels and a pair of shafts, is that what you want? Then you can push or pull the cart as you like.' Jessie nodded thoughtfully, and Mr Rogers scribbled on his paper once more.

'When will it be ready?' Jessie asked eagerly. 'The sooner I get a cart the better.'

'It'll take a day or two to find the timber.' Mr Rogers pursed his lips and the lines around his mouth deepened. 'When I say "find", I mean purchase, you understand?'

Jessie understood very well. Mr Rogers would scout round at the backs of houses for wood and then he would bargain with one of the street traders for old out-of-shape wheels. Still, he would make the cart sturdy and reliable, of that she had no doubt.

Ruby came into the passageway. 'What the 'ell's goin' on out 'ere, Jessie?'

'Mr Rogers is going to make me a cart.' Jessie's smile was gleeful. 'Don't you think that's a good way to improve my business? I'll need to pay out some money but I'll be quicker on the rounds.'

'What do you mean, "pay out some money"?' Ruby looked askance at Mr Rogers. 'I can't believe you're going to charge this young lady for doing a bit of scrounging.'

'Well,' Mr Rogers said, 'I'll do fair by Miss Jessie. I'll just need a little something to buy the timber and the wheels.'

Ruby slapped his shoulder and dust rose from his coat. 'You'll do no such thing! You get to work on that cart right now and there'll be no money changing hands or I might have to put up the rent.'

'Women!' He let himself out of the house with a scowl of discontent. 'I'll do my best, and that's all I can promise.'

'I want to see the results, and soon,' Ruby called after him. She took Jessie's arm. 'Now, come in and tell me how you're getting on.'

'I've got no furniture in the house, just upturned boxes, but it'll be comfortable enough when I find some curtains to put over the windows.' A thought struck her. 'I should have told Mr Rogers to get some boxes to make the cart.'

Ruby winked. 'He's there ahead of you, love. He won't pay out a penny for the wood or the wheels, you rest easy. You'll have your cart by this time tomorrow or Mr Rogers will feel the weight of my hand.'

In the kitchen, the kettle was boiling noisily, steam issuing from the spout and spitting into the fire. Ruby warmed the pot and made some tea. 'Sit down for five minutes, Jessie.'

When they were both settled, Jessie propped her elbows on the table. 'I really mean to make this business work. I'll soon have twice the round I had before.'

Ruby nodded. 'I know what you want, Jessie, but don't overdo it. You've no one but yourself to rely on, remember.'

'I won't overdo it, Ruby, and when I have the use of a cart, there'll be no more carrying heavy pails back and forth across London. I'll be up at the crack of dawn and selling my milk when only the servants are about.' She paused. 'Where's Non?'

'She's gone to see her son. I gave her money for a cab because she looked too poorly to walk all that way.' Ruby shook her head. 'The girl's a shadow of herself, poor thing, out of her mind with grief.'

'Well, she loved Mr Caradoc with all her heart. It's

so awful to think he's no longer with us.' Jessie spoke in a whisper as though frightened someone would hear her. 'I still can't believe it. Things like that don't happen to the Jones family.'

'Bad things happen in any family. Money don't protect you from harm, Jessie, though it's sad that a man in his prime should die like that, swept away by a river.'

'And there's the baby. He'll grow up without a father.'

'Oh,' Ruby said, 'from what I hear Mr George Jones is very well off. The infant will have everything he needs.'

'I wonder if Mr Jones will let Non see her little one.'

'Why shouldn't he?'

'Mr Jones is a right bully and Non says he grudges even a hold of little Rowan. Still, the boy will have a good upbringing, no doubt about that.'

Ruby sighed. 'I suppose you're right, but a baby needs his mother – and I'll have a few words to say to Mr Jones if he turns awkward. Anyway, there's nothing we can do now but let Non know we care about her.'

Jessie nodded. As always, Ruby was right: what Non needed now was her friends.

'What do you mean, he's not here?' Non stood in the hallway of the elegant London house and looked at the housekeeper who stood like a sentinel in front of her. 'I'm the boy's mother and I want to see my son.'

'Well, I'm sorry, Mrs Jones, but his grandfather has taken him on a trip abroad.'

'Abroad, but where?' Non persisted. 'Just tell me where that man has taken my son.'

'I'm not privy to that sort of information, madam. I'm a servant and do as I'm told.' She sounded as if she would have helped Non if she could. 'That's all I can tell you.'

From the drawing room, Non heard the sound of women laughing. She took a deep breath, walked to the door and flung it open. She recognized George Jones's sister, Prudence, who stood up abruptly and looked at her as if she was some beggar who had walked in from the street. Non was suddenly angry. 'I want to know where my son is.' She crossed the room and stood directly before Prudence. 'I'm married to Caradoc and I'm Rowan's mother. I think I deserve an honest answer. Where has my father-in-law taken my child?'

'How dare you intrude into my home and bother my guests?' Prudence said. 'I don't have to answer to you, my girl. You might have married Caradoc by some trickery or other but now he's dead, God rest him, and you are nothing to this family.'

'I'll stay here all night if I have to,' Non said. The ladies looked at Prudence, waiting with breathless silence to see what her reaction would be. Prudence called the housekeeper, who was still hovering in the hall. 'Fetch the footmen. I want this intruder ejected from my house forthwith.'

Non stared defiantly at the older woman. 'If you do that I'll make such a fuss that your neighbours will think I'm being murdered. Is that what you want?'

Prudence took her arm and hustled her into the hall. 'Look, I don't know where George has taken the boy, but I can tell you that he'll be back in town tomorrow. Call again then and you can make your threats directly to him. Now, please be good enough to leave me in peace. This affair has nothing at all to do with me.'

Non nodded. 'Very well. But I *will* come back tomorrow – and every day until I see my son.'

She was pushed to the door and then she was outside

the pillared doorway. Slowly, she walked back towards Treacle Lane. It was a few miles away, but Non had walked all the way from Wales to London.

She made her way through the broad streets and airy squares of some of the finer parts of London and by the time she reached the east of the city, her legs were trembling. She had wanted so badly to see her baby son, to hold Rowan in her arms, to kiss his cheek and look down into the eyes that were so like his father's. She leaned against a wall and took a deep breath. Perhaps the walk would prove too long for her, she should have heeded Ruby's advice and taken a cab. The sooner she was home and in her bed, the sooner it would be morning and she would see her son.

'What's wrong with the boy?' George Jones looked pleadingly at the doctor, who had come to the apartment in Paris in the middle of the night.

'It is probably nothing at all. Children develop a temperature with the slightest ailment. I could give you a powder to soothe him. You're taking him home to England tomorrow, are you not?'

George nodded. 'Give me the powder, and my man will pay you for your services.'

When the doctor had left, George called the nurse, who looked doubtfully at the powder, but she took the child and rubbed most of the contents of the little package into Rowan's gums. Then she rocked him until he fell quiet.

George nodded in approval. 'Good,' he said. 'Now you can put him to bed. Rest is the best thing for a sick child, but watch him through the night in case he becomes restless again. If he wakes, give him a little more of the powder.'

'Very well, sir.' The nurse sounded doubtful and George looked at her enquiringly.

'What is it?'

'I think this powder is a little strong for a child so young, sir.' She smelled it. 'I think there's some substance derived from the poppy – opium, sir.'

'Well, the doctor must know what he's doing so just get on with it, woman.' He needed a drink. Perhaps it had been a mistake to bring the boy away from London where he could depend on a doctor to give him a sensible answer to his questions. But he'd had to come: he'd heard that Manon had arrived in London, which meant she'd failed to find Caradoc. He supposed his flight had been as much to avoid hearing the bad news as to keep his grandson with him. Well, tomorrow he would be at home and everything would be resolved.

In the morning, George rose early. He had just finished dressing when there was a loud rap on the door of his room. He guessed it would be a maid with breakfast. 'Come in,' he called, and the door flew open to admit the nurse. Her cap was askew, her hair sticking out from under it in unseemly disarray.

The horrified expression on her face told him something was badly wrong. 'What is it?'

'Come and see, sir! It's the boy! He's not himself!'

George followed her to where his grandson was lying. He bent over the bed and saw, by the pallor on Rowan's face, that something was indeed very wrong. 'Send for the doctor at once.' He hardly heard the nurse run from the room. He was bending over Rowan trying to wake him. 'Come along, my dear child,' he said, taking his grandson's cold hands in his own. 'Wake up, Rowan, open your eyes.'

There was no response and panic flared in George.

'Please, God, don't take him from us,' he whispered. 'Don't let me lose my grandson as well as my son.'

He waited anxiously for the doctor to come. The time dragged as he chafed Rowan's little hands, as though he could bring the blood flowing back into them.

At last the baby opened his eyes – blue, just like his father's – and for a moment he stared up at George. Then he gave a soft sigh and his eyes closed again. George didn't need a doctor to tell him that Rowan was dead.

CHAPTER TWENTY

Morgan rode at the head of the herd, guiding the drove along St John's Road and into Smithfield market. His second in command, Harold, drew level with him and pointed towards the crowded pens. 'It looks like we're the last ones to get here,' he said unhelpfully.

'Of course we are! We've had so many delays – you didn't think the rest of the drovers would wait for us, did you?' Morgan was aware he sounded irritable but it had been a long journey. A horse and several cattle needed reshoeing, and as he was the smithy as well as the leader of the drove he had been forced to put the animals into the halfpenny fields while he worked. He was tired of droving, Morgan thought. As soon as he got home he would give notice to Mr Jones and take up his role as smithy again.

He rode to the edge of the square and surveyed the scene. He stood up in the stirrups and searched the area for room for his cattle and at last spotted a few empty pens. 'Harold, here!' He watched as the drovers prodded the reluctant cattle into the remaining small spaces. 'You stay with the beasts while I find us lodgings for the night.' He became aware that Flora was staring at him, her knitting needles in her hands, waiting for some sign that he noticed her. He felt a dart of guilt. He was taking advantage of Flora's affection for him.

'*Duw*, looks like Jed Lambert has caught us up,' Harold said. 'See?' He pointed with his whip. 'Good-looking cattle he's got there. Beside them, ours look scrawny.'

'We didn't stay long in the finishing fields,' Morgan said. 'It was either fattening the animals or missing the market.' He took pity on Flora and beckoned to her. 'Come with me. You can find a place for the three women who want to travel home, and the ones who are staying in town can find their own lodgings.' He held out his arm and swung her up into the saddle behind him. She clung to him, and he felt the softness of her breasts against his back. He winced. How could he tell her he didn't love her now that he'd tasted her sweetness? Flora was gentle and kind. She'd learned some harsh lessons in life but she still had the eagerness of youth.

'I don't want you to make me any promises you can't keep,' she said. It was as if she'd read his thoughts. 'I know you're in love with Non, will always be in love with her, and I won't be a burden to you.'

Morgan didn't reply as he guided his horse into the crowded streets. He stopped outside a lodging-house. In spite of the inevitable grime on the windows, the place looked decent and respectable. Flora slipped from the saddle. 'I'll go in and ask for rooms.' He watched her push open the door and disappear into the darkness.

He dismounted and rubbed his horse's neck. The animal was tired and would benefit from a night spent in a comfortable stable. 'It's all right, old girl,' he said softly, 'you'll soon have somewhere to put your head down.'

Flora reappeared and gestured to him. 'There's two rooms to rent,' she said. 'That'll do for the five of us.

It's cheap and clean, and I've told the landlord you'll pay a small deposit right away.'

'Well, you'll have to share the room with the women, Flora. I don't want anyone gossiping about you.'

'I think I lost my good name a long time ago,' Flora said wryly. 'I won't do anything to embarrass you, mind.'

Morgan swung into the saddle. 'Here's the money to pay for the rooms. I'll ride back to Smithfield to see to the cattle. You'll be all right until I come back, won't you?'

Flora nodded. 'Aye. Don't worry about me. I've not travelled the drovers' roads without learning to look after myself.'

He left her, and his thoughts returned to Non. Perhaps she, too, was in London now, if she'd given up the search for her husband. It was tragic that she'd lost him so soon, but she was young, resilient: she would rebuild her life, and then there might be a place in it for him.

The summer was almost over and the days were cooler, bringing a breath of autumn into the air. Caradoc sat in the kitchen watching Gwenllyn baking bread for supper. She was lithe and lovely, her sweet face engrossed as she bent over her task. She was a woman whom any man would want for his wife. He longed to take her to his bed, but the idea that he might not be free to put a ring on her finger still plagued him.

She met his eyes and her hands stilled. They looked at each other for a long moment, then she pulled a cloth over the dough and placed it in the hearth. She washed her hands and came to him, her face resolute. 'I've fallen in love with you,' she said softly. 'I want you for my own.'

He got to his feet, took a step towards her and hesitated. Gwenllyn came into his arms and pressed close to him. He smelled the sweet scent of her hair, felt the softness of her body. He was aroused, hungry for a woman's love.

She took his face in her hands. 'Kiss me.'

Slowly, his mouth came down on her lips, full and petal-soft. He was hardly aware that he had picked her up and was carrying her to the bedroom. She clung to him, her mouth against his neck, and he was filled with sensations he could no longer control. He was past reasoning with himself: his old life was gone and it was time he entered wholeheartedly into the new one.

'I love you,' Gwenllyn whispered again.

They lay on the bed together and he began to undo the neck of her gown. She helped him and soon she lay naked beside him. 'Your skin is like alabaster,' he said. 'You're so beautiful, Gwenllyn.'

She drew him to her. 'No more talking. Just hold me and kiss me. Make me yours for ever.'

He raised himself above her, and forgot everything but the need to pleasure her. She was sweet beneath him and he moved gently for fear of hurting her, then lost himself in the old rhythms of love. She was so young, so willing, and he knew that now there could be no turning back to his old life, whatever it had been.

Morgan sat in the kitchen of the lodging-house and drank the beer that Mr Quinn, the landlord, had provided. He could hear Flora's laughter as she sat in the front room with the other girls. She was wise, kind and passionate enough to make most men happy, yet now that Non was a widow, free of any ties, his hope was reborn that one day he would have her as his bride.

'Cattle selling well?' the landlord asked, pouring more beer into Morgan's mug. 'I hear the market's busy this week.'

'I've sold most of my animals,' Morgan said, 'but I've had to let them go for less than I'd hoped because they didn't spend enough time in the fattening fields.'

'I don't suppose the owner will be pleased to hear that.' The landlord sat down astride a barrel. 'Mr George Jones, is that right?'

'How did you know?' Morgan sipped his beer and watched the man carefully. He seemed too interested in a matter that had nothing to do with him.

'Oh, I get to know the faces of the drovers – I make a point of going to the market, watching the sales. I need a new pony, one that's broken in, and Smithfield is the best place round here to buy a good 'un. Barnet's better, but I don't want to travel so far. I was wondering if you could get me a little bit off the asking price.'

Morgan shook his head. 'I didn't have any horseflesh for sale on this run but I could point out a good animal and make sure it's well shod, if that's any help.'

Mr Quinn sighed. 'I've seen these market days come and go all my working life. I've rented rooms and provided victuals for the drovers, yet no one ever offers me a good deal.' He sounded disgruntled. 'Even Caradoc Jones was a hard nut to crack, and him the owner's son. He could have given me a bargain, if he'd a mind to. There's some say that he didn't drown in the river after all.'

'Well, take it from me, Caradoc Jones is dead. I saw him fall into the river, saw the horse trample him. Rumours are strange things – they grow as if they have lives of their own,' Morgan said abruptly. 'He's dead, believe me,' he repeated, but the landlord didn't look convinced.

'Jed Lambert was in here the other day and he saw the whole thing too.'

Jed, that man had been trouble from the day he was born. 'Well, I wouldn't take what he says to heart,' Morgan said. 'He was probably hoping for a few drinks on the house.'

'Well, I dunno about that. He sounded very sure of himself.' Mr Quinn rubbed his ragged beard. 'Though I did give him some of my good brandy, now you come to mention it. Another bit of gossip I heard,' the landlord went on, 'was that Mr George Jones is in London with his grandson. Some tragedy has happened there, too, though I'm not sure what. We hear a lot of gossip from the drovers.'

Morgan sat up straight. 'And Mrs Jones, the baby's mother, have you heard anything of her?'

'Only that she's living somewhere round Treacle Lane with that Ruby what's-her-name. Some say Mrs Jones is here to cause trouble, but memories are short. A couple of years ago she was a heroine. She helped heal the sick at St Bartholomew's hospital.' Mr Quinn got to his feet. 'Well, I've customers to serve but I'll come back a bit later and we can talk about the price of a pony. By then you might have thought how I can get one cheap.'

'Is Jed Lambert staying here?'

'No, but he's only a few streets away. He's lodging with that Ruby too. Why? You going to see him?'

'I might pay him a visit.'

When the landlord was serving other customers, Morgan finished his beer and left the inn without telling Flora. He didn't want her with him in case there was trouble. Jed was well known for his flying fists.

Treacle Lane was only a brief walk away from the inn where he was lodged and he stared up at Ruby's three-storey house, wondering if Non was inside it. It was getting late and he was tired after the last long stretch on the drovers' roads, but he couldn't wait until morning to speak to Jed Lambert.

Ruby answered the door to him. 'Morgan! Come in! It's good to see you again. Have you come to see Non? She's angry and upset because that George Jones has taken young Rowan away to some foreign place without a word of warning. I've put her to bed with some of her medicine, and I don't want her disturbed.' She drew him along the dark passageway. 'She's been back and forth to that big house but they won't answer the door to her. She's hardly eating and I fear for her health if she goes on like this.'

As they entered the kitchen Morgan saw Jessie sitting by the fireside, her head bent over some knitting. When she glanced up a smile of welcome spread across her face. 'Morgan! There's lovely to see you.' She bundled away the knitting and stood up to hug him. 'It's lovely to see old friends again. Did you know our Albie's back too? He looks fair worn out – he's been on the road with Jed Lambert. Picked his pocket, the silly, and Jed caught him so he had to pay him back. Jed got all the work he could out of Albie before he'd let him go – even now we're afraid he'll change his mind.' She sat down again. 'He's made Albie stay with the cattle at Smithfield, mind, so I haven't even seen him yet. What do you want to talk to Jed about?'

'Nothing important,' Morgan said. 'Just some business.'

'And you'll be happy to see Non again, I'll bet a shilling.'

'That can wait until morning,' Morgan said. 'It's Lambert I've come to see tonight.'

'Well, have a hot toddy with us.' Ruby fussed around

153

him. 'Come and sit here, in my chair. Put your feet up and I'll bring you a drink.'

Jessie leaned across the table, eager to gossip. 'I've got my own business now,' she said proudly. 'I've got two milking cows and I'm renting a house until I can afford a place of my own.'

'You're doing well, then?'

'Aye, well as can be expected. Instead of carrying the pails of milk on my shoulders I've had a cart made for me. It's so much easier, see?'

'Good for you, Jessie.' He forced a smile. 'Have you a sweetheart yet?'

Jessie shook her head. 'But I've plenty of work to keep me out of mischief. I'm going to have Albie to help me, once Jed lets him go.'

Morgan heard the front door open and tensed as he heard Jed Lambert's voice and his boots ringing down the narrow passageway.

'He's had enough to drink by the sound of it,' Ruby said.

Jed came into the room unsteady on his feet. He peered at Morgan and his mouth twisted in anger. He slumped into a chair. 'What you doin' here, smithy? Not taken him in as a lodger, have you, Ruby?'

'Now, don't start, Jed,' Ruby said warningly. 'Any bother and you'll be out of my house.'

'I didn't come to quarrel with you,' Morgan said. 'I wanted to ask you some questions, that's all.'

'What questions?' Jed's voice was surly. He clasped his hands together so tightly that his knuckles showed white.

'Why are you spreading gossip about Caradoc Jones? You know damn well you didn't see the accident, so why rake it all up again? It will only upset Non if she hears about it.'

Jed grimaced. 'The man's dead. What 'arm is there in talking about 'im?'

Morgan resisted the urge to take him by the scruff of the neck and shake him. 'Well, are you going to stop spreading gossip to Quinn the landlord?'

'What's it worth if I tell you?'

'It's worth saving yourself the beating you'll get if you don't tell me,' Morgan said.

Jed shrugged. 'I don't know nothing about Caradoc Jones and don't want to. If I was telling the landlord stories, it was just to get a drop of brandy on the house, see?'

Morgan studied the man's face. His words were plausible enough: he'd certainly tell a pack of lies if he thought it would get him something for nothing. 'Are you sure you haven't seen him, Lambert?'

'Course not. The man was drowned, everyone knows that. I didn't see him anyway.'

'I'd better be going, then. I need a good night's rest,' Morgan said, and added, 'It's time you let Albie go his own way.' He glared at Jed. 'You've had more than enough out of the boy, understand?'

'Aye, I understand.'

Out in the street Morgan walked briskly towards the inn. The lamp-lights were shimmering on the wet road and Morgan cursed: the animals that were left would look even skinnier with the rain soaking their hides.

He went straight to his room. He had to ponder Jed Lambert's words. What if he *had* seen Caradoc? But it was impossible. Caradoc would have returned home if he was alive. He had a great deal to lose if he stayed away from Five Saints.

He had only just snuffed out the candle when there was a timid tap on the door. 'Who is it?'

The door opened and Flora came into the room.

'*Duw*, it's dark in here. Haven't you a light, Morgan?'

He relit the candle. Flora was standing at the foot of his bed. 'What is it?' He knew he sounded impatient, but he was tired and rattled by the idea that Caradoc might still be alive.

'It's bad news,' Flora said. 'I'm sorry, Morgan.'

'What are you sorry about? What have you done?'

'It's more what *we*'ve done. Morgan, I'm going to have your child.'

Morgan closed his eyes. What a fool he'd been. Well, there was nothing for it now: he'd have to make an honest woman of Flora and marry her.

CHAPTER TWENTY-ONE

Georgina sat in the conservatory as Clive stood over her, his face dark. 'So, my dear, you won't leave your lover and come back to me?'

'That's right, so it's no use your pestering me.'

'Well, I won't take no for an answer. You are my wife, or have you forgotten that?' There was no response so he changed tack. 'I know I was wrong to leave you, but I want you back, my love.'

'Well, I don't want you.'

'Not even though your lover has abandoned you?'

'He isn't here because he's looking for a place for us to live. He only wishes for us to be together. Somewhere quiet where you won't find us.'

Clive laughed unpleasantly. 'I'm not letting you out of my sight, madam. And you've seen the last of your paramour. By now he'll be far away from you, a married woman!'

'You don't know Matthew. He's not cut from the same cloth as you.'

'That's plain to see. He's a labouring man and I am a gentleman.'

Georgina looked at him with loathing. 'I wish you were dead.'

'That would be too convenient, wouldn't it, my dear?'

'Why don't you go away?' Georgina said. 'I don't love you, I never did – and what do you hope to gain by coming here? I still haven't any money of my own.'

'Your brother is dead and you are now heiress to a fortune. I'd be foolish to stay away from my lawful wife in those circumstances, don't you think?'

'My father won't leave me his money. He'll leave all he has to Rowan, so I'm as badly off as I was on the day you left me.'

A strange expression came over Clive's face. 'You don't know what's happened to your nephew, then?'

'Father has taken him to France and, as far as I know, he hasn't come back yet.'

'Well, your dear little nephew is no more. He died of a fever and your father is a broken man.'

'I don't believe you! How would you know that?' Georgina was shocked. She'd resented the child, but she knew her father doted on him. He couldn't be dead. Clive was lying.

Clive looked at her, his face a mask of triumph. 'I know a great many things that you don't, my sweet. You thought I was ruined when they took my house from me, didn't you? Well, you were wrong, and when the furore died down I returned to London to see to my other business interests.'

Clive sat down and stretched his legs out before him, his hands thrust into his pockets. 'I still own a few lodging properties. You and your family never knew about all my financial interests.'

'If you owned property, why did you run away?' Georgina asked.

'You're not very clever, are you? I ran because it suited me. I didn't want a penniless wife, and I wanted to keep quiet about my smaller properties in case my creditors seized them. I'd bought them under an assumed name, you see. What the eye doesn't see, the heart doesn't grieve over.'

'I can't believe the baby is dead. Surely Papa would have come home by now if he was.' She stared at him for a long moment, trying to sum him up. 'I don't think you'd recognize the truth if it hit you in the face.'

'The brat is dead.'

'Why haven't I heard from Papa, then?'

'Do you ever listen to what I say? Your father cannot face the truth. He took the boy away and blames himself now for the child's death.'

'Aunt Prudence would have written to me, if what you say is true.'

'There's talk of a doctor attending the child, prescribing too much medicine.' He glanced at her. 'I don't think the brat's own mother knows about it yet.'

Georgina took stock of the situation. If what Clive said was true she was the sole heir to her father's fortune and she and Matt would never want for anything. But there was still Clive to deal with.

'You won't get rid of me with a few pounds.' A thin smile curved Clive's lips. 'I can see exactly what you're thinking and I won't be fobbed off.'

'I hate you,' Georgina said. 'I wish I'd never set eyes on you. You never earned an honest penny in your life and, what's more, your prowess in the bedchamber left much to be desired!'

Clive moved swiftly. He grabbed her chin, his fingers biting into the soft flesh. 'You lie!' He ground the words out and spittle came from his clenched teeth as his hand gripped even more tightly. 'I tried to teach you how to be a good wife but you're frigid. I've had better bedfellows from the lower orders than you, my dear wife.'

Georgina tried to push him away, but he held her

fast. His free hand grasped her breast and she cried out. 'You're hurting me, Clive, let me go.'

But he pressed her back into the seat and attempted to lift her skirts. 'You are my wife and you'll not deny me my rights.'

'Not here,' Georgina gasped. 'We'll go upstairs into the bedroom. I don't want to be taken like a kitchenmaid.'

'Why not?' he sneered. 'You have the morals of one.'

His fingers were bruising her cheeks, the heel of his hand pressing on her throat. 'I'm going to have you if it's the last thing I do,' he growled.

'Let me go!' She tried to scream, but he clapped his hand over her mouth.

Suddenly the door crashed open and over Clive's shoulder she saw Matt standing there, a pick handle held aloft. Slowly he brought it down and she heard the sickening crack as it hit Clive's skull. He fell against her, blood running from his mouth.

Matt dragged him away and Clive slumped on to the floor. Then she was in Matt's arms, clinging to him. 'You've killed him, Matt! Oh, dear Lord, what are we going to do now?'

He stood there holding her, his cheek against her hair.

'Oh, Matt, what have we done?' Georgina wailed.

Matt took control. 'I'll bring the horse and carriage to the back of the house and get rid of him. I'll clean him up and make it look as if he had an accident.'

He left her alone for a few minutes while he fetched the carriage and then she watched him wash the blood from Clive's head. She helped him support Clive as they walked out into the cold night air and somehow, between them, they put him into the carriage.

'Go back inside,' Matt said quietly. 'The servants

might be watching. Let them think your husband is drunk. Don't allow anyone into the conservatory until I've cleaned it.'

'But, Matt, they will wonder why I haven't called the footman for help. Why would I allow you to deal with my husband?'

'To salvage your pride, Georgina. They will believe you are ashamed of his drunkenness.'

Georgina watched as Matt drove off, then hurried to her room and changed out of her bloodstained clothes. She tore up her gown and petticoats and pushed them into the fire. Eventually, when she'd stopped shaking, she went into the drawing room and sat down.

She began to cry. It was all so awful, Clive trying to force himself on her, then the dreadful sound of the wood connecting with his skull. Worst of all, if Clive was telling the truth, Rowan was dead. It would break Papa's heart.

When she felt more composed, she rang for the housekeeper. Almost immediately the woman was at the door. 'Please send one of the girls to build up the fire for me, and then you may all retire for the night.'

'But, Mrs Langland, we heard strange noises and the footman saw you and Matthew the gardener help your husband into the carriage. Is anything wrong?'

'My husband was drunk,' Georgina lied. 'Just go to bed, all of you. I want to be alone.' The housekeeper bobbed a curtsy and left her. Shortly after, one of the maids came in and banked up the fire with fresh coals.

Georgina waited until she had left the room, then put her hands over her eyes.

At Ruby's house Non stared out of the window, watching two cats fighting over a piece of offal on the cobbled roadway of the narrow court. Her head was clearing.

The despair was still there – she had lost the man she loved – but it was time she accepted that Caradoc was gone for ever. Now she must concentrate on her son. Rowan was all she had left of Caradoc. She must bring him home and raise him in a way that would have made her dead husband proud.

When Ruby came into the room Non could tell from her pallor that something was wrong. 'What is it?' She got to her feet and grasped Ruby's hands. 'Tell me, is it bad news?'

'There's a footman at the door. He's been sent by your father-in-law and he wants you to go with him straight away.'

'Perhaps he's had news of Caradoc,' Non whispered. 'Or is my baby sick?' Fear constricted her throat. 'Oh, Ruby, tell me everything will be all right.'

'Bless your heart – of course it will. I expect the baby's got a cold or a fever and you're needed to give him medicine. Come on, let me help you with your shawl.'

The carriage belonging to George Jones's family was too wide to enter Treacle Lane but was waiting in the road at the top. Non hurried towards it. 'Can't you tell me what's wrong?' she asked the footman, but he shook his head, opened the door and helped her inside.

All would be well, she reasoned. Ruby thought Rowan must need medication and perhaps George had softened his attitude towards her methods of healing the sick. Even so, fear settled inside her like a stone.

As the carriage jogged along the narrow streets on the east side of town and into the broader squares where the wealthy lived, Non told herself that Rowan would be all right.

She was welcomed into the house in Bloomsbury by George Jones himself. He took her hands and she saw at once that he'd been weeping. 'What's the matter?' she said. 'Tell me quickly. Is it Rowan?'

'Sit down, my dear.' George held her hands tightly. 'I should have called for you before but I've been so ill with grief and I couldn't think of anyone but myself.'

'It's bad news, isn't it?' Non's mouth was dry.

'The worst. Rowan is dead.' He looked away from her stricken face. 'He was taken ill in Paris. I had a doctor to see to him, but there was nothing to be done. Our dear child is gone from us for ever.' He wiped his eyes. 'All I could do was go straight to Five Saints to bury him.' He looked at her, appealing for her to understand. 'Georgina became ill too, when she heard the news about Rowan.' He was silent for a moment. 'She has had troubles of her own to deal with. The housekeeper told me Clive Langland had been there and had threatened her. He had to be taken away drunk.' He rested his hand on Non's arm. 'But ill as she was, she still paid the proper respects to Rowan, believe me.'

Non was hardly listening. She felt she couldn't bear any more pain. Her son had died and she hadn't been with him.

'The boy had a Christian burial, Manon.'

'He's gone, buried, and I haven't even said goodbye to him.' Non stared at her father-in-law with unseeing eyes.

'I can't tell you how much Rowan's death grieves me,' George said. 'I would give my own life to bring him back.' He put his hands to his head. 'What sins have I committed that I've lost my son and grandson in only a few months?' He fell on his knees before her. 'I've wronged you, Manon. I took your son away from you and now I'm being punished for it. May God forgive me, because I'll never forgive myself.'

163

Without a word, Non left George Jones kneeling in the grand drawing room with tears streaming from his eyes.

Outside, she saw nothing of the tall, elegant houses; she was blind to the flowers in the gardens. She was living in a nightmare world where all she could see was the face of her son, alive and smiling, so like Caradoc. Well, he would be with his father in heaven now. But the thought didn't bring her comfort. She was alone in the world. The two people dearest to her were gone for ever.

CHAPTER TWENTY-TWO

Jessie was proud of her new cart. Her rounds took just as long as before but at least her shoulders were spared the weight of the pails. Now she stopped in a Bloomsbury square and waited for the maids to come with their jugs. She felt proud and happy, a real businesswoman at last.

One of the maids Jessie knew came out of the pillared house at the edge of the square and smiled as she held out her jug. 'You're doing well, Jessie. A new cart an' all.' She was from the same village as Jessie, and spoke to her in Welsh.

'Doing my best, see? Got any news, Bronwen?' Jessie dipped her ladle into the pail and poured the milk into the jug.

'Aye, there's been such goings-on by here.' Bronwen's voice dropped to a hushed whisper. She crossed herself solemnly, although she was as much a chapel girl as Jessie was. 'There's been another death in the family.'

'Oh, God bless us,' Jessie said. 'Another? What's happened? Old Mr George Jones, is it, or Miss Prudence? The two of them are getting on and must be shocked at the loss of Caradoc.'

'It's worse than that. It's the poor babba, Rowan. Took abroad, he was, by his grandfather and fell mortally sick there.'

Jessie thought of Non, who would be out of her mind with grief. She'd lost her husband and now her child.

'Poor old Mr Jones is beside himself, crying and moaning. It's getting us all into a terrible state, I can tell you.'

'What about Non?' Jessie asked. 'What sort of state must she be in? I'll have to go and see her, once I've finished my round.'

'I'm sorry to say there's bad news about your round, too.'

'What do you mean?' Jessie asked. 'What bad news?'

The maid heaved a sigh. 'Well, there's a cowman calling now, brings the animals with him and milks them on the doorstep so the milk is really fresh.'

'Well, my milk is fresh and you're still buying from me. Perhaps some of the others in the square will too.' Jessie spoke bravely but she'd taken hardly any money that day, proof that Bronwen was right.

'I'd better go back to my kitchen,' Bronwen said. 'They'll be screaming at me if I stay any longer.'

The day dragged by for Jessie, with only a few sales, and at last she admitted defeat. Several of her buckets were still full of milk that was rapidly turning sour in the sunshine. She went home, tiredness creeping through her. She lifted the pails from the cart she had been so proud of and set them on the bench, wondering if her business would fail before it had properly begun.

It took her some time to wash the pails and clean out the shed, and then she went into the house. She made up her mind to see Non when she felt better. She would fight to the end to keep her business going.

Later that night there was a knock on the door. Jessie looked up from her accounts and snuffed out her candle. No point in wasting good tallow. It was still half

166

light outside in the yard. She opened the door and screamed with delight when she saw Albie standing on the step.

'Jed Lambert has let you go! Come here,' she put her arms round him, 'and give me a big squeeze. I'm so glad to see you.'

Albie held her tightly and kissed her forehead. 'Well, I thought Ruby had given me a warm welcome but this one beats it.'

'Come inside. I've got some bread and cheese in the larder. Are you hungry, Albie?'

He laughed. 'I've been at Ruby's – you don't think she'd let me go out without a square meal, do you?'

'I'm so glad to see you. Tell the truth, I've been a bit lonely without Fred and his family, living in a house by myself.'

'Well, I'm here now and I can help you with the business. That's what we planned. You haven't changed your mind, have you?'

Jessie shook her head. 'No, but I'm worried, Albie. Another cowman has taken over most of my round in the squares where the rich people live. Bronwen Pugh told me he drives his cows to the doorstep so folk can see the milk is really fresh. I had to throw good milk away today because it was turning sour.'

'Well, there are other parts of London where a milk-maid could be busier than a dipper at a summer fair. Why don't we move the business to Whitechapel?' Albie pushed his sleeves above his elbows. He'd grown, Jessie noticed. His weeks on the trail had made a strong man of him. 'Why Whitechapel?' she asked.

'It's a good spot,' Albie insisted. 'There's watermen, coal shippers, tradesmen a-plenty, and they all need fresh milk. I've heard tell that the Jewish people are taking the trade in old clothes from Monmouth Street down to Cutler Street. I tell you, Whitechapel is one of the busiest parts of town – and I should know. I've dipped in many a pocket round there. And if we moved near Whitechapel, you wouldn't have to walk so far every day.'

'Well, if you're sure, Albie, we could try it.'

'Course we could, and it'll be all right, you'll see. I always thought you were silly to walk right across town to Bloomsbury anyway.'

'I don't know about that. I've liked the walk around there,' Jessie protested. 'It's where Fred built up his round.'

'Well, as you said, there's competition for it now. Look, Jessie, I'm a Londoner born and bred, and I know where you can make a good living. Trust me.'

'Well, what about this house?'

'You're only renting it from Fred Dove. You haven't bought it, have you?'

'No.' She smiled wryly. 'I'm not even paying him rent. He said he'd charge me when I made a profit.'

'Well, that'll be a long time coming.'

'All right, no need to rub my nose in it.'

'Look,' Albie said. 'Write to him, tell him what's happened and he'll be only too glad to see you getting on in your own way. Don't worry about leaving the house. He could let it to a lot of lodgers instead of just one. That way he'd make good money.'

'I suppose you're right. But where would we live?'

'Well, we can share a place, and I'll work with you on the milk.'

'I don't know.' She was worried that Albie meant to share her bed, and she wasn't ready for anything like that. Her arrangement with him was business, plain and simple. 'We can't do that. Folk would talk about us.'

'Not if we rent a room each for now. Later we can take a house and let rooms like Ruby does. Whitechapel's full of people needing a place to live.'

'But I haven't much money saved. I don't know if I could afford to rent, even in Whitechapel.'

Albie winked. 'Well, I have a little put by. I didn't waste my time when I was on the road with Jed Lambert,' he said, and held up his hands and waggled them. 'Look, I promise I'll be decent and hardworking, no more dipping, no more lying and cheating. I'll be a reformed character.'

In spite of herself Jessie smiled. 'I'll believe that when I see it.'

Albie was staring at her and Jessie sensed his need. He wanted her – and he wanted what she couldn't give him: her love.

Non sat in her room at Ruby's house and mourned her son. She kept seeing Rowan's dear little face, felt his plump fingers touching her cheek, and felt as though her world had ended.

She became aware of knocking, of voices in the narrow passage, then Ruby was opening the door. She felt a moment of panic: she couldn't face visitors, not yet. But it was Morgan in the doorway, twisting his hat in his hands, his face showing profound sadness. 'I'm so sorry, Non,' he said, holding out his arms to her.

With a moan she went into his embrace, and rested her head on his broad shoulder. 'I'm so glad you've come, Morgan,' she said. 'I don't know if I should go home to Wales or stay in London. Either way I have to make a living. I can't expect my friends to support me indefinitely.'

'Take your time, Non. There's no need to make up your mind just yet.'

'Rowan is buried at home in Five Saints, and I haven't yet visited his grave.' She looked up at him. 'Will you take me to Wales, Morgan, and then, if I decide to come back, will you travel with me?'

'I'll be glad to, Non. I planned to go back anyway.' He released her. 'I'm to be married. Flora and I are to be wed as soon as possible.'

He didn't look like a man ready to be joined in marriage with the woman he loved, Non thought. 'Are you happy, Morgan?'

She had voiced the question without thinking. 'I'm sorry. I shouldn't have asked something so foolish.'

'No,' he said flatly. 'I'm not happy, Non, but I'm ready to do the honourable thing and put a ring on Flora's finger. She's expecting my child.'

Non sighed. 'I'm sure you'll grow to love her, Morgan. Flora is a fine woman, hard-working and honest. I'm sure she loves you or she wouldn't be having your baby.'

'We'll all go back to Wales together, then. When do you want to travel?'

'Any time that suits you – straight away, if you like. How long will it take us to get there?'

'With a decent wagon and pair, and if we stick to the good roads, about four days.'

Non nodded. 'I've enough money put by to pay for it all.' She looked down at her hands. 'My father-in-law is giving me an allowance. He's going home too, and he wanted me to travel with him, but I can't help blaming him for Rowan's death. If he hadn't taken my boy to Paris, if I'd been called in to nurse him with my own remedies, he'd still be here today.'

Morgan made the arrangements for the journey, and before long Non was saying goodbye to Ruby. She clung to her for a long moment.

'Promise you'll be back,' Ruby said, with tears in her eyes.

'I promise.' Non felt it didn't matter where she lived now: she had no home, no ties.

The trip was accomplished without difficulty. Non was silent for most of the time. Occasionally Flora would tempt her to eat, but otherwise she sat in the wagon feeling only her grief. The days passed in a haze of unhappiness.

Five Saints was unchanged. The solid houses and green fields surrounding them should have brought Non comfort, but she felt as though she belonged nowhere.

Morgan booked them into the Greyhound Lodge, a fine old inn fitted with dark wooden furniture and heavy curtains. A cheerful fire burned in the grate, but its warmth could not take the chill from Non's heart.

Morgan was always at her side, and Flora was with her too, but always in the background. She was wan and quiet, and Non shook off her desolation to make an effort to talk to her. 'Come to my room after supper, Flora. I'll be glad of the company and perhaps you will too.'

'We both need someone to talk to.'

Non went to sit in her room and watch the blazing coals in the fireplace. She thought of the times when she'd been happy, when her husband and son had been alive. Those days were gone now and soon, when she had seen her son's grave and prayed beside it, she would have to pick herself up and make a life for herself. She would sell her herbal remedies to folk who couldn't afford a doctor, try to do some good in the world. But she would be lonely.

There was a gentle tap on the door and Flora peered in. 'Is it all right for me to come in?'

'Of course. Come and sit by the fire. You look as if you need a good rest. The journey must have tired you.'

Flora closed the door and sat on the opposite side of the grate. 'You don't want to scold me for being a bad woman, do you?' Flora's eyes were moist. 'I've held two men in my arms and the first made me believe I loved him, but Morgan has shown me what real love is. Now,' she swallowed hard, 'I'm tying him down and I'm sure it's not what he wants. I've been such a fool, falling for a baby, but I got carried away by my love for him.'

'Don't blame yourself, Flora. None of us is perfect. I'm sure Morgan cares about you, and I wish you well in your marriage.'

'I'm not too blind to see one thing, though,' Flora said softly. 'I'll never be first in Morgan's heart because you will always be his greatest love. But he's a good, honourable man and I think I can make him happy.'

'He's my friend,' Non said. 'Morgan has always accepted he will never be more than that to me. I love Caradoc, and no one could ever take his place.'

'You've had terrible things happen in your life,' Flora said, 'but you can still do so much to help others with your remedies.'

'You're right,' Non said. 'I should be getting back to work, in London, where there's great need for medicine folk can afford. At least by making it I can help others.'

'It will be good for you to move back,' Flora said gently. 'All your friends are there. I'll be married to Morgan in a few weeks' time, and I don't know where we're going to live. His house was rented and while he was on the road the landlord let it to someone else, but we'll be all right.' She paused. 'And I'll try my best to help if ever you need me.'

'That's kind of you, Flora. I'm tired now, so I think I'll go to bed and sleep.'

The next morning, standing in the graveyard with the clouds an ominous purple over her head, Non felt alone, even though Morgan and Flora were just a step behind her. She was grateful to her friends, and warmed by their love, but all she wanted now was to be alone with her son.

CHAPTER TWENTY-THREE

Georgina arrived at her aunt's London house with her servants, only to find that her father and Aunt Prudence had gone to Wales to visit Rowan's grave. In a way it was a relief: she needed to be alone to think things through.

She had left home on impulse, fleeing from Clive's death. She didn't look on it as murder – Matt had been protecting her, he hadn't meant to kill Clive. He had been so brave, clearing up the evidence, which proved how much he loved her. She'd told him to continue working at Broadoaks as though nothing had happened. She had asked what he had done with the body, but he had refused to tell her. It was better that she knew as little as possible, he had said, so firmly that she had not questioned him again.

She spent several days alone at the Bloomsbury house, keeping to her room for the most part, worrying about Clive's death. And she wanted Matt. She missed his dry wit, his love, and, most of all, his strong body in bed beside her. She was no longer interested in buying fashionable clothes: all she wanted was Matt. She was relieved when Aunt Prudence returned home. At least now she would have company, and in a few days she could go home.

'It was dreadful, Georgina!' were her aunt's first

words. 'I hated the drive to Wales, I hated the bleakness of the land there, and the little grave was so sad it tore my heart to shreds.'

Georgina took her aunt's hands. 'Never mind. You're in London now, back where you belong. What about Papa? Why didn't he come with you?'

'He's distraught. Poor George feels the baby's death was his fault. He keeps saying he shouldn't have taken Rowan to Paris and if only his daughter-in-law had been there the baby would have lived.'

Georgina agreed grudgingly with her father. Non might be a scheming hussy but she knew how to cure folk with the herbs she boiled, the roots she infused and the creams she made. 'We don't know what would have happened if Papa had stayed at home,' she said. 'It's not right that he should torture himself. It's not his fault, of course it's not.'

'Well, *we* know that but poor George will go on blaming himself, whatever we say.'

'Will he be coming to London?' Georgina asked. 'I don't like to think of him all alone at Broadoaks.'

'Neither do I,' said Aunt Prudence. 'Do you think you should go home to be with him? You can return to Town when he's feeling better.'

It was the perfect excuse to go home to Matt. 'I'll leave in the morning,' Georgina said. 'Will you send someone to make the arrangements for me?'

Her aunt nodded, fingering the jet necklace that hung over the bodice of her black gown. 'It will be done first thing. Now, Georgie, I hear Clive has paid you a visit. Have you seen him since he came to you at Broadoaks and behaved so disgracefully?'

Georgina felt the cold hand of fear clutch at her heart. 'No. Is he likely to come here?' She knew she mustn't arouse her aunt's suspicions.

'I couldn't say, dear. That man is a law unto himself. He's a scoundrel and you are well rid of him.' She frowned. 'Now, don't consider letting him return to you. I know life as a deserted wife isn't easy, but you're better off without a man like him.'

Georgina breathed a sigh of relief. Her aunt wasn't suspicious about Clive. Perhaps, with luck on their side, she and Matt would be safe.

Jessie continued her round as usual, calling at the big houses in Bloomsbury, offering her milk, but at last she admitted Albie was right. It was time she moved to Whitechapel.

As she pushed her cart across London she made up her mind to let Fred Dove know she had to leave his house. But it had begun to feel like home – even the lack of furniture didn't bother her – and outside there was a yard big enough for the cows. What would she find in Whitechapel?

When she got home Albie was already there. He took one look at her face and, without a word, began emptying the pails of milk down the drain. Jessie sat on the box in the kitchen and began to cry.

When he had finished, Albie came in and took her into his arms. 'Don't, Jessie. You'll make a fine businesswoman, you'll see. Folk will be clamouring for the good milk you can sell them.'

'I know you mean well, Albie, but it was my dream to live in this house and build up a fine business here. I'm frightened of working in Whitechapel – no one knows me there, and there's so many beggars that I doubt folk will have the money for milk.'

'There's plenty of people who want milk and are willing to pay for it,' Albie said stoutly. 'I'm a

176

Londoner to the bone and, believe me, I can sniff out a good opportunity when I see one.'

'What do you mean?'

'Well, you know what I told you about the old clothes market in Monmouth Street moving to Cutler Street? Well, you'll have a good round there. Just come with me for a day and you'll see.'

'I suppose it wouldn't do any harm to look,' Jessie said.

Albie smiled at her. 'Look, don't write to Fred for a few days. We'll stay here and I'll take you on the rounds until you know your way about. Then I'll look for rooms to rent with a yard at the back so we can keep the cows in a decent shed.'

'But will folk want animals on their doorstep?'

'There's so much going on there, they won't notice another cow or two. You'll see I'm right when we get there.'

Jessie felt a flicker of hope. Perhaps she might yet see her dreams come true. She kissed Albie's cheek. He drew back quickly. 'What's wrong?' Jessie asked, surprised. 'Aren't we friends?'

'Yes, we are, but I'd like us to be more than that – so don't play with me.'

'I'm not!' Jessie said. 'Look, Albie,' she swallowed hard, 'I thought I was in love with Fred Dove but then I discovered I wasn't. Now I'm going to take everything day by day. I need you, Albie, as a friend to help me find a new round. I'd be lost on the streets of London without you. For now will that be enough?'

He nodded slowly. 'All right. Tomorrow I'll take you to Whitechapel and we'll look for customers. There's a crowd of Irish living in the area and a lot of Jewish people in the Leman Estate. It's a nice, respectable place with some big houses.'

'Thank you for standing by me, Albie. You're a real friend,' Jessie said humbly.

Albie grinned down at her. 'And friendship is a good place to start any love affair.' He tweaked her nose, and she wondered how she would have managed without him.

In the morning, Jessie followed Albie along the small streets and narrow courts of Whitechapel. She was surprised to discover that Whitechapel high street was broad and lined with coaching inns – far different from what she had imagined.

A woman carrying a basket of fruit picked her way through a flock of sheep and a man was driving a few cattle along the road; their udders were full and they were bellowing mournfully.

'See the haycarts at the side of the road?' Albie said. 'They're heading for the market just to the left of the street.'

Jessie was dazzled by the scene. 'It's so busy here and the buildings look respectable,' she said.

'Away from the main streets it's different,' Albie told her. 'The yards and courts are dark, dismal places, but I dare say even there we'd find a customer or two for our fresh milk.'

'Are we going to live here?' Jessie asked, heart sinking at the thought of leaving Fred's sunny house for one in the maze of streets here.

'We'll have to,' Albie replied. 'Better to be on the spot than travel across town every day.' He smiled. 'I'm no cowman but I reckon we'd end up with buckets full of curds and whey by the time we'd bumped the cart this far.'

'I suppose you're right,' Jessie said. 'Can we go home now? The noise and the smell of the cattle are getting on my nerves.'

'Bleedin' 'ell, Jess. After all the times you've walked the drovers' roads behind a load of cattle you complain about Whitechapel high street?'

'Ah, but we were out in the fresh air. The cattle didn't smell so bad then.'

'You slept many nights in barns with them, didn't you? You should be used to animals.'

Jessie sighed. 'You may be right – but let's go home, Albie, and tomorrow or the next day you can find us lodgings here.'

She was glad to leave the noisy high street, and walked silently beside Albie trying to imagine living in Whitechapel. Her heart wasn't in it but she had no choice: she had to earn a living and so did Albie – if he stopped dipping as he'd promised he would.

It was good to be back at Fred's house with the yard outside and the cattle contentedly munching the grass. She sat on her box, with Albie on the floor, his long legs crossed. 'Remember what we talked about earlier,' he said suddenly, 'about us being friends?'

'Yes?' She thought she knew what Albie was going to say.

'I know you don't love me,' he went on, voice flat and unemotional, 'but it makes sense for us to share a room.'

'Why can't we have two like we said?'

'Well, it would be cheaper to have one room,' he said reasonably. 'We'll be in lodgings for a while until we find an empty house to rent.'

Jessie swallowed hard. 'But, Albie, people would think we were married.'

There was a world of longing in his eyes. 'Nothing would give me greater pleasure than to marry you but I know you don't want to marry me. I wouldn't lay a finger on you, Jess, you must know that.'

179

'Let me think about it,' Jess said slowly.

'Aye, but don't think for too long. We'd be better off doing the planning now so that we can move as soon as possible.'

Suddenly Jessie saw the sense in what he was saying. 'All right,' she said. 'We'll share a room. You make the arrangements as soon as you can.'

He didn't leap up and take her in his arms as she'd imagined. He just smiled, and Jessie saw that he was young and handsome – willing to work hard too – and that was the most any woman could ask for in a business partner and friend.

Georgina sat fretting in the conservatory. To be back at Broadoaks wasn't the joy she'd hoped for. Her father was ill and stayed in his room. He was still guilt-ridden and sick at heart about Rowan's death too.

There had been little opportunity for her to spend time with Matt even though he had stayed at his post, working among the trees and plants in the grounds. Sometimes she felt she could scream with the boredom of it all. She had been home for almost a week before she found a chance to see him alone. In a blaze of autumn sun she walked to the greenhouse and saw him inside, his sleeves rolled up above strong forearms. She closed the door behind her and put her arms round him. 'I've missed you, Matt,' she said, nuzzling his neck, 'I thought I'd die if I didn't see you.'

He kissed her passionately and she responded, aching for him to make love to her, but it was too dangerous. She drew away a little. 'I think we've got away with it, Matt,' she said breathlessly. 'No one has missed Clive.' She laid a finger over his lips as he began to speak. 'It will be all right, you'll see.'

'I'm not sorry he's dead.' Matt stroked her cheek.

'When I think of the way he treated you I could kill him all over again.'

'Well, he's gone out of our lives now. It's only a matter of time before everyone will assume he's died naturally and I'll be a free woman.'

Matt's fingers were tracing the line of her jaw now. 'Free to marry me.'

Could she give up her position as a respected society lady to marry a gardener? Georgina wondered. Did she love Matt enough for that? Somehow she doubted it.

CHAPTER TWENTY-FOUR

He held the axe aloft and let it fall on the piece of wood he was chopping. Sweat dripped from his brow and he rested for a moment, watching the spiral of smoke rise from the cottage's chimneys. It was about time he accepted that his old life had gone for ever. This was his life now, with the sweet girl inside the house. He should be the happiest man alive, yet he couldn't shake off the niggling belief that he had a wife and maybe children somewhere else.

'Craig!' Gwenllyn was coming towards him, skirts billowing in the breeze. 'I've some cordial for you.' She settled herself on a fallen tree. 'Come and rest. You've been out here for hours.'

He sat beside her and pushed back his hair. 'Don't worry about me, I'm much better now and my leg is almost completely healed thanks to your wonderful care of me.'

'You should still be taking things easy. You had a terrible accident and I'm lucky to have you.' She touched the scar at his temple. 'It was a wonderful day when Nanna and I found you washed up by the river.'

'I wonder if anybody searched for me along the bank.'

'Well, your clothes – or what remained of them – were soaking wet, so I think we must have been the first to spot you. And no one else was in sight.'

'I must have been washed a long way down the Wye,' he said, 'and I know I'm lucky to be alive, but I feel anxious about having an easy life here with you. All I do is milk the cows, feed the hens and chop logs for the fire. Perhaps it's about time I did some travelling, tried some of the border towns to see if anyone knows me.'

'You're not ready for that yet,' Gwenllyn said softly. 'You were born a gentleman, we know that, and you work like a good labouring man. I'm proud of you, Craig, and I couldn't manage without you now.' She leaned against his shoulder. 'And I won't have to manage without you. We're going to be married soon, aren't we?'

He sighed. 'Yes, but I wish—'

'Don't wish for anything but a peaceful life here with me.'

He took her hand and kissed the palm. 'I hope I'm not cheating you, Gwenllyn. What if I remember one day that I have a wife and family? You don't know anything about me, yet you've taken me on trust all this time.'

'I love you, Craig. I want you with me for ever and I feel in my heart that we are meant to be together.' She pulled his head down to hers and kissed him, lips hot, and he could only enjoy the sensations that pulsed through his veins.

He drew her down on to the grass and opened her bodice, his fingers seeking out her breast. As he caressed her he felt her respond to him, and he moved aside her skirts.

'I love you, my darling,' she said huskily. 'I want you so badly I could die.' She lifted herself up to him and as he joined with her she gave a little gasp. 'Oh, my darling Caradoc.'

The name struck him like a blow, and the passion

drained away from him. He rolled off her and lay looking up at the sky. It was very blue, with wispy clouds. 'My God!' he said. 'My name is Caradoc. How did you know?'

Gwenllyn's face was suffused with colour. 'I didn't!' she said. 'It just came out – it didn't mean anything. It's so much like Craig – it was just a mistake.'

He tried to think past the haze in his mind, to connect something with the name Gwenllyn had called him. 'Damn!' He thumped the grass. 'If you know anything about me, for pity's sake tell me.'

She clutched his hand. 'I know only that you came out of the river and that I love you so much I could die of it.'

'You must know something, Gwen,' he said softly. 'Wasn't there anything with me, in my clothing?'

'There was nothing, nothing at all.' Tears splashed on to her clasped hands. 'I'm sorry I called you the wrong name but I don't know why I did.' She gulped back a sob.

He drew her into his arms and she clung to him. Now he felt ashamed. 'Don't cry any more. I dare say the name means nothing – perhaps it belonged to a friend or a cousin, I just don't know.'

'Craig, I can't bear it when you look so worried, so lost! But you're safe with me. Please don't be angry with me again because I can't bear it.'

'I'm sorry,' he said. 'I wouldn't hurt you for the world.' He kissed her, then stood up and drew her to her feet. The mood for passion had gone, and when he looked up into the sky the sun was sinking below the horizon. Suddenly it seemed like an omen.

Morgan and Flora were married quietly in the small church that crouched into the craggy side of Kilvey

184

Hill, looking down on the small township of Swansea. Afterwards they went to the cottage Morgan had rented for them, and Flora, with the gold band on her finger, felt she was the luckiest woman in the world.

That night they slept in separate beds, and Flora cried herself to sleep. It served her right. She knew Morgan didn't love her, that their marriage would never be more than a bargain, yet she had given herself to him and fallen for his baby. Many men would have said they had been tricked into marriage, but not Morgan: he was a gentleman, a man of his word. He would bring up his child with a glad heart but he would always be longing for another woman, who would never be his wife.

The day after the wedding, Morgan left her to go on the trail with a fresh herd for Smithfield market. Flora knew he would be gone for more than a month and felt sick at heart.

She sat in their cottage and wondered how long it would take him to forgive her for falling pregnant. Not that he'd reproached her in any way – he'd been kind and considerate – but he'd had the look in his eyes of a man who longed to be anywhere but with his bride.

She got to her feet at last and looked round her, wondering what to do. The cottage was spotless but perhaps she should take down the curtains and wash them to freshen the colours. And there were windows to polish and floors to scrub.

She worked all day, washing, drying and ironing, but the misery wouldn't go away. She was not used to staying indoors, but the days were shortening and soon, she told herself, the droves would be over for the year. The Morgan would be at home with her – and the baby.

She hoped she was carrying a son – a man like Morgan needed a son. Her heart lifted. Once they had

185

a family Morgan would accept his lot with patience and dignity. Slowly, one day, he would come to love her.

'When and where are we going to be married?' Gwenllyn asked. She had asked him the same questions for days now, and Caradoc was reluctant to answer her. He saw her look up at him as they walked down the hill towards the riverbank – the river drew him endlessly: it held the secrets of his life. The truth about his past lay somewhere in the depths of the Wye, he was sure.

'It's difficult, Gwenllyn. How can we get married while I don't even know my own name? Perhaps it would be better if we waited for a while longer.'

Gwenllyn shook her head. 'We can be married in the little chapel in the village. We'll make up a name for you.'

'If we marry I want my first name to be Caradoc,' he said. 'I've come to feel that it *is* my name. Perhaps you'll call me that now.'

'All right, *cariad*. You can be any name you choose. What about Rees for your surname?'

It didn't sound familiar but Rees was as good as any other name, he thought. 'We'll have to talk to the minister,' he said cautiously, 'ask him if the marriage will be legally binding if I use a new name.'

'No!' Gwenllyn's face was suddenly pale. 'Don't say anything about it to the minister – he might refuse to marry us.'

'Well, then, perhaps we *should* wait a while.'

Gwenllyn looked down at her shoes. 'We share a bed and I'm worried I might fall for a baby.' Her eyes met his. 'I know the village folk don't care about me one way or another,' she slipped her hand into his, 'but I would feel better if we made our promises before God. Surely that can't be wrong?'

'All right.' He gave up the unequal struggle. He wanted to bed Gwenllyn and it was only fair that he put a ring on her finger. So what if he had been married in another place and at another time? His life was now at Gwenllyn's side, sharing her hearth and her board as well as her bed. 'We'll be married as soon as it can be arranged.'

Her smile was radiant. 'You won't be sorry, my darling. I'll love you as you've never been loved before. I promise I'll be the best wife a man could have.' She squeezed his hand.

'I've no money that I'm aware of and I'm living on your generosity. That's not a very good start to a marriage.'

'It's all the marriage I want,' she said softly.

He stood at the waterside, looking down into the river, and heard the faint bellow of a bull, then a horn sounding on the still air. Something stirred in his mind.

'Come home now,' Gwenllyn said quickly. 'I'm chilled by the wind.' She put her arm through his and drew him away. 'Let's go and see if the blackberries are ripening.'

Reluctantly, he allowed her to drag him away from the water's edge. Perhaps she was frightened of the river, afraid it would suck him in to its depths again. He smiled. 'Come on, then, Gwen. Let's have some toast and honey and sit by the fireside like an old married couple.'

'I'd like nothing better,' she said, eyes gleaming with mischief, 'except that after our toast and honey, we'll go early to bed instead of sitting by the fire.'

He bent and kissed her parted lips. She was so eager for him, asking nothing of him but his love. Well, he would give her all the love he was capable of and yet, he knew, there would always be a secret part of him that she could never reach.

Jed Lambert watched as the two figures merged in the distance. They were kissing. She was a beautiful girl and he, well, he was Caradoc Jones, son of George Jones, and mourned by all his family, including his dear wife Non. But she wasn't his dear wife any more. It seemed that Caradoc didn't remember his past – or maybe he didn't want to.

There was money to be made out of the situation, he was sure. But who should he talk to? George Jones would probably have him beaten half to death, force him to tell everything, and he'd gain not a penny.

There was Miss Georgina, a flighty piece, and on her father's death she'd inherit everything. She had most to lose if Caradoc was found. She would probably pay him well to keep the knowledge to himself.

He was impatient to get the drove over and done with. He was still a long way from London and Smithfield market. He shook the reins, urging the horse into a gallop. He had ridden ahead of the drove to arrange accommodation for the night and planned to take a room at the Lamb and Flag, where the food was good and the beds were clean – and, with luck, there'd be a buxom serving girl to share his.

He headed up the steep incline to where the inn was perched on the brow of the hill. Down below him the winding river was silvered by distance and sunlight.

Strangely, he missed young Albie: the boy was a good storyteller and he had enlivened the long hours on the roads with his talk of London and the rich pickings to be had. It seemed a damned sight easier to steal for a living than to ride along the drovers' roads until your bones ached.

At the inn, the landlord came to the door to welcome him. 'Good evening to you, Jed,' he said. 'I thought I heard the sound of the horn in the distance. Want a bed for the night, do you?'

'I do that, Joshua, and a woman to share it with.' He slid from the saddle and held out his hand. 'Good to be here again.'

'Same old Jed, straight to the point. I suppose you can wait for a woman until you've had a meal and some beer, though.'

'Just about.' Jed followed the man indoors and sat on one of the wooden benches.

'I hear old Dai's putting up his prices for grass.' Joshua was pouring beer into a tankard.

'Not again? Farmers have a rich enough living as it is without putting up the price of grazing. *Duw*, if the price of grass gets any higher it won't pay me to bring the animals this way at all.'

'Don't say that. We'd miss you and your talk. What's happened to the young boyo, that Albie? He was good for a laugh.'

'I let him go,' Jed said. 'He couldn't forget his pickpocket ways, stealing from his own.'

'Shame, but I enjoyed his stories. Anyway, I'll send Mali to serve you, nice new young wench, see?' Joshua winked. 'Don't say she's never been bedded but she's fresh and clean. I think you'll like her.'

'Broken the filly in yourself, I'll wager.'

'Maybe, maybe not.'

Jed leaned back against the warm wood of the bench. Tonight all his appetites would be satisfied, and his mouth creased into a grin when he saw young Mali bring a foaming tankard towards him. Her eyes were

189

bright, her breasts bounced enticingly beneath her dress and Jed licked his lips in anticipation. The trip wasn't going so bad and when he got back to Wales he'd go and see Miss Georgina Jones and make her pay a good price for his silence. If luck was on his side, he might never again have to suffer the hardships of the drovers' roads.

CHAPTER TWENTY-FIVE

Non tore the reddish-brown leaves of the pellitory plant into shreds and mixed them with a little honey; beside her stood a small glass of muscadel which she spooned slowly into the bowl, covering it with a clean cloth. She would leave the syrup to stand for half an hour to ferment, then it would be ready to use.

'Good thing you came back to London, Non. I don't think I could stand the pain in my teeth if you didn't keep feeding me that medicine.' Ruby sat near the fire, a rag filled with salt tied to her swollen cheek. 'Supposed to help is this salt lark but it don't do much good. Jokin' apart, though, it is good to have you back where I can keep an eye on you.'

Non forced a smile. 'Well, I'm glad to be here with my friends, and there was nothing to keep me in Wales.'

'Now don't go feeling sorry for yourself, girl. You've a good head on you – you could make a living for yourself anywhere in the world.'

'I know I shouldn't feel sorry for myself but I can't help it sometimes. I feel so alone.'

'Well, look at me,' Ruby said, 'all on my own for years. Plenty of men around, my lodgers to start with, but I haven't met anyone I could fall for. You've had a great love, and I know it seems cruel that he and the child have been taken away from you, but that's life, Non. There's nothing we can do about it.'

'I know that.' Non smiled suddenly. 'I'll try to put my grumbles away but you stop giving me your home-made philosophies or I won't give you any medicine.'

Ruby patted her arm. 'You're a good, brave girl, and you have a lot of grieving to do, but some day you'll find happiness again, I'm sure.'

Non didn't believe she could ever be happy again but she had to count her blessings: she had her friends around her, she had her health, and there was nothing more she could ask for in this life.

'You know Albie's going to live with Jessie?' Ruby said. 'She's not very keen on the idea but it'll be cheaper for them – and she won't be bothered by young layabouts. She's pretty, she's got a business, and she'd be a good catch for any man. Albie needs to look after her, now they're moving to Whitechapel.'

'I think she does love Albie.' Non warmed her hands at the fire – the weather was chilly, with a bite of autumn in the air. 'I don't think she realizes it, but she's bright and lively when she's with him.'

They sat in silence for a few minutes. Ruby pointed to the bowl on the table. 'Isn't that ready yet? My jaw feels it's going to burst. My teeth feel so bad I could almost pull them out myself!'

Non strained the liquid through a clean rag, squeezing the cloth to extract every drop of juice from the mixture. 'This will have you feeling better in a couple of minutes. Drink it slowly.'

Ruby sipped it. A log fell in the grate, sending sparks up the chimney. 'Do you know – I think the pain's going already.' She took off her bandage and held it towards the fire. 'When I've warmed this I'll put it back on. I know I look a sight in it but I'll try anything to make the pain go away.'

'Try getting someone to take your teeth out, Ruby,' Non said drily. 'That's the best remedy of all.'

'It's all right for you – you're not the one who 'as to suffer the agony of *that*! Let's talk about something else to keep my mind off my aches and pains.'

'The drovers are coming to Smithfield on Friday,' Non said. 'I wonder if I'll see Morgan. I hope so, he's always been like a brother to me.'

'Well, you're not like a sister to him. He's in love with you but you're too daft to see it.'

'Caradoc is the only man I'll ever love. I'll never marry again,' Non said.

'It will get easier to bear. No pain lasts for ever.' Ruby touched her cheek tentatively. 'Except toothache!'

Jessie followed Albie up the stairs of the tall house in Leman Street, relieved that a kindly Mrs Levy had let them a room at the top of the house. She was still unhappy moving away from Fred's pleasant house but she knew Albie was right – she would never earn enough of a living to pay Fred back for all his generosity. As it was, he'd let her keep the cows: it would cost him more to ship them over to Ireland than the worth of them.

'There's only one bed, Jess,' Albie pointed out, 'but I can sleep on a chair.' He winked at her. 'I wouldn't say no to a share of the blankets, though.'

Jessie put down her bag. The room was unexpectedly light and pleasant, but the houses in Leman Street were owned by folk who made a successful living. Albie had been right about the area. Old clothes hung all along the street, tidy respectable ones, some a little out of fashion but made from good cloth and clean. She might buy some for herself – her wardrobe, if it could be called that, consisted of two gowns and a threadbare coat.

'Did you hear what I said, Jess, about us sharing the blankets?'

'Albie, we're friends, and I'm happy for us to live together and make a respectable living. Of course we'll share the blankets. But not the bed – we've got enough to think about as it is. It's not going to be easy. This room is pleasant and respectable but the cows will be a few streets away and we have to find rent for their yard as well as our room.'

'Well, we'll be up early tomorrow, do the milking then, start earning right away.'

Jessie felt panic grip her. True, she possessed the handcart and two good milking cows, but she had no money and Albie had nothing but what he'd stolen from gullible visitors to London. How could she hope to make a success of a business with so shaky a foundation?

But it was too late to change her plans now. She was committed to paying Mrs Levy the rent every week and she had to keep the animals fed and watered. She had obligations and it would need all her wit to pay her way.

Albie would help with the heavy work, lifting the pails on to the cart and washing them after the round, but he wouldn't be bringing any money in, unless he went back to dipping – and that was the last thing Jessie wanted. She was afraid he would be caught again.

'I'm starving.' Albie's voice broke into her thoughts. 'What if I go out and get us a pie each?'

Jessie looked round the room: the fire was the only place where she could cook some stew, or boil a piece of ham. 'We'll buy something in tonight but we can't afford to spend money like this. Tomorrow, when the round's finished, I'll go to the market, get some meat and vegetables and make us a proper meal.'

'I can do that while you're out,' Albie said quickly. 'I'm a dab hand at cooking.'

'When have you done any? Not at Ruby's, I'll bet a shilling.'

'You're right! I never cooked a morsel at Ruby's, but when I was on the trail with Jed Lambert I learned to cook on an open fire.'

Jessie sat down and eased off her shoes. 'Go on, then, and get the food. Talking about eating has made me hungry.'

Albie stood in the doorway. 'It's going to be all right, Jessie. We'll make a good living between us, you'll see.'

When he'd gone, Jessie sat looking into the fire. It was getting dark, but she wouldn't light the candle yet. Candles cost money. Suddenly her fears crowded in on her: what if she didn't succeed and they ended up in a debtors' prison? She thought of the days she'd spent with Fred Dove, happy days when she worked hard but didn't have to keep a business afloat.

By the time Albie returned with the pies Jessie was almost asleep. She had to be up early in the morning to find some customers, so as soon as she'd eaten she'd go to bed.

'Lovely and hot, Jess. They smell good, don't they?'

'I'll get us some plates.' The tall cupboard in one of the alcoves looked as if it might contain crockery and cutlery, but when she opened the door there were only empty shelves. 'We'll have a picnic,' she said. 'It won't be the first time I've eaten a pie with my fingers.'

The meal was good, freshly cooked. 'I caught the pieman when he'd just taken them out of the oven,' Albie said.

'Well, make the most of it,' Jessie said. 'Tomorrow we'll have boiled chicken and perhaps a few potatoes. You'll have to go out and buy some plates and cutlery.'

'Sounds good to me,' Albie said, smiling.

When supper was over, Jessie watched him rake out the fire. 'I'll light it first thing so you get up to a warm room,' he said.

'Don't worry about me,' Jessie said. 'I faced enough sharp mornings when I was on the drovers' roads. We'll leave the fire until later in the day – we'll have to save on coal.' She went over to the table and peered into the tin jug that stood on it. 'I'll have a wash before I go to bed,' she said slowly, wondering how she could undress without embarrassing them both.

Apparently Albie caught her train of thought. 'I'll go for a bedtime stroll.' He licked his fingers. 'I can wash once you're in bed.'

Jessie undressed and washed quickly in the cold water. She thought again of living in Fred's house. A whole house to herself – how fortunate she'd been. But all that was behind her. She slid into bed. The newly washed blankets smelt fresh and she was happy that Mrs Levy kept a good supply. She snuggled down, pulling them up to her chin. It was almost dark in the room now and soon her eyes closed.

She heard Albie come in, heard his strangled cry as he bumped his shin on the table leg, and turned her back so that he could undress. Then the bed springs creaked as, to her surprise, he settled in beside her. It was too late to argue with him, she thought. She was so tired that the effort of sending him to sleep on the chair was too much to contemplate.

'Goodnight, Albie,' she murmured.

CHAPTER TWENTY-SIX

Georgina walked beside Matt across the fields behind the house, far enough away from Broadoaks that they would not be seen together. She stopped beneath the sheltering boughs of a tree and looked up at him, her eyes alight with happiness. 'Everything is going to be all right for us now,' she said. 'No one has thought to ask where Clive Langland has gone.'

'It's not been long since . . . Perhaps no one's missed him yet.' Matt was frowning. 'I can't believe I killed him.'

Her smile faded. 'He was attacking me – you did the only thing possible, Matt, so try not to think about it.'

'I struck out without thinking.'

Georgina took his hand. 'Forget about Clive. I don't think anyone in the world would care what happened to him. He was one for travelling here, there and everywhere, and eventually people will assume he's dead and that I'm a widow.'

'What good will that do us, though?' Matt said unhappily. 'I know you wouldn't want to marry me. I'm too far below you.'

'Clive boasted to me that he owns property in London. It would come to me once he was assumed dead.'

'You're rich enough already, Georgina. You don't need more money.'

The hint of disapproval in his voice stung her. 'I'm not rich, Matt. I live at Broadoaks because my father allows me to. As I've already told you, I have no money of my own so there are no rich pickings to be had from me.'

'Georgie, you know that's not what I want. I earn a decent living as a gardener and I can work anywhere. I could keep both of us quite comfortably.'

'Well, I'm not ready to give up everything. My father's money should come to me and he would cut me off without a penny if he had an inkling that I'm involved with you. Matt, I can't marry you while my father is alive.' She was pleased she'd thought of such a good excuse.

He put his arms round her and kissed her throat. 'I only want you, Georgie. I don't care about money, you know that.'

She released herself from his embrace – she couldn't concentrate while he was so close to her. 'I do, and it's part of why I love you, Matt, but I have to be careful.'

'Not if we were married, showed the world we're in love. Why would you have to be careful then?'

Georgina tried to think of the right answer. 'Look, no one knows Clive is dead, so we can't marry at the moment anyway. And Papa has suffered so many blows lately that I couldn't bring myself to hurt him again. I know your worth, but he would think you're not good enough to marry into the gentry.'

'Your father is rich and clever, but he was a working man when he was young. We all know how George Jones rose from dealing in cows to become the owner of the Bank of the Black Ox. His achievements make poor folk like me feel we might be successful one day.'

Georgina laid her hand over her forehead. 'Don't talk about it any more, Matt. Let's just enjoy our moments together while we can.' She wound her arms round his neck and drew him close to her. 'I love you, Matt. I didn't know what love was until I met you.' She ran her hand down over the strong taut muscles of his chest and lower to the buttons on his trousers. He was hard against her hand and she smiled up at him. 'You want me and I want you, Matt. Let that be enough for now.'

Jessie was glad that Albie was at her side on her first delivery round the streets of Whitechapel. He was right: many folk were pleased to have the milk brought to their doorstep. After a few hours, almost all the supply was gone.

'We're doin' all right, ain't we?' Albie said, his smile wide, eyes alight, 'and once you get used to the round I can find some other work and bring in extra money. We'll be all right, Jess.'

'Just so long as you don't go back to your old trade,' Jessie said sternly. 'I need you, Albie, like I've never needed anyone before.'

He lifted an empty pail to the back of the cart and looked at Jessie with a light in his eye that was unmistakable. 'Now, don't go getting the wrong idea,' she said quickly. 'I need you as a friend, now, is what I meant.'

'I know.' Albie sounded subdued.

Jessie was suddenly sorry for him. 'I do love you, mind, but not in the way you'd like. I'm sorry, Albie. I don't want to be anyone's wife yet.'

'But we can let people think we're married, can't we?'

'Yes, if that's what you want, though Mrs Levy hasn't asked us any particulars of that sort, has she?'

'Well, not exactly.' Albie looked shamefaced. 'I told

her in the beginning you was my wife – I don't think she'd have given us the room otherwise.'

'Oh, well, I don't suppose it matters,' Jessie said. 'Perhaps one day we'll tie the knot – who knows?' She smiled, making a joke of it. She might be happy as an old maid, she thought, dressed in lace and silk and being served by respectful servants.

The cart jumped over a stone and the pails rattled, bringing Jessie back to the present. 'Let's get on with selling the milk before what's left turns sour.' She smiled up at Albie and pinched his cheek.

He swiped away her hand.

By late afternoon, the milk was all gone and Jessie was heartened by the success of her first day. Although she missed the broad squares of Bloomsbury the people she met on her new round were friendly and cheerful.

Albie led the way as they went home through the narrow courts. 'There's something I want to show you, Jess,' he said, a mischievous smile playing round his mouth.

'Tell me!' Jessie said. 'I'm tired and I want to get home.'

'Look over there.' He pointed to an open-fronted shop on the other side of the street. 'We're in Golden Lane, and do you see what that place over there is?'

'It says "Cow-keeper" over the door.' Suddenly she didn't feel so tired. She crossed the road and peered inside. 'Perhaps one day I might have a shop like this and serve my customers without having to walk till me feet hurt.'

'Aye, and if it's up to me, it won't be long coming,' Albie said. 'And now let's get home. I'm starving.'

'You're like a little boy, always thinking of your belly. If you go on buying us pies we'll both be too fat to walk the round.'

200

'Go on, Jess, just one more night. We're both too tired to cook now, aren't we?'

'Oh, all right.'

Albie placed his hands on her waist. 'Anyway you got no need to worry about getting fat – you're made like a doll.'

'Go on with you!' She began to push the cart over the cobbles, listening to the clanking of the empty milk pails. Her first day on the new round hadn't been too bad at all.

Georgina was looking out at the rolling green fields beyond the Broadoaks gardens. She hadn't seen Matt since early that morning: he'd been dispatched to Swansea by the head gardener to fetch some rare plants for the greenhouses.

She hated the frustration of meeting Matt in the fields like a common serving wench, but what was the alternative? She could hardly run off with him even if she wanted to: her father needed her – and he would never allow an alliance between his daughter and a gardener. Georgina knew, too, that she could never be the wife of a man without money.

Matt didn't return until late in the evening, and by then Georgina was imagining all sorts of things: he'd been hurt in a brawl, or he'd found a pretty girl to take to his bed. She sat through dinner in a fever of impatience. She needed to see Matt, to talk to him, to make him promise he would love only her.

The moon was silvering the pond when at last she could slip from the house and make her way to the spot near the greenhouse where she and Matt usually met. Her heart was beating fast as she hurried across the lawn, glancing behind to make sure no one was watching her. Her satin slippers were not the ideal footwear for outdoors but she hadn't wanted to arouse suspicion by putting on her boots.

She reached the shadow of the greenhouse and paused to catch her breath. A figure stepped out of the shadows and Georgina went forward, eager to be in her lover's arms.

'Good evening, Miss Georgina. You're just the person I've come to see.'

Georgina started. 'Jed Lambert! What are you doing skulking around my garden?'

'I could ask the same of you, except that I have more urgent things on my mind.' He came forward, his face suddenly becoming clear in the moonlight. 'I know your secret, you see.' His voice was like silk. 'The secret that you and your "friend", the gardener, want to keep to yourselves.'

Georgina's mouth dried. 'How could you know anything about me or one of the gardeners?' Her heart was thumping so loudly now she thought he must hear it. At all costs, she must keep calm.

'Oh, I mean a particular gardener by the name of Matthew.'

She bit her lip to stop herself screaming at him to go away. Anger would accomplish nothing. 'What do you *think* you know about me?'

'I've kept a watch on you, on and off, for some time.' He laughed quietly. 'I've seen quite enough to assure me you'd pay well for my silence.'

She clutched her throat. He knew that she and Matt had got rid of Clive – why wasn't Matt here now to help her deal with him? 'So you want money,' she said, her voice flat as though she had no interest in the proceedings, even though her life depended on his silence.

'That's exactly what I want,' Jed murmured.

'I haven't any here now – you must know that,' she said.

'Your father is a rich man and he must keep some in the house, hidden in a safe place. Get it for me or I'll walk up to the house and tell everyone about your goings-on.'

Suddenly Georgina took her courage in both hands. 'Once you've done that your little game would be over and you'd get nothing. It's not in your interest to tell anyone about what you've seen.'

'But it's very much in yours if I don't, isn't it, Miss Georgina? I'm telling you, I could cause such a scandal. You'd be in all the papers, you and your lover. You'd never be welcomed at the houses of respectable people, would you? Your lover would be dragged away from here too. It would be better if you paid me now.'

Georgina was flustered. How much *did* he know? 'You saw me and Matt, and you saw us with Clive? What did you see?'

'Enough,' he said sharply. 'Fetch the money or I'll shout it from the rooftops and you and your lover will be finished. I think your father's had enough misery for the time being without you adding to it.'

'Wait here.' Georgina ran back to the house, her thoughts spinning. She dared not refuse to pay the man – she could imagine the laughter, the insults that would be directed at her for being in love with a common gardener.

She knew where her father kept the key to his desk and opened the drawer with shaking fingers. There was a bag of gold sovereigns inside and some notes from his bank. How she would explain their disappearance was something she'd think about later. She hurried back to the garden and, for a moment, thought Jed Lambert had disappeared. Then he moved out of the shadows, and she wanted to kill him. But she had one death on her conscience already – she couldn't bear another.

'Here.' She thrust the money into his hands. 'There won't be any more.'

'I think you might change your mind, Miss Georgina,' he said smoothly, and slid away into the darkness, leaving her shaking, wondering what other threats he might make. He seemed so certain that she'd pay for his silence.

Then she heard soft footsteps and shrank against the greenhouse door. Perhaps he'd come back – but it was Matt who came from the shadow of the trees into the light from the moon. 'Oh, Matt!' She threw herself into his arms. 'Matt, something terrible has happened.' She put her head into the warm hollow of his neck and began to cry.

Jed was deep in thought as he rode away. Georgina Jones had seemed really frightened, as if she had more than a simple love affair with a gardener to hide. What had she said? Had he seen her and the gardener with Clive? She must have meant her husband, Clive Langland. Jed urged his horse into a gallop. He was on to something here, something big, which meant that a lot of money was coming his way.

CHAPTER TWENTY-SEVEN

As Flora entered the forge the heat struck her. She wiped her face on her apron. 'I've brought you something to drink.' She watched as Morgan hammered a horseshoe into shape, sending sparks flying in all directions. He nodded, and continued with his work. They had been married for only a few weeks, but she had hoped they would become closer, more like husband and wife should be. 'Morgan,' she said softly, but he continued to hammer the glowing piece of metal as though he hadn't heard her. 'Please, Morgan, don't be angry with me.'

He put down his hammer. 'Why should I be angry with you?'

'Because I fell with your baby. I didn't want it to happen.'

He rubbed his forearm across his face and sweat gleamed on his skin in the ruddy glow from the fire. 'We're both old enough to know the risks of lying together – you can't take all the blame.'

'But you feel trapped, don't you, Morgan? You wish you'd never met me.'

He sighed. 'Don't torture yourself, Flora. We're married now and that's an end to it.'

'And you're going to punish me for the rest of my life!'

'What do you mean?'

'You don't come to me in bed, you never hold me or kiss me. I was good enough for you before, so why aren't I good enough for you now?' Flora's temper was rising. 'I'm weary of being treated like I'm nothing to you. I'm your wife and soon we'll have a child together, yet you don't behave like a husband. You don't act like a normal red-blooded man. Tell me the truth, Morgan, do you find me repulsive?'

Morgan looked at her. 'Do you really want to hear the truth?' His voice was hard.

'I suppose I do.' She met his challenging gaze.

'I don't love you, Flora, and I'm sorry to be harsh but I'll never love you and you know why.'

'Because Non is your perfect woman? Why, Morgan? She fell for a baby by Caradoc Jones. She was no better than me, even though she did marry him.'

'But Caradoc loved Non. He wanted her for his wife.' He took up his hammer again. 'Look, Flora, I'm not angry with you and of course I don't find you repulsive. I made my decision to marry you and bring up our child with you, but don't expect much more of me.'

'You slept with me before we were married, before I fell for the baby. What's different now?'

'Don't keep worrying at it, Flora. Some things are best left unsaid.' Morgan began to hammer the horseshoe again and she watched him, loving him, the strength of his shoulders, the way his muscles came into relief as the hammer hit the metal. The way his dear face was covered in sweat. She loved him so much it was almost like a pain.

He put down the hammer and took up a pair of long pincers. He grasped the horseshoe and dipped it into a barrel of water where it hissed and spat like an angry cat. Defeated, Flora left him alone. She stood outside for a moment in the fresh air, staring across Swansea to where the industries flourished along the banks of the river Tawe. Morgan had done well by her, she couldn't deny it. He'd rented a good solid house, across the valley from the steaming manufactories along the river-banks; he'd bought good furniture and even a cradle for the baby. He was a good husband in all respects but one: he did not love her.

She felt the tears burn in her eyes. She wanted him so much and it hurt that he would not lie in her bed with her. Perhaps her gently swelling stomach put him off, the heaviness of her breasts. Didn't he realize how vulnerable she was now and shouldn't he be comforting and reassuring her that she was still a fine wife for any man?

She turned to the kitchen and stared into the fire. She needed to build it up if she was to bake a game pie for supper. She would make a cup of tea first – she needed something to comfort her: the pain of Morgan's rejection was becoming almost physical.

She made her tea and gazed around the neat kitchen, at the spotless floors, the well-scrubbed table, the chairs. She was a good wife to Morgan: she did her best to feed him well, to build up his strength after a hard day in the smithy. When spring came he would take to the road again, following the drovers' trail to London, but by then she would have her baby to care for and wouldn't be alone.

The thought galvanized her into action and she put down her cup. She'd make Morgan the finest pie he'd ever tasted. She would prove to him that she was a good wife. She put her hands together and looked up to heaven. 'Please let him love me, however long it takes.'

★   ★   ★

Jessie trundled her cart along the rough roadway. She'd built up a good trade around Cutler Street and even in some parts of the Leman Estate. She turned into one of the narrow courts where a queue waited for her. Her spirits rose: the ragged poor of the back-streets were waiting for her to bring them milk.

'Stop dreamin' and give us a jug of milk.' An old man grinned at her toothlessly.

'All right, Barnie. Let me catch my breath.' She gave him his milk and looked at the rest of the people waiting to be served. Some carried jugs, cracked and chipped, some bowls, but all were willing to pay her for the milk that might be their only nourishment that day.

Albie appeared at her side. 'I thought I'd come and help you finish up.' He smiled down at her.

'Two love birds if ever I saw 'em.' Barnie's eyes twinkled. 'Wait till you been married a few years – he won't come running after you then.'

'Behave!' Jessie said sternly.

'Come on, you lot up the front, we 'aven't got all bleedin' day!' a woman called from the back of the queue. 'Stop chattering, Barnie, and let the dog see the bone.'

The crowd laughed good-naturedly and Jessie set about filling up the various containers. At the end of the line a small girl looked up pleadingly at Jessie and held out a none-too-clean bowl. 'Can I have a little milk for my ma, please?'

'Have you got any money, my lovely?' Jessie asked kindly. The child shook her head and Jessie glanced at Albie. He nodded and she filled the bowl with milk. 'Here,' she said. 'And there's some money to buy your ma some bread.'

The child didn't smile, but she took the money and

the milk and disappeared into one of the courts like a shadow.

'Well, that's us finished for the day,' Jessie said. 'How about going home now?'

Albie took the shafts of the cart and pushed it along the cobbles. The milk pails clanged.

'Go easy, Albie, or you'll lose one of the wheels and dent my pails into the bargain.'

She followed him as he wound his way through the back-streets. Her feet ached as they'd never ached before, not even on the long walk from Wales to Smithfield, but then she'd had soft grass under them instead of the hard roads of London.

It was a relief when the Leman Estate came into view, the houses in a dignified row, windows glinting. 'It's good to be home,' Jessie said softly.

'You wait!' Albie said. 'Once I get you inside our room I'll throw you on the bed and kiss you till you forget to be tired.'

'Don't you dare – or I'll hit you so hard you won't know whether you're on your head or your heels.'

Albie laughed and wheeled the cart to the yard at the back of the house. 'You go in,' he said, 'and put your feet up. I'll wash the pails and see to the cows.'

Jessie went into the house and took off her boots. She made a face at the mud that had transferred to her hands. Barefoot, she climbed the stairs to the attic room where she and Albie lived.

Once inside, she washed quickly in cold water from the jug, then sank on to the bed. The bag at her waist jingled with the coins she'd collected during the day. It had been a good day for takings. Some would go towards the rent and some towards fodder for the animals. Still, one day she'd make a decent living, have a whole house to herself and a backyard big enough to keep the animals in. One day. Now, lying on the bed in the small room she shared with Albie, she felt that that day would be a long time coming.

Flora woke to the sun shining through the bedroom window. She looked at the empty pillow beside her and realized that all her words to Morgan had been wasted. He had no intention of sharing her bed. It wasn't so much that she wanted him to make love to her, at least not straight away, but she could have done with his strength and warmth, the security of having him near.

She got up and washed quickly, then pulled on her clothes. Even though the sun was out there was a chill in the air, and she shivered as she tied an apron round her. She caught sight of herself in the mirror. The rise of her stomach was noticeable now – she felt fat, ugly and frightened. She remembered the first time she had fallen for a baby by one of the drovers. Thomas had been a married man and she had been fool enough to believe him when he said he'd leave his wife for her. She laid her palms against her stomach as though to protect the child inside. She had miscarried her first baby after taking some potion to rid herself of it, and had been so sick afterwards that she had almost died. It had taken a lot on Non's part to make her better again. This time she would guard her baby, nourish it – and when she held a healthy son in her arms, surely Morgan would come to love her.

It was midnight when the first pains woke Flora to the awful realization that something was wrong. She gasped as her belly contracted, then lifted the blankets and saw the blood staining the sheet.

'Morgan!' she cried. 'Morgan! Help me – please help me!'

He stumbled into the room, his eyes heavy with sleep. 'What's wrong? Are you sick?'

'Get help, Morgan! I'm losing the baby.'

'I can't leave you alone.'

'Go! I need a doctor or a wise woman, anybody who can help me through it.'

She heard him drag on a pair of trousers, then he was running down the stairs and she heard the front door slam. She was alone with her pain and anguish.

She lay for what seemed a long time in her blood-soaked bed, then people were in the room, an old woman with kindly eyes and a young one with her sleeves rolled above her elbows.

'Let's have a look at you, girl.' The old woman lifted the sheet. 'The baby is coming away from you – there's nothing more sure than that.' She looked at Morgan. 'Bring some water from the kettle for me to wash your wife, and some sheets and cloths – anything clean.'

Morgan went out of the room and Flora began to cry. 'My husband – I want him with me.'

'He'll be back in a minute. Anyway, men only clutter up the room at a time like this, guilty at what they've put their woman through.'

But Flora wanted to hold Morgan's strong hands, wanted him to look at her with love.

He returned to the room, his face pale and anxious. She held out a hand and he came to sit beside her, engulfing her cold fingers in his. 'You'll be all right now, Flora,' he said. 'You've got a good midwife to look after you.'

The spasms came again, racking her whole body with pain. She cried out and Morgan bent close and kissed her cheek. 'Be brave, Flora, it will soon be over.'

'The baby,' she said. 'Our baby is lost.'

'You're a strong, healthy woman, Flora. We can have others.'

'But this one was unwanted. Losing it is a punishment on me for all the wrong I've done.'

'Don't say that.' Morgan clasped her hand tighter. 'You don't deserve to be punished for anything.'

The hours passed slowly as the pain tore at her. Morgan was still at her side, his hair ruffled, holding her hands.

'I'm sorry,' she whispered.

He rested his cheek against hers. 'Just hold on and I'll be here at your side.'

'Do you love me just a little bit?' she asked.

'I love you very much.'

She smiled. The pain was receding now, she felt warm, cosy, and very tired. She saw the old woman look at Morgan and shake her head. Flora knew then that she was going to die. Somehow it didn't seem to matter. But she must comfort Morgan. 'Thank you for everything, my love,' she heard her voice whisper. 'I love you, Morgan, and I'll always love you. Perhaps, if God is kind, we'll meet again in eternity.'

He was fading away from her. 'Goodbye, my darling,' she said. And then, as her life ebbed away, he kissed her and all the rainbows in heaven came to bear her to her rest.

CHAPTER TWENTY-EIGHT

Non combed her hair and put it up in a bun, pinning it tightly so that her unruly curls would stay in place. She hurried downstairs and picked up her basket of herbs. 'Ruby, I won't be long,' she called.

Ruby appeared in the hallway and beamed at her. 'Guess what's happened?' She pointed to her mouth. 'Another blasted tooth 'as come out, thank Gawd.'

Non smiled. 'Well, that's a mercy, I won't have to keep giving my precious medicine to you. Now perhaps I can go out and make a living for myself.'

Ruby gave a big sigh. 'I'm getting long in the tooth all right. Soon I'll only have my gums to chomp on.' She smiled, revealing a gap of blackness where her teeth were missing.

'Go on, now get on with your selling, keeping busy is the best thing for you right now.'

Non nodded. 'That's all I can do. I've got to stop feeling sorry for myself and get on with life.'

'That's the spirit. There's a lot of folk depending on you.'

Non stepped out into Treacle Lane and shivered. It was cold and a fine rain mingled with the fog that seemed to hang like a curtain over the houses. It was a day when folk would keep to their own homes, and that suited Non. Hopefully she would find bored wives at home who would spare her a little of their time.

She lifted her cloth and looked into her basket. She had packets of dried parsley and thyme, which rustled when she touched them, several bottles of angelica syrup, and essence of blackberries, which was good for the winter miseries.

Suddenly she glimpsed a man in the crowd – his hair was light, his features sharply defined. He looked so much like Caradoc that she dropped her basket and stopped to catch her breath.

'You all right, dear?' A tall old man in a good cloth coat and shiny hat stopped beside her. 'You look a little pale. Shall I call you a cab?'

'No, I'm all right,' Non said breathlessly. 'I just felt a bit faint.' The man helped her pick up her basket of medicines, then slipped it on her arm. He put his arm round her waist and it dawned on her that he was trying to rob her. 'All I've got is a few shillings,' she said. 'Please don't take that from me.' His grip on her grew tighter and she struggled with him. 'Get away from me!'

Suddenly there was a flurry of arms and legs, and the man staggered and fell to the ground. The young man who had thrown him down was on top of him, snatching back Non's purse.

As he stood up, Non recognized him. 'Albie!' They watched as the man got to his feet, straightened his collar, replaced his hat and walked away as though nothing had happened. 'Albie, you came in the nick of time.'

'Just as well I did,' Albie said. 'He was a fine wirer. He'd have had the clothes off your back if I hadn't been here to help you.'

'Oh, Albie, it's good to see you,' Non said. 'We've been wondering how you and Jessie are getting on.'

214

'I was on my way to see you and Ruby. Jess and me have set up house together – well, not a whole house, of course, just a room – and the milk round is going well. What are you doing out on a day like this? You'll catch your death.'

'I thought I'd try selling my medicines, but I've had such a shock I'll go home.'

'Come on, then,' Albie said. 'You're not fit to be on your own, especially on a day like this.' He led her through a street she'd never seen before. 'Take my arm,' he said. 'You're as pale as anybody fresh put in the ground. That thief upset you more than I thought.'

Non shivered. 'It wasn't only that,' she confided. 'I thought I saw Caradoc.' Her voice was little more than a whisper. 'I know he's gone from me, but I saw a man just like him.'

'Hush now, it's all right, I'm taking you home. You can go out and sell your herbs when you're a bit stronger.'

She was glad when they reached Treacle Lane. Albie guided her into the kitchen, and Ruby was all of a fuss as soon as she saw the state Non was in.

'Bleedin' 'ell! What's 'appened?' Ruby took the basket and put it on the table. 'Have you been run down by one of them mad drivers?'

Non shook her head. 'I just felt a bit faint and then this man came along and . . .' Her voice trailed away.

'A thief looking like a gent picked on her,' Albie explained.

'We'll all have a toddy and she'll soon feel better.' Ruby bustled about making the drink. She handed a cup to Non, who sipped, then gasped as the heat of it caught her throat. She set the cup down. 'It was lucky Albie came along and saved me.'

'I was coming to see you all.' Albie sat astride a chair.

'I wanted to tell you that me and Jess are settling well. We're snug as anything in our little place in Leman Street.'

'Well-off folk live there,' Ruby said. 'How can you and Jess afford it?'

'Well, we're doin' all right with our milk, sellin' it to the toffs and the poor folk. Once Jess is all right on her own, I'll find a job for myself and then I'll set her up in her own cow-keeper's shop so she won't have to walk the streets.'

'Good for you, Albie,' Non said.

'How many rooms you got?' Ruby pushed the kettle on to the fire and folded her arms across her chest.

Albie looked abashed. 'Just the one. It's all we needs for now.'

'Well, watch you don't make Jessie fall for a baby.' Ruby's voice was stern. 'She's young yet and so are you.'

Albie's face reddened. 'We're not . . . Well, you know what I mean. I respect Jess and one day I'll marry her. There will be time enough to think of getting babies.'

'Very sensible,' Ruby said drily. 'But the winter nights are coming and you'll be snuggling up together to keep warm. That'll be enough to tempt all the saints in heaven.'

'Leave him alone, Ruby.' Non smoothed Albie's hair away from his face. 'They're doing their best to earn a living and I'm proud of them.' She felt better: the toddy had warmed the pain in her chest into a bearable ache. She saw again the man with the bright hair, the man who had looked like Caradoc, but Caradoc was in heaven with their son and the sooner she got used to life on her own the better.

Georgina stood in the doorway, watching her father alight from the carriage with mixed feelings. He'd been to London again, trying to find peace, but she had known he would come back to Five Saints sooner or later. 'Papa.' She put her arms around him. 'Papa, you're so thin!' she exclaimed. She saw now that he had the face of an old man. 'Papa, come and sit by the fire. You look so tired.'

He took her arm and they crossed the hall to the drawing room. Once inside, he slumped into a chair and rubbed his red-rimmed eyes. 'I feel as if my world has ended,' he said. 'I only have you now, Georgina. You won't leave me, will you, even if your husband comes back to you?'

She put her arms around him. 'I won't leave you, Papa. I'll never be with Clive again, so don't think it.' She felt the irony of her words. 'He's gone out of my life for good, Papa.'

Her father settled back in his chair, his eyes closed. Georgina knelt beside him and held his hand. 'I love you, Papa – you know that, don't you?' she said softly.

His eyes flickered open and a brief smile touched his mouth. 'I know you do, *cariad*, and I'm grateful, make no mistake about it.' He waved his hand as if to encompass the house. 'This will be yours one day, my girl. Everything I own will be yours – but we'll have to think of a way to stop Clive Langland getting his hands on any of it.'

'Try to rest now, Papa. I heard that Clive has gone overseas to the other side of the world. He won't come back.' She hated lying to him, but he'd suffered enough without her adding to it. 'Perhaps you should go to your room and rest,' she added. 'I'll tell one of the maids to build up the fire and she can turn back your bed too.'

He nodded gratefully. 'That would be best.'

Georgina saw her father to his room, and when he

was settled she pulled the blankets up around his chin. He was quite unlike his usual confident self. He had grown old and tired.

As soon as she could, Georgina went into the garden in search of Matt. He was in one of the greenhouses and she was glad of the warmth after the chill outside. 'Papa is home.' She didn't touch him and he kept a respectable distance, in case one of the other gardeners saw them together.

'I know. I saw the carriage draw up. How is he?'

'Not well.' It had hurt her to see him so changed. 'He's still blaming himself for little Rowan's death.' She gulped. 'I think he even blames himself for what happened to Caradoc.'

'How can he when Caradoc was miles away, crossing the Wye?'

'If Papa hadn't been so keen to separate him from his wife, Caradoc would probably be alive and well today.'

The greenhouse door opened, and Georgina glanced round, expecting to see one of the gardeners.

'Evening, Mrs Langland, or should I say "*Widow Langland*"?'

'What do you want?' Georgina said sharply, as Jed Lambert came forward, his face twisted into a gloating smile.

'I know it all now. I've put two and two together and worked it all out. I wondered why you gave me money so readily. You had only to deny the love affair between you and your gardener and everyone would have believed you. But you got rid of that husband of yours. He's never been seen since he left your house. I spoke to one of the servants and she told me Mr Langland was practically carried out of here, blind drunk. But he wasn't drunk, was he? He was dead – and you two got rid of him. So, Widow Langland, I want money.'

'I'll pay you,' Georgina said quickly, 'but my father is at home now and he won't put up with your demands. He'd have you beaten within an inch of your life if he knew you were blackmailing me.'

'Well, aren't you uppity, Widow Langland?'

'Why do you keep saying that?' Georgina asked impatiently. 'I said I'll pay you and I will, as soon as I can get some money.'

'Ah, but the stakes have gone up.' Jed came and stood near her. Matt moved forward. 'It's all right, I don't want any trouble – but I do want paying.'

Matt took him by the collar, his clenched fist against Lambert's throat. 'What makes you think I won't do away with you?'

Jed Lambert eased himself out of Matt's grip. 'Too many gardeners about the place.'

'Just go away,' Georgina said sharply. 'I'll need some time to get the money, but I'll do it as soon as I can.'

'All right. You have a few weeks. I've business in Smithfield, but when I come back there'd better be something here for me.'

Georgina watched him saunter out of the green-house. 'I don't think we're ever going to have any peace now. I just wish that man was dead.' She looked at Matt with tears in her eyes. 'I'm so frightened, Matt.'

He took her in his arms. 'I'll stop him bothering us, one way or another. You can count on it.' His voice was like steel.

Albie walked along Leman Street and into the house. He had news for Jessie. He'd found a job with a saddlemaker who was willing to train him, as long as he didn't expect too much pay. He took the stairs two at a time.

She was sitting in their room, her face pale, and alongside her stood two strangers.

'What's going on, Jess?' Albie felt a prickle of fear run down his spine.

The men looked him over. 'We've had a complaint,' one said. 'A Mr Spencer claims you robbed him of a valuable purse.'

'You must be mistaken,' she said. 'Albie works with me on the milk round.'

The men ignored her. 'Were you near Treacle Lane three days ago?'

'Well, yes, I was visiting old friends. What's wrong with that?'

'On the way you came upon a lady and gentleman speaking together. You pushed the man to the ground, robbed him and gave him a black eye into the bargain.'

'You don't understand.' Albie looked at Jessie. 'I wasn't doing anything wrong. The man they're talking about was trying to rob Non Jones.'

'Well, you'll have to come with us to answer some more questions.' The men looked at him more closely. 'This isn't the first time you've had dealings with the law, is it?'

'I swear I wasn't up to anything. The man who attacked Non was a fine wirer – he knew what he was doing and he's the guilty one, not me.'

'Well, we'll decide that.'

One of the men grasped Albie, then the other, and they frogmarched him out of the door. The last thing Albie saw of his home was Jessie with tears streaming down her face. Suddenly he was angry: just when he was going straight, some mealy-mouthed villain had ruined it all. 'I'll be back, Jess,' he called. 'I'll sort it out and then I'll be home.'

CHAPTER TWENTY-NINE

Caradoc woke to the sound of rain beating on the window. He glanced across at Gwenllyn, and saw she was still asleep. He slipped from under the blankets to look outside. The valley was covered in mist and the river could no longer be seen, but he could imagine it, wide and deep, going he knew not where through the land. But he had known the Wye in all its moods, he was sure of it.

'Come back to bed, sweetheart.' Gwenllyn's whisper shook him out of his reverie. 'It's cold without you.' She looked so beautiful, lips parted, slender hand held out towards him. How could he resist her?

He pulled back the sheets and looked down at her breasts, full and inviting in the early-morning light. He took her in his arms and she clung to him. 'I love you so much, *cariad*,' she said. 'I don't think I could live without you.' She pulled his head down and her lips parted warmly. He made love to her slowly, and when it was over, he lay beside her, holding her hand. He loved her, desired her, but a voice murmured in his mind that their affair was doomed.

'You've gone all quiet, my lovely,' she said softly. 'You do love me, don't you, Caradoc?'

'Yes,' he said. 'I do.' Then he tickled her waist and she laughed. She was warm and rosy with the afterglow of lovemaking, but something stirred in his mind, another woman, another moment – a great longing for he knew not what.

'You've slipped away from me again,' Gwenllyn said. 'The past is dead. We must make the most of what we have now.'

'It's time I got dressed and lit the fire downstairs. We can't lie in bed all day.' He slid away from her, frustration washing through him. His memories seemed close to the edge of his mind but faded as soon as he tried to find them.

Later, with the fire blazing up the chimney, he pulled on his coat and let himself out. The grass was spiked with dew that glistened against the green. He breathed in the autumnal air and tried to calm his racing mind. Somewhere near the river he would find himself. He would remember what his life had been about, who he was. And yet, as he strode down the hill, that moment seemed a long time coming.

He heard the sound of hoofs – muffled but coming closer – and he stood quietly, waiting. The rider came into view, hat pulled close down to keep away the rain.

The man reined in his horse. 'Morning,' he said. 'Rotten day to ride the trail.' He looked down at Caradoc. 'Days like this I want to give up the roads for good and settle back home in Swansea or even Five Saints.'

'You're Jed Lambert, aren't you?' Caradoc said. 'We've spoken before. You must be riding ahead to book a field for the beasts and a bed for yourself. No sleeping outdoors in weather like this.'

'I'd certainly like shelter tonight,' Jed Lambert said evasively.

'I've watched the movement of cattle through

the river and learned from it,' Caradoc said. 'Are the droves finished for the season?'

Jed Lambert nodded. 'I won't be taking to the road any more this year – perhaps never again, if my plans work out.'

'And what plans are they?' Caradoc asked with mild interest.

'Oh, I expect to come into money any day now.' He smiled, but his eyes remained cold. 'Where do you fit in round here? Landowner, are you?'

'Why would you think that?'

'The way you talk. You must be well educated too – strange to meet a man like you shut away in a place like this.' He indicated the rugged countryside that surrounded them.

'It's as good a place as any.' Caradoc knew he sounded defensive. 'And I like the peace and quiet of the countryside.'

'That's a good enough reason to stay here.' Jed's eyes were half closed, as though he was waiting for some reply. After a moment he shifted in the saddle. 'I'd better press on,' he said. 'There's some real work waiting for me once I get home.' He urged his horse into a gallop with a quick cut of his whip and Caradoc watched him ride away. The conversation had made him realize the idleness of his life, his lack of purpose. Why was he submissively accepting Gwenllyn's charity? It was about time he shook himself free of the apathy that had held him for months.

He should be travelling to the places Jed had talked about – Swansea, perhaps, or Five Saints. The drove must have set out from there. Why hadn't he thought of that before? The answers to the questions he asked himself perpetually might be found in the place where the cattle drove began.

He was feeling stronger now. His head still ached sometimes but his bones had mended, and the work he'd been doing had strengthened him. It would be hard to leave Gwenllyn, even for a short time, but she must understand that now he had to have answers to the questions that continually raced through his mind.

He began to walk back towards the cottage where she was waiting for him.

Jed's brush with Caradoc Jones had been interesting, he thought. It was clear the man still had no idea who he was or where he came from. That suited Jed. If Caradoc stumbled upon the truth about himself, it might prove difficult to get money out of Georgina. The old Caradoc would have had nothing to do with blackmail: he'd have employed a lawyer to get his sister off the hook. Jed knew he'd better go back to Five Saints now and make sure of the money.

Jessie had finished her round and stood still, for a moment, staring at the empty milk pails. She felt lonely and afraid for the first time since she had come to live in London. She hadn't got over the shock of Albie's arrest. She began to lift the pails back on to the cart.

''Ere, Miss, let me help you with that.' A boy of about ten lifted a pail and Jessie recognized him as one of her customers from the poorer courts and lanes.

'What's your name?' she asked, as they put the last ones into the cart.

'Ma calls me Dan.' He brushed his hands against his ragged jacket. 'Me dad's in Newgate, though he's an innocent man.'

'A good friend of mine has been taken there,' Jessie said. 'Is it a very bad place?'

'The worst,' Dan said. 'Is your friend called Albie? The one who helped you on the milk?'

Jessie nodded. 'He's been taken by the constables for something he didn't do.'

Dan made a grimace. 'Me dad's always getting taken away for things he didn't do. Ma says the crushers've got it in for him. But,' he added, 'your Albie'll be taken to the magistrate first. Then he'll get sent to the sessions at the Old Bailey but after that he might get off free as a bird, if the right people speak up for him.'

'I should have thought of that,' Jessie said. 'I can ask my friend Non Jones to see the police. She's honest and respectable and it was her Albie saved from the thief.'

'There you are then, Miss. Shall I come with you on your milk round until your man comes back to you?'

'I'd be very grateful, Dan, but I can't afford to give you much money. Now there's no Albie to help, I'm struggling as it is.'

'I wouldn't want paying,' Dan said. 'A jug of milk for my little sisters will do.'

Jessie held out her hand. 'Right,' she said, smiling, 'and I'll be glad of the company.'

Dan walked back with her to Leman Street. 'You must have long pockets to live 'ere.'

'Me and Albie have one room at the top of the house. It's a bit expensive but I'm near where my cows live and where my milk round starts.'

'Sounds good. I'll see you in the morning.' Dan faded into the fog and Jessie heaved a sigh of relief. Thank goodness for Dan! He was only a boy but he was strong and willing and he seemed to know a lot about the law. Later she'd go to see Non. Non would speak up for Albie – she'd do all she could to help, Jessie was sure of it.

When she let herself into the broad passageway of

the tall house, Mrs Levy bustled out of the dining room and stood with her hands folded across her chest. 'I'm sorry, Jessie,' her voice was stern, 'I can't let you have that room any longer.'

'But why not? The rent is paid till the end of the week.'

'So it is, but Mr Levy says we can't have the wife of a criminal living on the premises. I'm really sorry, Jessie, but you'll have to go at the end of the week.' She leaned forward. 'And you're not married, you and Albie, are you?'

Jessie couldn't lie. 'No, but we aren't doing anything wrong. We don't sleep together.'

'I might have overlooked that, but now Albie's been taken into custody . . .'

'That's all right, Mrs Levy. I'll soon find something else.' She didn't know where she could go, though: her takings were down because she was slower loading the cart, and wheeling it on her own took longer because she didn't have Albie's strength.

After supper, Jessie made her way towards Treacle Lane. The sooner she saw Non the better. It was a good thing she'd met Dan, but sad that a child should know how the constables worked.

She tried to imagine Albie facing a magistrate who knew nothing about poverty and she felt like crying.

Non answered the door to her knock, and smiled. She was smaller now, and her cheekbones stood out sharply. 'Come in. Ruby's got the kettle on the boil so we can sit and have a talk.'

It was warm in the kitchen: the fire was blazing and the floor so clean Jessie feared to walk on it. Ruby hugged her. 'It's about time you came to visit,' she said. 'I've been dying of toothache for weeks.' She looked closely at Jessie. 'Something's wrong, isn't it?'

'It's Albie,' Jessie said. 'He's been taken by the constables.'

'Oh, no!' Ruby said. 'The boy hasn't been up to his tricks again, has he?'

Jessie turned to Non. 'It was that man – the one who tried to rob you. He's told the constables that Albie knocked him down and tried to rob him.'

Non's hands flew to her mouth. 'Oh, Jessie, that's so unfair, Albie was rescuing me! *I* was the one being robbed.'

'Well,' Jessie licked her lips, 'if you could go to the constables or the magistrate and say what really happened he should be set free.'

'Of course I'll speak up for Albie. I'll go first thing in the morning. I'll wear my smartest clothes and present myself as Mrs Jones, daughter-in-law to Mr George Jones. Then the constables might take notice.'

'Well, that's clever of you, Non,' Ruby said. 'You got a fine voice and a string of long words and I know you'll make a good impression.'

'I knew you'd help, Non,' Jessie said. 'Poor Albie must be so frightened – he could be in Newgate by now among all those murderers.' She wanted to tell Ruby she'd been thrown out of her lodgings, but Ruby had enough to cope with: her rooms were all full to bursting and Jessie couldn't add to her burdens.

Ruby shook her head. 'I don't know what the world's coming to. Albie's picked many a pocket in the past and now he's been taken in on a false charge. Who'd believe it?'

'Never mind, we'll soon have him back.' Jessie settled more comfortably into her seat, happy that her friends were looking after her. When Albie was free, she would hug him and hold him, and tell him how much she'd missed him.

The next morning Dan was there at the start of her round. He grinned at Jessie and took a handle of the cart. 'Let me push it for you.'

'Get away, there's not much meat on your bones as it is. You fill up the jugs – I hope you've got clean hands.'

Jessie pushed the cart along Leman Street, waiting for her usual customers to come and fetch their milk but the doors remained closed. Slowly, it dawned on her that news of Albie's arrest had spread.

'What's up with people?' Dan frowned. 'No one needs milk today by the look of it.'

'They don't want to buy it from me,' Jessie said. 'Albie's been taken by the constables for thieving and hitting a man, but he's innocent.'

'Aye,' Dan said drily. 'My dad was innocent every time but it didn't do 'im any good.'

Jessie saw the resignation on his face and despair settled over her. 'Come on, let's go to the back lanes. I don't think my customers there will let me down.'

The queue of people waiting for milk stretched further into the mean courts than usual. 'They'll have heard of Albie's arrest,' Dan whispered. 'They think you're one of us now, see?'

'One of us?' Jessie asked.

'Aye. Your man's in prison and that makes you one of the crowd. Don't you know anything?'

Dan started serving the milk.

'Give them plenty, Dan, it'll only go sour if we keep it,' Jessie told him.

All too soon, the customers had gone and Jessie still had four full pails. 'You take plenty for your family, Dan,' she said, 'and I'll see you in the morning. Where do you live?'

'Top of the rag shop in Cutler Street, the one that sells boots as well as clothes.'

'You're nearly home, then.' She watched him walk away, careful not to spill his milk, and tears brimmed in her eyes. She fought against them. She had good friends and soon Albie would be back. Together they'd build up a new round and a new life.

CHAPTER THIRTY

The morning sun shone weakly through the mist. Caradoc caught Gwenllyn coming back from feeding the chickens and knew this was the time to talk to her. He tried to pluck up the courage to tell her he was leaving but it was hard: she was happy, her eyes sparkled, and she held out her arms to him. 'What is it you want to say?' she asked softly. 'I know there's something on your mind. I've something important to tell you too.' She looked up at him coyly. 'I think I already know what you're going to say.'

'No, you don't,' Caradoc said. 'Look, Gwen, this isn't easy but I have to say it. I'm going to leave you for a while, go back along the river to Swansea and see if my roots are there.'

'But you can't!' Gwenllyn's lips trembled, and he took her into his arms, guilt tearing at him, knowing how much he was hurting her.

'I'll come back for you, but I wouldn't be a man if I didn't try to find answers to all the questions that burn in my mind.'

'But why do you think anyone in Swansea would know you? The way you talk you could be from anywhere – London, perhaps.'

'When I hear a drove crossing the river Wye, the sound of the horn, the barking of dogs, something

230

stirs in me. I'll come back, I promise.'

'You said you'd marry me, or have you forgotten about that?'

It seemed heartless to leave her alone, but the trip to Swansea or Carmarthen on a good horse wouldn't take more than a few days. 'I don't want to leave you but how can I go on allowing you to keep me in food and clothes – even the roof over my head? How can I marry you, not knowing my own name?'

'I need you, Caradoc.' Gwenllyn swayed towards him. Her face had drained of colour.

'What's wrong? Are you ill?' He picked her up and carried her across the garden, then pushed open the front door with his foot.

When he sat her down, her eyes flickered. 'Just get me some water.'

'Perhaps I should fetch the doctor.'

She cupped his face in her hands. 'There's no need, Caradoc. I know what's wrong.' She took a deep breath. 'It's what I wanted to tell you, what I was so excited about.' She seemed uncertain of what to say. 'Caradoc, I know this is the worst time to tell you, but I'm carrying your child.'

He stared at her, unable to speak, his emotions in turmoil. That Gwenllyn might be expecting his baby was something he'd never considered. Suddenly his plans to leave her faded away. Much as he wanted to go, she couldn't be alone at a time like this.

It was as if she'd read his mind. 'If you need to leave, then that's what you must do,' she said dully. 'I'll be all right on my own. Nanna and I managed without a man to take care of us.'

'I can go to Swansea another time.'

'Go now,' she said, her voice faint. 'I don't want to hold you against your will. But come back soon in case something goes wrong. These first months are when women miscarry if they're going to.'

He knew then that he couldn't leave. She needed him now as he had once needed her.

'I can't leave you at a time like this,' he said, and held back a sigh. Thoughts of finding his roots nagged at him, but winter was coming and Gwenllyn would be heavy with child by then. She could not be expected to feed the hens, dig the garden, chop logs for the fire.

He kissed her cheek. 'I'll be here to look after you for as long as you need me.' His words were brave, but hope of finding his identity was vanishing.

Morgan hammered the horseshoe with heavy blows, as though that would alleviate the pain that had been inside him since Flora had died.

He felt so ashamed. She'd been his wife, carrying his child, and he'd been cruel to her, telling her he'd never love her. Perhaps the shock of those words had caused her to miscarry and lose her life. It was only when she was on her deathbed that he had taken pity on her, and said the words that she'd longed to hear.

He gave a bellow of rage and threw down his hammer. He couldn't be alone any longer with his thoughts. He'd leave his work – he had very little to do at the moment anyway, now that the cattle droves had ended. There was a steady flow of horseshoes to make but nothing that couldn't wait. He would go to London, see Non, tell her his troubles. She was wise: she would listen to him, and she would be kind.

It took him just an hour to prepare for the ride across the Welsh hills. He knew the different routes by heart. He knew the rivers, the Wye and the Severn, too, and when the sky heralded bad weather. At least he would be doing something other than punishing himself with his thoughts.

He set out at first light. It was a chilly morning and the valleys were lost in mist. He reined in his horse for a last look at the house. It was there that Flora had died, and his words hung in the air like devils that would destroy him. He turned his back on his house and the forge and rode on towards the wild, rugged hills.

Gwenllyn lay in bed, watching the light and shade that dappled the curtains. She put her hands on her flat stomach and prayed for forgiveness. She'd lied to Caradoc, told him she was with child. If only it were true! But she couldn't let him go: she knew that when he reached Swansea someone would know who he was and she couldn't allow that to happen.

He came into the room with a glass on a tray. 'Here's some cordial for you. How are you feeling now, Gwenllyn?'

'Still a little weak and faint,' she said. She looked at him with hungry eyes, admiring the breadth of his shoulders as he bent over her. He held out the glass and she took it in trembling hands. 'You're so good to me,' she said. 'I'm sorry I've ruined your plans, but you can go to Swansea in the spring when the weather is kinder.'

'I'll stay with you until the baby is born,' he said. 'When will that be, Gwenllyn?'

'I don't know exactly.' She hated lying to him. 'I think I've missed two of my monthly courses so I suppose the baby will be born in April or May.'

'We'll wait until it is a few months old and then we'll go to Swansea together.'

'How will we find our way?' Gwenllyn asked fearfully.

'In the spring the droves will begin again and I can ask one of the drovers to draw me a map.'

'But it could be a wasted journey,' Gwenllyn said. 'And how far is it? You can't expect me and a baby to ride a great distance.'

Caradoc ran a hand through his bright hair. 'I don't know – and perhaps I'm wrong. It could be I came from Gloucester or even, as you said, London.'

'Why don't you go to London, then?'

'Something teases the edge of my mind. I think the key to my whole life is in South Wales.' He kissed her cheek. 'Anyway, we'll spend the winter here and wait for the birth of the baby. Then we'll decide where to begin my search.'

Gwenllyn bit her lip. How was she going to keep up the pretence that she was expecting his child?

'Go on, you,' she said, 'I know you've work to do.' She forced a smile. 'I'll have to rely on you when the baby comes.' She was tying him to her with invisible bonds, but she couldn't let him go. She just couldn't.

When he left her, she was suddenly overcome by the enormity of what she'd done. She'd lied to Caradoc all along, destroying the evidence of his identity. Now she was hoping to keep him with another tissue of lies. Her hands went over her eyes and she began to cry.

CHAPTER THIRTY-ONE

Jessie packed her few possessions and carried them down the three flights of stairs to the hall. Mrs Levy was waiting for her. 'I'm sorry about this, Jessie, but my husband is adamant. We're respectable people and we can't be seen to harbour criminals.'

'I understand,' Jessie said, 'and thank you for finding out where Albie's been taken. I've a friend who's hoping to prove his innocence.'

'Well, that's good.' Mrs Levy handed her some coins. 'This is what I owe you from the rent, and there's a bit extra to tide you over. I'm sure you'll make a success of your milk round. You're a hard-working girl and deserve to make a good life for yourself. Where are you going to stay?'

'At a house off Cutler Street. Dan, the young boy who's been helping me, says I can lodge there until I find another room of my own.'

Mrs Levy clucked her tongue. 'That's not a good place for a young lady to live.' She folded her hands over her bosom.

'I've no choice,' Jessie said. 'I'm grateful to Dan and his family for taking me in.'

'Well, then, off you go, and keep your chin up, Jessie.' Mrs Levy saw her to the door, and Jessie hitched up her bag on her arm and stepped out into

Leman Street. It was a cold day and Jessie shivered. As Mrs Levy closed the door, Jessie wondered how she would make ends meet with only a few customers to buy her milk. Still, once Albie was released, they could build up a new round together.

Cutler Street was busy even at this hour of the morning, crowded with people handling the second-hand garments, peering at collars and cuffs, picking up hats and boots, haggling over the prices. Jessie's spirits rose. It wasn't going to be as bad living in the crowded poor streets of London as she'd thought.

When she found Dan's house, she almost ran away. The windows were open and a fearful stench seeped out into the road. She considered asking Ruby if she could sleep in her kitchen for a few days. But Ruby already had a young lad sleeping on the kitchen floor. No – and Jessie knew she should be grateful that she wasn't going to sleep in the street.

'Jessie!'

She turned to see Dan trundling the cart towards her. 'I milked the cows like you showed me and I've sold nearly all the milk.' He stopped beside her. 'Mind, I didn't get as much from them as you do.'

'You've done well,' Jessie said. 'What time did you get up this morning?'

'I don't know but it was still dark, and I was a bit frightened of the cows, they're so big, but as soon as I got milking they seemed to know I was being good to them.'

'Well,' Jessie said, 'I found a gem when I found you.'

'It was *me* that found *you*,' Dan said, his grubby face creasing into a smile. 'Come and meet my ma – I've told her all about you.'

He pushed the cart into the alley beside the house and tied the wheels together with thick rope. 'Don't want it to go missing. Thieves and cut-throats come down 'ere for clothes.'

Jessie followed him up a flight of rickety stairs. The smell of stale food and urine was worse the higher she climbed. She passed an open door and saw what looked like a heap of tattered clothes until a young child sat up and she realized the room was full of ragged people.

'That's where the bad smell comes from,' Dan said, his skinny arm round Jessie as though to protect her from it. 'Come on, we live at the top of the house and my ma is as clean as can be.'

Jessie dumped her bags on the landing outside Dan's rooms and tried not to breathe in the fetid air. She knew now how fortunate she'd been to live in Leman Street, in a clean room and a respectable neighbourhood.

Dan's mother greeted her as she stepped through the door. She had brown paper tied round her forehead and smelt strongly of vinegar. 'Come in, Jessie. I've got a bad head today and vinegar helps it a bit. You've been good to my boy and you're welcome to share what little we've got.'

'Thank you, Mrs . . . ?'

'Jest call me Ma, everyone else do.'

'I've got some money,' Jessie said. 'I'll be able to pay my way.'

'Well, that'll be nice. Sit down somewhere that's not piled high with children or clothes.'

Gingerly, Jessie pushed some old coats from a broken-backed chair and put her bags on the bare floor. 'It's kind of you to take me in,' she said. 'I'll try not to be a nuisance, and I'm sure I'll find a new room soon.'

'You can stay as long as you like. One more won't make any difference to me.'

Jessie wondered who else lived with Ma and Dan. There were three cramped rooms, filled with children and old clothes. 'I'll be out of your way first thing in the morning on my round.' She patted Dan's thin shoulder. 'I'll have my helper with me, and he'll make sure we find new customers, won't you, Dan?'

'I liked milking the cows.'

'They're gentle animals,' Jessie said. 'I've walked from Wales to London with a whole herd of them. Good as gold, they are, so long as no one frightens them.'

'I won't frighten them,' Dan said quickly. 'I think they're getting used to me. I'll go and wash the pails now so they're ready for the morning.'

'I'll come with you,' Jessie said. 'I have to go back to the yard anyway and feed the cows.'

'You sit down, girl,' Ma said. 'Let the boy do some work. I'll get us a bit of bread and cheese, and we can drink some of that milk you've given us.'

Jessie wanted to get out of the house, but Ma was gesturing her back into her seat. She sank down and looked longingly after Dan. She could hear him clattering down the stairs and wanted to burst into tears. She seemed further away than ever from being a success.

'There.' Ma put a plate in front of her with a good bit of cheese and a hunk of bread. 'Eat that and you'll feel better. No one feels good on an empty belly.'

Jessie picked up the bread. 'Thank you, Ma,' she said. 'There's kind you are. One day I might be able to repay you.'

'No need.' Ma flapped a hand. 'You just eat and ease your bones. Let our Dan help you. I've never seen him so keen to work before.'

Jessie tried to smile, but the bread tasted like

sawdust. She thought of Albie and felt she was as much of a prisoner as he was. Still, she had been taken in by a respectable, honest family and for that she must count her blessings.

Non pulled her hat into position and stared at her reflection in the mirror. 'Do I look respectable enough to persuade a judge to let Albie go?'

'You look like a proper lady.' Ruby tugged at the back of Non's coat. 'You're too thin, girl. I wish you'd put some flesh on your bones – you don't eat enough to keep a bird alive.'

Non squared her shoulders. 'I'd better get off. I'm going to see one of the magistrates, a Mr Cousins.' She paused. 'He was kind enough to reply to my letter, and that's encouraging.'

'Let's hope so. How did you find out about him?'

'His wife is one of my customers, a nice, respectable lady. I was able to help her with one of my syrups.'

'You'll go far, Non Jones, so long as you get your strength back.'

'Well, I'm building up a little band of regular customers.' Non tweaked her hat again: it still didn't seem to sit right on her thick hair.

'You look lovely. You'll make a good impression on this Mr Cousins, especially if his wife puts a word in for you.'

'I think she's already done that – he wouldn't have agreed to the meeting otherwise. Wish me luck.'

'You don't need it. You've a good head on you and know how to speak nicely.'

Non hoped she'd find her way to Mr Cousins's house without too much trouble – she didn't want to arrive late for her appointment or flustered from having to rush. She rehearsed in her mind what she would say to him. She had been the victim in the struggle with the thief. Albie had only intervened when the man had tried to steal her money. She hoped she could convince Mr Cousins that she was telling the truth. It was possible Albie would be released at once, but if not she would ask permission to visit him in prison.

She found the house off Giltspur Street with little difficulty. She could hear the faint sounds of cattle protesting in their pens at Smithfield market and a sense of loss swept over her. The market reminded her of Caradoc.

The house was solidly built, the front door imposing, the brass fittings gleaming. A maid opened the door to her and bobbed a curtsy when Non gave her name. 'Mr Cousins is expecting you,' she said, backing away to allow Non to come inside. The hall was large and airy, good pictures hung on the walls and a rich carpet reached from the door to the staircase.

She was kept waiting for a few minutes, and twisted her hands together nervously. She didn't know what to expect but she hoped Mr Cousins was as kindly as his wife. At last the door to a book-lined study opened and a tall, white-haired man beckoned her forward. 'Mrs Jones.' He held out his hand and she took it, feeling his fingers curl with reassuring strength round her own. 'Come into my study and tell me how I can be of help to you.'

'As I explained to Mrs Cousins,' Non said, 'my friend has been arrested for something he didn't do.'

'Well, sit down and tell me what happened.'

Non recounted the tale of how she was being robbed and Albie had come along in time to defend her. 'So, you see, he was not attacking the man. On the contrary, the man had accosted me.'

Mr Cousins took some details of Albie's appearance,

240

where he lived and what he did for a living. He looked up at Non and made a wry face. 'Unfortunately your friend has a reputation with the bench,' he nodded, 'quite a reputation. He hasn't been an honest citizen until now, has he?'

'Well, whatever he's done in the past, he's innocent of the charge against him this time.' Non clasped her gloved hands together. 'And I have here a letter from another friend, Jessie, telling you how Albie repaid someone he'd robbed by working for him until the debt was cleared. Please say you'll help, Mr Cousins.'

'I believe you're the widow of Mr Caradoc Jones, cattle drover,' Mr Cousins said quietly, as he took the note from her, 'and the daughter-in-law of Mr George Jones, owner of the Bank of the Black Ox.'

'That's correct, sir,' Non said.

'Well, you seem a respectable young woman, so I will take all the facts into consideration and see what I can do to obtain your friend's release.' He held up his hand, as Non opened her mouth to thank him. 'I can't promise anything,' he said. 'I might not be presiding over the case, but I'll do my best to help.'

He rose to his feet and Non realized the interview was at an end. 'Thank you for your time. How much do I owe you, Mr Cousins?'

He smiled. 'Just give my wife some more of that syrup you make. Her temper is much better since she started taking it.'

As soon as she left the study, the door closed behind her and a maid appeared to show her to the door. As she was about to leave, Mrs Cousins came into the hall. 'Mrs Jones.' She took Non's arm and drew her into the drawing room. 'I want you to meet my friends,' she said. 'I think you'll find some new customers among them.'

Non was surrounded by ladies who all talked at once, until Mrs Cousins held up her hand for silence. 'Now I suggest I persuade my husband to rent a little shop for you. It would be much more convenient for you than travelling all the way across town from Treacle Lane.'

Non was alarmed. 'But I haven't the money to rent a shop.'

'No one is asking you to pay.' Mrs Cousins smiled warmly. 'I want to be your patron. You deserve some help – you're very gifted in what you do. I don't know how I'd cope without your medicine now.'

'Thank you, Mrs Cousins, but I'm building up a good list of customers. My name is known now and I'm happy working as I do.'

'Oh, but it would be so convenient if you had a shop in a good part of London. You'd have even more customers then. Think about it, my dear. Now sit down, take some tea with us and tell us about your cures.'

Non did as she was told, and hope trickled into her mind. At least she could earn her own living and wouldn't have to take charity from anyone. Kind as Mrs Cousins's offer had been, Non had no intention of accepting it. Still, this meeting had already brought her some new customers and, more importantly, Mr Cousins might be able to free Albie. She settled back in her chair and talked to her prospective customers with a feeling of excitement that had been missing for too long.

CHAPTER THIRTY-TWO

Jessie soon became used to the bad odours of the tall house off Cutler Street. Even the people on the second floor greeted her now when she came in from her round. She warmed to them, and gave them any milk she had left over. About twelve people lived in the one room, a mixture of men, women and a few children. They seemed to have nocturnal habits, only leaving the house when darkness fell. But, she told herself sternly, what they did was no business of hers.

Her round still consisted mainly of the poor, who waited in a ragged group for her to bring milk to them. Dan had spread the word about the good cheap milk Jessie had to offer, and the length of the queues had grown accordingly. He was used to the cows now, pushing them easily into place above the pail to milk them.

'Jessie,' he said one day, as he trundled the cart along the narrow alleyway that led home, 'you won't change when Albie comes out of prison, will you?'

'What do you mean?' She smiled at him knowing full well what he meant. 'If you think you're going to get out of working for me you can forget it. I need you and I'll go on needing you.'

His grubby face brightened. 'I'll work hard, you know that, and I won't need paying – the milk you give Ma every day makes up for the hours I put in.'

'Look, Dan, I owe your ma more than the price of some milk. I'm able to pay my way now and I've been offered the use of a field for the cows where they can graze for nothing. It's a bit out of the way, but I don't mind that. Think of it, Dan – I won't have to buy fodder for them and that'll save me a few pennies.'

'Who's offered you grazing for nothing? Sounds suspicious to me.'

'Well, you know we've got some of our customers back in Leman Street – I was talking to Mrs Levy, remember?' He looked bemused. 'Well, Mrs Levy's husband owns a big piece of land a few miles away. It's perfect, Dan. The animals can graze there, Mr Levy says, so I can pay your ma rent and still put a bit aside for the future.'

'You mean when Albie comes out of jail, don't you?'

'Yes, I suppose I do. But I'll still need you, Dan. When I've got enough money I'll rent a shop so that customers can come to me instead of me pushing the cart to them.'

'I push it more than you do,' Dan said indignantly.

'Come to think of it, I suppose you do.' Jessie patted his shoulder, but he shook away her hand self-consciously. 'I don't know what I'd do without you.'

And she meant every word. If Dan hadn't been pushing the cart for her she'd never have sold so much milk. And the round had taken longer this morning, which meant the list of customers was longer.

Dan peered into the pails. 'Not much milk left today,' he said, with pride. 'See? I'm lucky for you – I've brought you new customers.'

'And I'm very grateful,' Jessie said, and hid a smile.

At the alleyway near the house, Dan lifted off the remaining half-full pail of milk. 'Take it up to Ma,' he

244

said, 'and as soon as you bring the pail back I'll get on with washing them all out.'

Non was taking medicine to Mrs Cousins and hoped she'd see her husband, the magistrate, too. As luck would have it, he was in the hall when she arrived, putting on his topcoat and hat.

'What's happening to Albie, sir?' She was too anxious to wait while the pleasantries were observed.

'I made a point of finding Jed Lambert, the cattle drover Albie worked for.' He smiled wryly. 'You may remember you brought me a note about him from your friend Jessie. Well, far from Lambert clearing Albie's name, he didn't have a good word for the boy. Albie robbed him of a lot of money and Lambert feels the debt is not yet repaid in full.'

'I know Jed Lambert only too well,' Non said. 'He's a villain himself. He must be doing this out of spite. Surely my testimony will be enough to convince a jury of Albie's innocence?'

'We'll have to wait and see – but the evidence seems to go against him. Albie might even face the rope.'

Non thought she was going to faint. She tried to fight off the waves of panic and somehow found her voice. 'Thank you, Mr Cousins, for listening to me, but whatever Albie has done in the past he's not guilty of this charge, I know that.'

'I'll put in a word on your behalf, but it doesn't look very hopeful for your friend.'

'Thank you,' Non said calmly, but she wondered if she would ever see Albie again.

A tantalizing smell greeted Jessie as she climbed the last flight of stairs. Ma had made a thick soup of peas and bacon, and the smell even blotted out the persistent odour of unwashed bodies from the rest of the house.

'We'll eat as soon as the boy comes in,' Ma said. 'I'm that proud of Dan. He's really shaping up, thanks to you.'

She platted the broken chair next to her. 'Sit down. The soup's simmering nicely, the bread is cut, so I got a minute to put my feet up.'

Jessie sat down with relief. She'd been working since early morning and now she was tired. Then her heart leaped in fear. She knew from Ma's expression that she had bad news to tell her. 'What's wrong?' she asked. 'It's Albie, isn't it? Tell me, Ma! What's going on?'

Ma reached out and took her hand. 'One of the lodgers from downstairs has just come out of Newgate. He's heard that Albie's likely to hang.'

Jessie slumped in the chair and its broken back dug into her flesh. 'Oh no, I can't bear it!'

'Well, we can't take it as gospel,' Ma said quickly, 'because Albie's case has still to be heard, but jest be prepared for anything, love. It isn't always justice that's done in them courts.'

Jessie's mind whirled. She imagined Albie swinging at the end of the rope, a spectacle for everyone to see. 'I'm going to Non. Perhaps she'll know more about what's happening than we do.'

'At least get some hot food in your belly first. Look at you! So thin and pale and – Jessie, wait!'

But Jessie was already on the landing, then running down the stairs – her heart racing and her mind clouded with fear. She ran through the dark alleyways, through rat-infested courts, and it didn't take her long to reach Treacle Lane.

Non answered the door and drew her inside. 'Come in and sit down. You've heard about Albie, haven't you?'

'It's true, then?' Jessie allowed herself to be led inside. 'You've been to see the magistrate again – what did he say?'

Non took her into the kitchen, where Ruby was already pouring tea. 'Sit down, Jessie, and I'll tell you what little I know.'

Jessie felt hope flicker and die as she looked from Non's sombre face to where Ruby stood, spooning sugar into the tea, avoiding her eyes.

'I thought everything was going to be all right,' Non began, twisting her hands. 'The magistrate, Mr Cousins, said he'd do what he could. I told him my story and he believed me, I know he did.'

'But?' Jessie asked, fear almost choking her.

'He's seen Jed Lambert. As a result Albie's to be sent for trial.'

Ruby set a cup of tea in front of Jessie. 'That don't mean they'll find him guilty,' she said.

But Jessie knew that a man sent to trial at the Old Bailey usually ended up on the gallows. She began to cry. 'I've made things worse for him. Why did I send Mr Cousins that note? What a fool I've been! I've got to see Albie – I can't let him go to his death without him knowing how much I love him.' Her words took her breath away and she realized in that moment that she *did* love Albie – very much. She hadn't even admitted it to herself before now.

'I'm sure that will be possible,' Non said. 'I'll speak to Mr Cousins.'

Jessie rubbed her eyes, trying to see through her tears. 'Why can't he believe Albie was helping you, Non?'

'I think he did,' Non said slowly, 'but it was Albie's past record and Jed Lambert that did the damage.'

'We can't let him die! We just can't! I love him so much and I never told him.'

'Look,' Non was stroking Jessie's hair, 'I'll see the magistrate again tomorrow and find out if we'll be allowed to see Albie.'

'I *hate* Jed Lambert!' Jessie said. 'I knew he was evil from the first time I took the drovers' roads with him. I wish I'd never written that note to Mr Cousins. Oh, Non, what am I going to do?'

'There's not a lot we *can* do but wait,' Non said. She was quiet for a minute. Then she said, 'But it might be possible to find a lawyer to defend Albie.'

'But Jed Lambert won't stay silent, I know that much about him. He's cruel and he'll relish blackening Albie's name. Unless . . .' – she stared at Non – '. . . unless we can find a way to keep him away from the court.'

'How can we do that? We don't even know the date of the trial, never mind where Jed Lambert will be on that day.'

'I'll think of something.' Jessie felt hope well inside her. 'Without Jed's accusations there's nothing against Albie, not once you've had your say. And they'll believe you, Non. You're honest and respectable – yes, the court will believe you.'

Jessie finished her tea. 'I'm going home now,' she said. 'You find out the date of the trial and I'll do the rest.'

'Be careful,' Non said. 'Don't land yourself in trouble.'

'I won't.' Jessie hugged her. 'I'll see you tomorrow when I've finished my round. By then you might have found out more from Mr Cousins.'

As Jessie walked home, her mind was racing. How could she stop Jed Lambert from appearing in court, even if she could find out the date of the trial? If she had to, she'd go and see Mr Cousins herself, tell him the whole story about Albie working to pay off his debt. He would surely be freed then, and she and Albie could live their life as it should be lived: as man and wife.

CHAPTER THIRTY-THREE

Jed faced the magistrate and stared at him defiantly. 'You've had the crushers to bring me here and I haven't done nothing wrong.'

'When I spoke to you last, are you sure you told me the whole truth, Mr Lambert?'

'What do you mean, sir? I'm only too willing to help if I can.' It didn't do any harm to butter up the magistrate.

But the man wasn't impressed. 'But the boy, Albie, he rode on the trail with you to pay you back the debt he owed, isn't that correct?'

'How do you know that?'

'So you were happy to take him on the road with you?'

'Well, yes. He had to repay me for thieving off me, didn't he?'

'And you trusted him?'

'I suppose so.'

'Trusted him enough to let him know that one or two of your sales were not quite legitimate?'

Jed shifted uneasily from one foot to the other. Mr Cousins had looked into his past and that made him uneasy.

'Do you think this is a case of let sleeping dogs lie, Mr Lambert?'

Jed knew when he was beaten. The London crushers were sharp, not afraid to use force if necessary, and he didn't want to put himself in any danger. It was better to let the young rat go.

'What if you withdraw your accusations and we call it a day?' Mr Cousins said.

'Aye, might be just as well. Albie'll be found guilty of robbing that defenceless old man anyway and you can't hang a man twice, can you?'

As Jed left the house, his gut twisted in anger. He hated the boy now, and the smug magistrate. Most of all he hated that bitch Jessie. This was all her doing! But for now there was nothing he could do but get himself back to Wales before the law pinned something on him.

Morgan rode steadily through the hills and up towards the Wye and the Severn. The wind was cold, driving into his face, but he rode hard and fast as though he could outrun the guilt he felt about losing Flora. He hadn't fallen in love with her, but they'd had a kind of love, a steady love, that might have been more binding than passion. He'd been cruel to her, making his feelings obvious. He should have pretended a little, if only to make her happy.

A hard rain began to fall, and Morgan decided to stop for the night. The Lamb and Flag inn was only about a mile away: he would rest there, change horses, then make the rest of the journey to London. Non would understand his guilt. She had lost the man she loved – perhaps they could comfort each other.

A fire burned in the inglenook and most of the local customers were huddled round it. Some of the men played cards; others sat in contented silence, away from the nagging tongues of their wives. How lucky they were, Morgan thought, to have wives to go home to.

'Well, Smithy, I didn't expect you to be travelling the roads at this time of year.' The voice was familiar and Morgan frowned. Jed Lambert was standing beside him with a tankard of beer.

Morgan said nothing and made his way to the bar where the landlord was mopping up spilt ale.

Jed Lambert followed him. 'I'm on my way back to Wales.' The man seemed determined to engage him in conversation, but Morgan turned his back on him. 'Bit of trouble up there in London,' Jed went on, 'concerns Non Jones and that slip of a girl, Jessie. Bit of bad luck what's happened to them, real sad it is, and Non not long a widow. Come and sit a while, and I'll tell you about it.'

Morgan felt a dart of fear. 'Has something happened to Non? Is she all right?'

'Get your beer and then we can talk,' Jed insisted.

Morgan had no choice but to sit with the man in a corner behind the door. He took a deep drink, then leaned back on the creaking settle. 'Are you going to talk to me or not?'

'Aye.' Jed paused with an infuriating smile and put down his tankard. 'Jessie's thrown in her lot with that Albie, and he's in trouble again. I tried to help him by taking him on the trail with me, but he's been a thief all his life and it's the rope this time. He attacked some old man.' Jed tipped back his head and drank his ale, deliberately keeping Morgan waiting. ''Bout time he was caught – he's been a thief all his life.'

'And Non?' Morgan's voice had an edge to it.

'Oh, she's well enough, but she's had dealings with the magistrate too. Seems she was mixed up in this theft case.'

'I can't believe that,' Morgan said. 'Non is honest as the day is long.'

Jed shrugged. 'Well, I saw her going into the magistrate's house and made it my business to find out what was going on. After all, that Albie stole money from me. He thinks he's paid off his debt by riding the roads with me – good to him I was, grew quite fond of him – but he deserted me as soon as he could. I owe him a hiding and I'll give it to him one of these days.'

'So Non is trying to speak up for Albie, is that all?'

'No, no, she was there when Albie attacked the old man. She even helped Albie get away, from the look of it.'

Morgan knew Non well enough to realize there was more to the case than Jed was telling him. 'Well, I'll be in London myself in a few days, and I'll have the true story from Non's lips.'

'You'll have to ride hard,' Jed said. 'Weather's not too good and the Wye and the Severn will be running high.'

'I'll pay the toll and go over the bridge or on the ferry,' Morgan said, irritated by the man. 'I can ride most of the way.'

'Rather you than me,' Jed said. 'I'm making stops at all the inns on the way to Swansea. Travelling in comfort, that's what I'm doing.'

'I didn't know you had that sort of money to waste,' Morgan said, glancing at Jed, who narrowed his eyes and regarded him with a look of spite.

'Oh, I've got money and more coming,' he said. 'You never thought I was good enough company for you, did you, Morgan? But when I'm rich, you'll have to show some respect.'

'I never liked you or your crooked ways – and as for you being rich . . .'

'Well, I'm better off than all the rest of you. What with high-and-mighty Non Jones selling herbs from door to door like some pedlar, and you so poor you have to ride hard without the comfort of overnight shelter, I don't think I've done so bad.'

Morgan put down his beer. 'Are you spoiling for a fight, Lambert?'

Jed pulled back a little. 'I was only saying how well I've done for myself. No need to take offence.'

Morgan got to his feet. 'Well, I'm not going to thank you for your company,' he said. 'I'd rather be with a rat than spend another minute with you.'

Jed swore in Welsh and Morgan leaned over him. 'Just guard that tongue of yours, Lambert,' he said, 'or I might feel the need to teach you a lesson.' He walked towards the bar and put down his drink, cursing himself for letting Lambert put him in a foul temper. The man was a liar, and full of evil intent. Morgan glanced behind him and saw the hateful look on Lambert's face. It was best to forget about him and what he'd said. Soon he would be in London and could find out the truth for himself.

Non was tired. She had walked the streets selling her medicines for what seemed hours and she'd done well with her new customers. The angelica syrup had all sold because people were making ready for the fevers that would come with the winter weather. Non longed to crawl into Ruby's house, sit in a chair and kick off her boots. She imagined toasting her feet at the fire. But she still had another call to make. She'd promised to talk to Jessie about Albie's trial.

Non found the house just off Cutler Street and was appalled by the poverty of the area. The fronts of the buildings were almost hidden by second-hand garments, and as Non made her way into the house she almost gagged at the smell. She wound her way upstairs, turning away from rooms filled with hordes of

254

shabby people, who stared at her with hopelessness in their thin faces.

Jessie opened the door as soon as Non knocked and drew her inside. 'Any news?' Her face was pale and her eyes huge. Her features had taken on a pinched look, and Non held her close, wanting to reassure her but knowing it was impossible.

'What's happened, Non?' Jessie led her to a chair near the grate. The fire was almost out and the room was cold. Non wrapped her coat round her and tried to find words that wouldn't worry Jessie.

'Mr Cousins has seen Jed Lambert – and sent him off with a stern warning to look to his own affairs – and Albie was taken to the rotation offices at his suggestion to be examined by another magistrate.'

'And what was the outcome?' Jessie's eyes were filled with tears. 'It's bad news, isn't it? He's going to stay in Newgate.'

'I'm afraid he'll be sent for trial. We'll have to wait for the outcome of that,' Non said quietly. 'Mr Cousins explained the procedure to me. When Albie goes to court he'll be able to give his side of the story and I'll back him up on that. Then the supposed victim, the old man who tried to rob me, will give his story and the judges will decide who is telling the truth. It means Albie will only face one charge. Jed withdrew his accusations so everything looks more hopeful.' Non took Jessie's hands. 'It will be a fair trial, Mr Cousins assured me of that, and we both know Albie's innocent.'

'But imagine him going to the Old Bailey – it will be awful! My little friend Dan knows about these things and he says nearly everyone who goes to the Bailey is put away or hanged. Oh, Non, how can I bear it?'

Non hugged her. 'It will all be cleared up soon. I

think my testimony will carry some weight, and Albie's story will be proved true.'

Even as she spoke reassuringly to Jessie, Non's heart fluttered with fear. She, too, had heard of how men and women were hanged publicly for the smallest offence because the judge believed the complainant.

'There, there,' she said, and clasped Jessie to her, 'everything will be all right.' But even as she spoke, in her heart she feared the worst.

Albie sat on the stone bed in his cell at Newgate and put his hands over his ears, unable to bear the prison noise – women and children crying, the screams of a man being whipped. He felt as if he had gone to sleep and woken up in hell. He got to his feet and tried to see outside, past the bars at the small, grimy window. He'd been a thief, yet it was for a crime he hadn't committed that he was in Newgate. He thumped the wall in anger.

The prisoner in the next cell uttered a string of curses. 'Shut up! I'm to hang at noon – can't I 'ave a bit of peace on my last day 'ere?'

Albie flinched. If the hearing went against him that would be his fate. He told himself to be calm as the man in the next cell began to keen. He closed his eyes in despair: how could he bear the suffering of his fellow inmates a moment longer?

But Jessie would get him out of this hell-hole. The thought of her brought him comfort and eventually he slept.

Albie was woken by screaming from the next cell. He stood on his bed and looked out of the window. It must be noon already. He couldn't see anything but the grey walls of the prison block facing him, but he could hear the roar of the crowd who had gathered to see a man hanged.

The roar grew louder and some of the crowd were clapping and cheering. Albie imagined the man dangling from the noose, his legs kicking as he struggled against the rope.

He sank on to his cold, hard bed and, though he told himself he must be brave and conduct himself like a man, hot and painful tears came spilling from under his closed eyelids and ran unchecked down his face.

CHAPTER THIRTY-FOUR

Jed arrived at his home in Five Saints under a downpour of rain. He slid from his saddle and led the horse to the stable. It was small and the walls needed work. The house was run-down too, but his landlord was unwilling to pay out any money to maintain the property.

But soon everything would change. Jed was determined that once he had all the money he could take from Mrs Georgina Langland he would have any house he wanted. He might even own Broadoaks, given enough time.

Old Mr Jones was a beaten man. He'd lost his spirit. He blamed himself for the death of his grandson and believed he'd lost his son too. Jed knew that Caradoc Jones was alive in a remote cottage a few miles from the Wye. He nursed the knowledge like a precious jewel.

He rubbed down his horse and flung a blanket over its back. Horses cost money, and Jed was always one to look after his investments.

The house was cold and he lit the fire in the kitchen. He didn't like looking after himself, but when he was rich servants would wait on him hand and foot. Why should folk like the Joneses have all the luxury when he was a hard-working man scarcely making a living?

He was too tired to eat – in any case, the bread in the

cupboard was mouldy and so was the cheese. He harboured a great resentment against the Joneses: they'd always expected a doffing of the cap and a bowing of the knee, but soon the mighty would fall.

He fell asleep in a chair, with the grime of the road still clinging to his clothes. His dreams were of the money he would make in bringing the Joneses to their knees.

Georgina made her way across the lawn to the greenhouse where she knew Matt would be waiting for her. She let herself into the warmth and saw him reflected in the glass.

'Matt,' she breathed, and he was at her side enfolding her in his arms. She kissed his neck and pulled his face towards her. His mouth was warm and she felt there could be no greater love on earth than theirs.

'My lovely Georgie,' he whispered, pulling her down on to the stone bench. 'I love you so much I could die for you.' He slipped her cloak from her shoulders and began to undo her bodice. Her breathing grew ragged – she wanted him so much that she could hardly contain herself.

When she was naked, he stared at her body for a long sensuous moment and Georgina was glad she'd borne no children to spoil it. She could see that Matt was aroused, but stopped herself reaching out for him. Past experience with him had taught her to be patient.

He ran his hands over her breasts, her hips, then slowly moved to her thighs.

Afterwards, she traced the outline of Matt's strong jaw. 'I love you,' she said softly.

'I know you do, and I love you, Georgie. Why don't we run away to live in Paris where Jed Lambert can't find us? We won't need much money. I can easily find

259

a job and we can forget all that's happened here, make a new start.'

'Silly Matt,' she said gently. 'I couldn't live in poverty. I've never even dressed myself, so how could I look after us when I can't even care for myself?'

'You could learn. Wouldn't it be worth it, Georgie?'

'I'd do anything to be with you, but be patient. When my father, bless him, leaves this world, I'll have all the money I could ever need. We could see Jed Lambert, pay him off – we could do anything we wanted.'

'Do you really think he would leave us alone? You're too innocent, my lovely. He would bleed you dry and he might tell everyone what happened to Clive Langland anyway.'

Georgina sat up and pulled her cloak round her. 'I can't leave now. What would Papa do without me? And if we did run away Jed Lambert would go to him and take money from him. As you say, he's not a man to give up easily.'

Matt sighed. 'I suppose you're right.'

'Perhaps Fate will be kind to us and Jed Lambert will meet with an accident.'

'No.' Matt got to his feet and adjusted his clothing. 'Bad as he is, I've enough on my conscience.'

Georgina looked up at him. His hair was silvered by the moonlight and his fine jaw and cheekbones were touched with light. He looked like an angel. 'Matt, we'll think of something. I can give Lambert enough money to keep him quiet for a while. Perhaps I should find someone to dig into his past . . .'

'And what will anyone find but a few shady horse deals? That's not going to bother a man like him.'

Georgina took a deep breath. 'What about concealing a murder? Why didn't I think of it before? Once I've given him money, and can prove it, he'll be an accomplice in a murder.' She chewed her fingernail. 'There will have to be a witness, a trusted member of the family – perhaps even my aunt Prudence.' A smile spread across her face and she held out her arms to Matt. 'Come here and give your clever girl a kiss. I think we've got him, Matt.'

When Jed woke, he took off his clothes and went to the stream at the back of the house to wash. He was filled with triumph. Caradoc Jones was still lost in a fog of confusion, and he could approach the Langland woman armed with that information. She would see sense then, realize that he could blow her world to pieces.

The water was cold and he whistled as he bathed. Everything good was coming his way, and he would celebrate with a night on the town. He'd find himself a willing wench, then eat and drink to his heart's content. Tomorrow he would ride up to Broadoaks and feast his eyes on the woman who would make him rich.

Later, he rode into Swansea and stopped outside the Old Castle Arms. The interior was hazy with pipe smoke, and Jed waved to the landlord to bring him a drink, then settled himself on a chair where he could face the room. Georgina Langland was a vixen and he didn't trust her for one minute, or her besotted lover. And he liked to look after his own back – no one else would do it for him.

Jessie pushed the cart towards home and heard the clank of the empty milk pails with satisfaction. The round was doing well now and the money coming in regularly. Lately, some of her old customers from Leman Street had come back to her, happy to buy fresh milk from a clean milkmaid. Some of the cow-keepers were not as careful about washing out the pails as she was and consequently the milk tasted sour the next day.

But Albie was still inside the grim walls of the prison and it was time she did something about it. So far she'd only spoken to Mr Cousins and she needed something to prove Albie's innocence. She'd start with the ragged people who lived in the house off Cutler Street.

Dan appeared from one of the courts lugging an empty milk pail. 'These pails are heavier than they look,' he grumbled as he lifted it on to the cart and brushed himself down. Jessie noticed that a couple of buttons were missing from his coat and the sleeves were too short for him, making him appear even skinnier than he was.

'The round's going well, Jessie,' he said, still puffing from the effort of carrying the pail. 'I think we'll soon be rich, don't you?'

'Well,' Jessie said, 'rich enough to buy you another coat anyway.'

Dan laughed, for a moment appearing like the child he was. 'Can I choose? Can we go down Cutler Street right now and have a look?'

'We'll clean the pails first,' Jessie said, 'and then we'll have a good look at all the coats in Cutler Street.'

'Hello, me darling. There's a sight to feast me eyes on!'

The voice was so familiar that Jessie whirled round with a wide smile. 'Fred Dove! What are you doing in London?' She caught his hands in hers. 'And how did you find me?'

'Hold on!' Fred kissed her fingers. 'I'll answer your questions one by one. I'm here in London because I came looking for you and I found you because I had the wit to ask for any pretty milkmaid working in the area.' His eyes crinkled into laughter and he held her close. 'I've spent months looking out for you, talking to cow-keepers all over London, and my patience has been rewarded.'

Jessie turned to Dan, who was staring, sour-faced, at the man for being so familiar with her. 'Dan, this is Fred Dove. I worked for him and his family when I first came to London. He was very kind and let me keep the animals so I could make a start on my own.'

Dan grinned. 'Well, I work with her now, Mr Dove, and so will Albie when he comes out of Newgate.'

'Albie?' Fred looked enquiringly at Jessie. 'You're not married, are you, Jessie?'

'Of course not,' Jessie said quickly, 'but Albie and me, well, we're . . .'

'That's a relief.' Fred took her hand again and kissed her fingertips. 'I'm a widower now, Jessie, and the only girl I'd want for a wife is you.'

Once she had longed to hear him say those words but that was in the past. Since then she'd made her own way: the business was beginning to grow and she wanted to prove herself capable of running it on her own. 'I'm sorry, Fred . . .' she began, but he held up his hand.

'Don't answer now. Sure I'm a big ox blurting out my feelings here in the street. Come on, Jessie, take me to your house – I'm looking forward to seeing the beasts again.' He grinned. 'Do you suppose they'll recognize me?'

'We're going to buy a coat for me,' Dan said sulkily. 'That's what you said, Jessie.'

'And so we will.' Jessie turned back to Fred. She couldn't admit she was living in a filthy rat-hole and that the animals were kept in a small, rented field.

'I'll come with you,' Fred said, with determination.

He took the shafts of the cart and began to push it along the road.

Jessie looked at Dan. 'I don't suppose it will do any harm if Fred helps us choose a coat, do you?'

'I don't like him,' Dan said gloomily. 'He'll want to change everything, make you marry him and work for him and, oh, everything's going wrong!' He ran away from her, his trousers flapping against his legs.

Jessie was at a loss as to how she should deal with Fred. He'd been so good to her that she couldn't just send him away.

'Look.' She stopped at the top of Cutler Street. 'I might as well be honest with you. I'm not making a fortune – I lost my comfortable room in Leman Street that I wrote to you about, and now I have to live in a lodging-house.'

'Sure, my colleen, I never expected you to be rich. I'd want you even if you hadn't a penny to your name.'

'But, Fred . . . I'll tell you everything.' She drew him along the narrow court where the tall house merged into the fog that had come down. She stood outside the door, smiling when Fred wrinkled his nose at the smell. 'This is where I live, and lucky enough I was to find it. If it weren't for Dan I'd be sleeping in the gutter.'

'Things can't be that bad.' Fred frowned in bewilderment. 'You've got a good round. Some of the customers are poor, I'll grant you, but you sell out of milk every day so you must be able to afford a better place to live than this.'

'I'm saving my money, Fred. One day I'm going to have a shop with a place for the cows at the back. I have ambition, Fred. I don't want to be beholden to any man.'

'Sure being a married woman is no disgrace,' Fred said. 'I love you, Jessie – I've always loved you. I had responsibilities before, but now I'm free to marry again. Why can't you just say you're willing, Jessie?'

'Because I'm not willing. I'll always be fond of you, Fred, but I can never love you. I love Albie.'

'Albie – is he the one in prison?'

'Yes, but he's done nothing wrong. He's innocent, Fred, and I've got to find a way of proving it.'

'Well, Jessie Price, you've come down in the world. You live in a hell-hole and you're waiting on a criminal. What's happened to you, girl? You're not the Jessie I once knew.'

'No,' she said sadly. 'I'm not, am I? Sorry to let you down, Fred, but I have to make my own way in the world now. Can't you see that?'

'I won't give up, Jessie,' Fred said. 'I'll wait for you for ever, if need be.'

Jessie hated to see the disappointment on his face. 'I'm sorry, Fred, but I don't love you.' She pushed open the door, aware for the first time in ages of the awful smell. Everything about the house looked and smelt worse than she had realized, but now she was looking at it from Fred Dove's point of view and he had never had to face the harsher side of life.

'Goodbye, Fred,' she said. 'I've made my choices in life and I mean to stick by them.' She left him then and walked upstairs, her mind calm. Fred's appearance had made it clear to her that she wanted Albie. He was the man she loved.

CHAPTER THIRTY-FIVE

Caradoc returned from his walk and stood at the door. He dreaded going into the cottage. It was getting more and more difficult to stay with Gwenllyn when every nerve in his body called out for him to go to Swansea. If no one knew him there he could try Brecon or Hereford. Only when he'd exhausted the fairly close towns would he travel to London.

Gwenllyn had prepared beef stew with fluffy dumplings, and as Caradoc washed his hands in the water barrel he could smell the enticing aroma. He realized he was hungry.

'You're working too hard,' Gwenllyn said, frowning. 'Your face is white as flour. You're not really over your accident and you should go easy on yourself.'

'The accident was months ago,' he said. 'My leg is almost mended and my arm hardly bothers me. It's just my mind that won't work properly.'

Gwenllyn put her arms round him and rested her head on his chest. 'Don't be so hard on yourself. Everything will come back to you one day.'

'I don't know about that,' Caradoc said. 'I thought once my body had healed my mind would too. But I've no idea how I got into the river or how I broke my bones. Was it a fall from a horse? If so, where was I going and where had I come from?'

'There, there.' Gwenllyn patted his back as though he was a child. 'Just eat your dinner and then you'll feel better.'

He moved out of her arms and sat at the table, irritated. She was trying to brush away his feelings of loss and frustration as though they were childish whims. Didn't she realize he could never be himself without knowledge of his past?

'The dumplings are good.' He tried to smile. These days, he was downhearted and it was growing more and more difficult to hide his feelings from Gwenllyn. She was with child and he should be helping and supporting her, not whining about his own problems.

As though sensing his feelings, she reached out and covered his hands with hers. 'I know it's hard, *cariad*, but you're safe here. You have everything you need, and me to love you.'

'I know,' he said, 'and I'm very grateful.' He cut a piece of beef. 'Good meat,' he said. 'Must have come from a well-fattened animal.' He lowered his fork. How had he known what made good beef? He felt like hitting his head against the wall to force the memories back. He continued to eat but his mind was racing. He tried to hold on to the possibility that in the past he'd been involved with cattle.

Gwenllyn's eyes were worried when they met his. 'I'm all right,' he said quickly, 'just a bit tired. As you keep telling me, I should rest more. Then, perhaps, my memory will return.'

'You won't leave me if it does, will you?' Her voice was trembling. 'I don't want to be alone, Caradoc. I couldn't live without you, not now.'

'Don't worry,' he said lightly. 'If I find I'm a rich businessman I'll keep you in comfort for the rest of your life – the baby too, of course.'

That night, Caradoc lay wide-eyed in the darkness, but the urge to sleep was too powerful to resist. When he woke in the morning he knew he had to put aside his restless thoughts and face the future with Gwenllyn and the baby.

Ruby looked carefully at Fred Dove. 'Are you sure you know Jessie?' she asked. 'You look too smart to be a cowman.' She had taken him in as a lodger the night before and as he'd paid in advance she hadn't asked too many questions. Now, however, in the morning light she had the chance to look him over.

'You must remember when she worked for me as my milkmaid,' he said. 'Sure she was good to me when my wife was poorly with the baby.'

The penny dropped and Ruby smiled in relief. 'I remember now! Course I do. Fred Dove, well, well.' She turned her head sideways. 'Good shoes, smart coat – I almost took you for a gentleman.'

'Sure I hope I'm a gentleman right enough,' Fred grinned. 'I'm going over to see Jessie today – I want to help her with the round so that she can move out of that terrible place where she's living.'

'What terrible place?' Ruby asked. 'I thought the girl had good lodgings in Leman Street.'

'She was thrown out of there, so she was. Once that Albie had been taken by the constables she was told to leave. Didn't you know?'

'Of course I didn't!'

'She's in a house near Cutler Street, a stinking hole, with all sorts of odd folk living there.'

'She must move here with me at once!' Ruby was agitated. 'Why didn't the silly girl tell me what was going on? And Non knows where Jessie's living! Why didn't she tell me?'

'Jessie must have told her to keep quiet about it. Too proud she is, wouldn't even let me help her, and haven't I loved her since I first set eyes on her?'

'We'll go and fetch her, then,' Ruby said. 'I'll not have her living near Cutler Street a minute longer.'

'But she'll be on her round now, so she will,' Fred said. 'Let the girl make her day's takings and then go and fetch her.'

Ruby pursed her lips. So, Jessie had been too proud to ask for help. Well, the girl was growing up and Ruby couldn't fault her for that. 'Have a bite of breakfast, Mr Dove, and later I'll bring Jessie home to where she belongs.'

Later that day Non hurried along Cutler Street. She had bad news for Jessie, and she wasn't looking forward to delivering it.

It wasn't long before she caught sight of Jessie, pushing her cart along the bumpy cobbles, with a young boy at her side.

'Non, what are you doing here?' Jessie hugged her. 'Have you got news for me?'

'Well, yes, but I don't think you're going to like it.' Before Non could say any more Ruby had rushed up to them, hat askew, skirts flapping. 'Jessie, you bad girl!' Ruby elbowed the boy out of the way and caught Jessie's arm. 'You're to come home with me and I won't take no for an answer.'

'But I can't,' Jessie said. 'I live here now and it suits me.'

'You're not going to live like a pauper,' Ruby insisted.

'But Ruby, it's close to my round and Dan helps me. You haven't met him yet, have you? Dan, this is my

269

friend Ruby. Thank you for the kindness, Ruby, and I'm grateful, but the answer has to be no.'

'You can't say that! At least come home with me to talk it over.'

Jessie appealed to Non: 'I'm doing all right, aren't I, Non?'

'Well, Jessie, you'd be better off living with Ruby, you can't deny that,' Non said. Jessie would need all her friends once she had heard the bad news.

'See here, Jessie,' Ruby said excitedly, 'that Fred Dove is looking for a decent place to keep the animals. He's got a good head on him and he's mad about you. The two of you could marry and make a fine business with the milk.'

'But I don't love him,' Jessie said. 'I don't want to be married to him. Please, Ruby, believe me, I'm all right as I am.'

'You stubborn girl, why don't you listen to plain common sense?' Ruby looked exasperated. 'Think it over anyway – you know you're always welcome in my house.'

'Thank you,' Jessie said, and held up her hand as Ruby opened her mouth to speak. 'I can come to see you later when the pails are washed and everything's put away.'

'Well, I suppose that will have to do, but shall I come in with you now and have a cup of tea?'

Non saw Jessie's hands tighten on the handles of the cart and knew she was ashamed to ask anyone into her lodgings. 'I must count my takings, and I've a lot of work ahead of me.'

'Jessie, I need to talk to you,' Non said. 'It's important.'

Jessie paled. 'Out with it, Non. I'm thinking the worst already so you might as well put me out of my misery.'

Non took a deep breath. 'I'm sorry,' she said, 'there's no chance of visiting Albie. His case comes to trial next week.' She saw tears brimming in Jessie's eyes. 'But I'm sure with Mr Cousins helping us he'll be found not guilty.'

'And if he's not, we'll see him shamed and hanged in front of anyone who cares to watch.'

'That's it! I'm taking you home,' Ruby said.

'I'll find a cab.' Non knew how Jessie felt: she'd also lived through the fear of losing the man she loved.

Non raised her hand as a cab came into sight and the driver slowed. 'Don't usually stop around here,' he grumbled. 'Where you going, Miss?'

'My friend is poorly,' Non said. 'We're taking her to Treacle Lane.'

The driver sniffed. 'All right, then. Let's be on our way before the thieves and vagabonds round here have the wheels from my carriage and the horse from between the shafts.'

Non sighed with relief as she helped Jessie into the cab. She put her arms round the girl and pulled her close. 'You've got friends, Jessie,' she said, 'and we're all going to do what we can to help Albie. Everything will turn out for the best.' But in her heart Non knew that it was doubtful Albie would ever be free.

CHAPTER THIRTY-SIX

Jed brushed down his horse with steady strokes. The animal was getting old and should be put out to graze but he had no money for a younger one. One day, though, and soon, he would have enough to buy a string of them, but he had to move quickly and wrest as much as he could out of the slut Georgina Langland. Then he could live like a gentleman all his life, but all in good time: for now he would have to take what he could get.

Georgina watched Matt working in the garden. He was covering the plants to protect them from the cold weather that was coming. Already the days had turned chilly and the mornings were dark and dreary. But Georgina was happy. She and Matt were meant to be together and no one, especially not Jed Lambert, would come between them.

'Oh, there you are, Georgina.' Her father had come into the drawing room. He looked thin and anxious, and her heart went out to him. 'The journey from London has tired your aunt and she has decided to rest in her room.'

'Papa, come and sit by the fire, you're looking so pale and tired. I'll travel with Aunt Prudence when she goes home to London. In any case, she's as strong as an ox.' She led him to a chair and he sank into it.

'I'm feeling so tired,' he said, 'and wondering what I've done to deserve all the ills that have befallen me.'

He looked up at her. 'Why did I have to lose my son and grandson? I keep asking myself but there's no answer. With you in a failed marriage I'll never have grandchildren now.' He sighed. 'I've never lied or cheated my way to success. I earned every penny of my money. Wicked men live on, while the good fall by the wayside. There's no sense to it.'

Georgina bit her lip – her father could be so insensitive. One of the maids came into the room and bobbed a curtsy. 'Excuse me, Miss Georgina, there's a – a man at the door who says he needs to speak to you.'

'What's his name?' Georgina felt a flutter of fear.

'Jed Lambert, Miss.' She wrinkled her nose. 'He smells of horse, Miss Georgina.'

'I'll come at once,' Georgina said, as her father rose from his chair. 'Don't bother to come to the door, Papa. This will be about a new pony I was after.'

'You're not dealing with the likes of Jed Lambert, are you?' George said. 'He's not an honest man.'

'Sit down, Papa. Let me deal with things my way. You do too much and at your age you should rest more.' Her skirts swished as she left the room. Jed Lambert was getting above himself: how dare he come to the front door?

He was standing outside tapping his riding whip against his boots, with a greedy smile on his face. 'Mr Langland,' he said, with a mock bow, 'how good of you to see me.'

'I've got your money,' Georgina said sharply. 'Come inside.'

She ran upstairs and knocked on the door of her aunt's room.

Prudence was seated near the window, her eyes closed. 'Are you awake, Aunt?' Georgina asked quietly.

Prudence opened her eyes. 'I am now. What do you want, Georgie? Can't you see I'm trying to rest?'

'I need you to witness something,' Georgina said slowly. 'I have to give a man money, and I want you to be there when he takes it.'

Prudence sat up straight, her eyes sharp. 'This can only mean you're being blackmailed.'

'Yes, but please don't ask any questions. It's enough for you to know that if this man were to spread his evil gossip it would harm all the family.'

Prudence rose from her chair and smoothed her hair into place. 'Very well. I shall be your witness, my dear, but I hope you know what you're doing.'

Georgina led the way downstairs to where Jed Lambert stood in the hall. He was pretending to be at ease, but his shoulders were stiff and the hands holding his hat were white at the knuckles.

Georgina gave him the money. 'Count it,' she said. 'It's enough for you to keep your mouth shut.'

'Maybe, maybe not.' Jed fingered the bag of gold.

'Well, you'd better make the most of it because that's all you're going to get from me.'

'What d'yer mean?' He stared from Georgina to her aunt and back again. 'If I want more I'll ask for it.'

'No, you won't,' Georgina said. 'You think you've got a hold over me – well, think again. You've taken money from me in front of a reliable witness and if the constable was to be informed you would be in a lot of trouble.'

'You'd be in more,' Jed said.

'And I'd pay a fine lawyer to get me off while you rotted in Swansea prison,' Georgina said icily. 'Now, go away and don't come back.'

Slowly Jed turned towards the door. 'Don't think you've heard the last of me,' he said bitterly. 'Keep looking over your shoulder because I'll be waiting to pounce.'

He slipped through the door and disappeared. Georgina should have been relieved that the danger was gone, but somehow she knew it was only just beginning.

Jessie pushed her cart through Leman Street, happy that most of her old customers had come back to her.

'Morning, Jessie.' Mrs Levy was standing on the doorstep, her jug in her hand.

Jessie filled it, watching the milk bubble against the cold china. 'I've moved back with Ruby in Treacle Lane now, and I'm comfortable there,' she told the woman, and took the coins Mrs Levy handed her. 'I made some good friends in the house near Cutler Street, mind.'

'Well, I'm sure you did. You're a nice girl, Jessie, and I know you're going to make a success of your business.'

'I hope so, Mrs Levy. My animals give good milk. I keep them clean and fed and it might sound silly but they're like friends to me now.'

'I'm sure.' Mrs Levy didn't look sure at all.

Jessie hung her measure on the hook at the side of the cart and picked up the shafts. 'I'd better be getting on,' she said. 'I've a lot of serving to do before my day's work is finished.'

'Ah, now, talking about serving, I know of a little cow-keeper's shop going nearby and I thought perhaps you'd be interested in renting it. I've got the address for you,' Mrs Levy went on. 'You can read, can't you, Jessie?'

'Yes, Mrs Levy, and I can do figures in my head too.'
She was proud of that: not every girl of her age could
work over books as she did.

Mrs Levy gave her the slip of paper. 'Now it's up to
you.'

As Jessie watched Mrs Levy return to her house, she
put the paper carefully into her purse. The shop was
round the corner from Cutler Street, near where she
used to lodge, and she decided to go straight away to
view it.

The building was respectable enough and the shop
was just an open front leading directly on to the street.
From there she could serve all her old customers and
probably some new ones too. There was a ragged
bundle in one corner and Jessie shook her head sadly.
Some folk would sleep where they dropped but she
would have none of that once she rented the place.

When she knocked at the side door, the landlord
looked at her suspiciously. 'I hope you don't mind me
calling,' she said, 'but Mrs Levy from Leman Street
said you're in need of a tenant for your shop.'

'I might be.' His eyes went to her cart and the milk
pails. 'Aye, you look respectable enough, and if Mrs
Levy's a customer you must be. I'd need five shillings
in advance, mind. I don't want you doing a flit after a
few weeks.'

Five shillings was a lot of money, Jessie thought.
Still, it would be worth it – the shop would pay for itself
after a few weeks. 'Can I think it over?' she asked.

'Let me know by tonight.' He closed the door, leaving Jessie to study the peeling paint and the worn
knocker.

When she reached Cutler Street Dan joined her. His
hair was dishevelled but his hands were spotless and he
was wearing a new coat. 'You look a little gentleman,

Dan,' Jessie said. 'You'll be even better if you smooth your hair down a bit.'

'Never mind me 'air,' Dan said. 'I got a message for you.' There was a sharp, eager look on his face.

'What is it?' Jessie's heart pounded. 'Is it from Albie?'

'Not from Albie but near as good as. One of the men from the lodging-house – you knows him, O'Flynn the pickpocket – he says he can get Albie off. He says he saw the whole thing, the gent trying to steal Miss Non's purse and Albie fighting him off. Says it was all over in a flash but none of it were Albie's fault.'

'I'll go and see him straight away. Will you finish the round for me, Dan?'

Dan swelled with pride. 'Course I will.'

Jessie made for the house where she had lodged until a few days ago. The smell of damp and filth was all-pervading and she realized how lucky she was that Ruby had given her a decent home.

Jessie lifted her skirts as she climbed the stairs to the landing and looked into the room where Mr O'Flynn lived. A baby was crying fretfully and a young woman, eyes sunk in their sockets, lifted it to her skinny breast.

A figure detached itself from the other occupants and came to her on the landing. He pulled the door shut behind him. 'The name's O'Flynn.' He leaned against the wall, which was running with damp. 'I might be able to help you, but it'll cost you.'

'How much?'

'Let's say a few shillings, shall we?'

Jessie's dream of running a shop dissolved. She summed up the man, then came to a decision.

'I'll give you three shillings.' She gestured towards his clothes. 'You'll need something respectable to wear if you're to convince a judge of anything so I'll give you two shillings more and I'll come with you to choose the outfit.'

'Don't worry about my clothes,' he said. 'O'Flynn robs and cheats the rich, but don't do anything to hurt his own kind. I'll get some clothes and I'll get young Albie off.'

Jessie gave him her morning's takings. 'This will do to start you off. Be ready because as soon as I know when we can see the judge I'll need you straight away.' Then she walked off. For all she knew O'Flynn would take her money and she would never see him again. She felt a pang as she thought of her missed opportunity. She couldn't afford to rent a shop now . . . or could she?

She made her way back along the street and gazed longingly into the empty shop. The counter was of fine, solid wood, the floors were covered with sawdust and at the back there was a yard where she could wash the pails and measures. The walls needed whitewashing and the whole place could do with a good scrubbing, but it was an excellent place to start her business. She knocked on the door.

After a time she heard dragging footsteps and a man cursed. The door was opened a crack and the landlord looked out at her. 'Oh, it's you. You taking the place?' he asked, rubbing his eyes. It was clear that he'd been asleep.

'Yes, I am,' Jessie said boldly. 'But I'll pay you two shillings a week in rent and I'll give you fresh milk every morning.' She glanced at the shop. 'I'll keep it as clean as a new pin.'

'What about the deposit?' the landlord growled.

'I got no deposit,' Jess said, 'but I'll do your cooking and clean your house. I'll be a reliable tenant and I'll keep vagrants away from the place as I'm late to bed and up at first light.'

'I don't know.' He stroked his chin. 'I wanted a good sum to put in my pocket . . . but a regular amount coming in would be handy, especially if you was to cook for me and run an errand now and then. Perhaps I should think it over.'

'You haven't got anyone else waiting to take it on,' Jessie persisted. 'It's been empty for some time, and it will get ruined if any old Tom, Dick or Harry sleeps in it as they please.'

'Oh, all right,' the landlord said. 'Take it over as soon as you like. And remember, in the morning I like a good breakfast of bacon and fried bread. Wait here.'

He shambled away, then came back with a key. 'This is to lock the back door so your buckets and things are safe. Now leave me in peace.' He closed the door.

Jessie swallowed hard. She'd won! She had a place of her own and soon, very soon, if justice was with them, she would have Albie back in her arms.

CHAPTER THIRTY-SEVEN

Caradoc stared into the fire, unaware of his surroundings. He could see through the flames a marble mantel with hares and dogs carved in relief. He felt fine cotton against his skin, saw a table groaning with hams and sides of pork. He knew there was another world out there, a world he used to inhabit.

'You all right, Caradoc?' Gwenllyn had come into the kitchen. 'You're very thoughtful.'

He felt as if he'd been woken from a deep sleep: the illusion vanished and he was once again a man without a past. 'I was thinking about you,' he said, taking her hand and drawing her on to his knee. 'I'm always thinking about you, Gwenllyn.'

'If that's a lie then it's one I like to hear.' She wound her arms round his neck and he felt her breasts press against him. Immediately he was aroused. Gwenllyn's touch always lit a flame in him and he wanted her with a passion that burned him up – so why did he always feel that something was missing?

'I love you, Caradoc.' She laid her cheek against his, and he smelt her clean scent. She was beautiful, she wanted and needed him – especially now a baby was on the way.

His arm encircled her waist. She was still slim with no sign of her coming motherhood. He laid his hand flat on her stomach. 'No one would believe you were with child,' he said softly. 'Your waist is still so small.'

She pressed her mouth against his and he realized she never spoke of the baby. Was there something she wasn't telling him? 'Surely you should be showing by now?' He held her away from him and looked into her eyes.

'I don't know. I've never had a baby before but I'm sure there's nothing wrong.'

'We'll have the doctor from the village look at you all the same,' Caradoc said. 'We can't take any risks with your health. Having a baby is a serious matter. Even I know that.'

Pain gripped him: he had held his own child close to his heart, he was sure of it. He tried to push the mist from his mind, his desire for Gwenllyn gone.

Gwenllyn knew him well, knew when the dark clouds came to haunt him. Now she slipped her hand inside his trousers and teased him until his passion returned. 'Take me to bed, Caradoc,' she said, her breath warm on his cheek.

He led her upstairs and she fell on to the bed in an attitude of surrender. He undressed her slowly. 'Oh, my love,' he murmured, 'you're so beautiful – I can't get enough of you.' He kissed her and she tasted sweet and wholesome.

Afterwards, he knew he should feel fulfilled, but some part of him was empty. Gwenllyn was a loving, beautiful, desirable woman but she was not *his* woman.

Later Caradoc took a walk through the village, seeking something that eluded him. The river Wye held the answer to all his questions. It was as though the water had washed him clean of his past and into a new future. A future he didn't feel right in.

Caradoc's first call was at the house of the midwife. He wanted her to examine Gwenllyn.

'I will, sir,' the woman said. 'I'm Mrs Pedlar, and I've seen you about our village but we never got to talking, did we?' She tied and retied her apron strings. 'I did hear that old Martha's granddaughter was with child but I haven't been asked to see her until now.' There was reproof in her tone. 'She should be filling out now and the child moving.'

Caradoc wasn't sure about that, but he said nothing. 'Come and see Gwenllyn this afternoon if you can,' he said.

As he walked further into the village he heard the sound of a hammer on an anvil. The arrival of the blacksmith was an event – the village was too small to keep a smith fully occupied. It was almost like a fair day: all the farmers turned out with wheels to be mended and horses to be shod.

He felt the roar of the fire and smelt burning leather. Then he saw the strong back of the man bent over the heat and a memory stirred. Caradoc watched for a while from the shadows of the shed until the crowd around the smithy thinned as he finished his work and Caradoc could see him clearly.

As though he had felt his gaze, the man turned and a look of amazement crossed his face. 'Caradoc Jones!' he said. 'I thought the river had taken you a long time ago.'

'You know me?' Caradoc was almost afraid to ask the question in case the man had mistaken him for someone else.

'Of course I know you. I'm Morgan the smithy! I've ridden with the Joneses for many a year and I'm on my way to London. The weather's been bad so I thought I might as well spend the night here.' He paused, and Caradoc saw him frown. 'What's happened to you? Everyone thinks you're dead, including your poor wife.'

'My wife? I don't remember anything about my past. All I know is that I came out of the river half dead and Gwenllyn brought me back to life.' He took Morgan's arm. 'Come with me, back to the house. We can talk for as long as we like and you can tell me all the things I should know.'

He saw Morgan puff out his cheeks. 'There's an awful lot to tell,' he said, 'and it's not all pleasant.'

As he walked back to the cottage with Morgan at his side, Caradoc felt as though a new life was beginning and that the man beside him, Morgan the smithy, held the key that would unlock his past once and for all.

'What's all this, then, Jessie, you so smart and ladylike in your new shop?'

As Mrs Levy held out her jug Jessie felt she would burst with pride. 'I'm doing it all for Albie,' she said. 'I want him to have a good living, something respectable to come home to when they let him out of prison.'

'Don't build your hopes up too high now, young lady,' Mrs Levy said. 'Justice is a funny thing, and sometimes it isn't even done.'

Those were words Jessie didn't want to hear, so she took up her measure and filled Mrs Levy's jug. A queue had formed and for a time Jessie was kept so busy that she could think of nothing but pouring milk and taking money. She was doing well but she knew it would take all she could earn to pay the landlord his rent and make enough to feed the animals. She wouldn't see much profit for a while.

Dan came round the counter, skirting the ever-growing queue of people – some of them respectable maids from the big houses. 'Doin' well, Jessie! By the time Albie comes home we'll be rich.'

'Have you seen Mr O'Flynn?' Jessie asked anxiously.

Dan shook his head. 'No, but if anybody can get Albie off it's O'Flynn.'

'What will he have to do, Dan? Will he speak to the magistrates or the judges or will he just have to go to the trial?'

Dan winked. 'There might not be a trial – better if there's not.'

'Why is it better?'

'If there's a trial it means Albie will have to face the jury. They can be real cruel, them juries, send a man to the gallows as soon as look at him.'

Fear clutched Jessie. She imagined Albie in a big hall somewhere being judged by people who didn't know him. 'He will be all right, won't he, Dan?'

'Course he will. You're not to worry.'

Later, when Jessie returned home to Treacle Lane, she sat in the kitchen near to tears. She missed Albie so much, his bright chatter, his loving looks.

Ruby came into the room with a tray of dirty dishes. 'Don't sit there moping, girl. I need a hand with all this work.'

'I'm so worried,' Jessie said. 'It sometimes feels as if Albie will never come back.'

'Of course he'll be back! You won't do him any good by thinking he won't.'

'I know you're right.' She forced a smile. 'I'll help you with the dishes and then we'll count my takings.'

'By the look of that purse you got there you're on your way to making a fortune.'

Jessie weighed it in her hands. It was heavy, filled with coins – it had been a good day for selling milk. But she would give it all up, the shop, the milk round, everything, if only she could have Albie at home with her again.

★　★　★

'You're not with child,' the midwife said bluntly.

Gwenllyn looked at her fearfully, wondering how she could lie her way out of her dilemma. 'But, Mrs Pedlar, I've missed my monthly courses. I must be with child.'

The woman shook her head doubtfully. 'Well, all I can say is I've looked you over well, poked and prodded your belly till my fingers are sore, and there's no baby in that womb.'

'I don't understand it,' Gwenllyn said. 'I wanted a baby so much.'

'That may be the trouble.' Mrs Pedlar looked at her shrewdly. 'Some ladies want a child so bad they make themselves believe it's happening.'

It was a way out. 'That must be it, then,' she said. 'I felt sick in the mornings, felt as though my belly was swelling, and I was sure there was going to be a baby for me and Caradoc.'

'Well, I still have to be paid for my time,' Mrs Pedlar said. 'I've come all the way up here, on my bad legs.'

As Gwenllyn paid the woman she heard the door latch lift and her heart sank. Caradoc would be sure to leave once he knew she was not with child. He would go searching for what he called his roots and leave her all alone. She tried to frame the words in her mind in such a way that he'd feel obliged to stay with her, but as soon as he walked in Mrs Pedlar said, 'You've planted no seed. There's no baby.' She pulled on her shawl. 'I see you've got company so I'll leave you in peace. If you need me again you know where I live.'

Gwenllyn became aware of another man standing in the gloom behind Caradoc. He took off his hat and inclined his head. Somehow Gwenllyn knew the charade was over: the truth had a way of coming out and she could see by the look on Caradoc's face that he'd found his past.

285

CHAPTER THIRTY-EIGHT

Georgina looked at Morgan the smithy as he stood in the sitting-room doorway. 'Are you sure it's my brother?' she asked. 'Caradoc has been missing for a very long time without sending word.'

Prudence came bustling out of the drawing room. 'What's going on, Georgina? What does this man want?'

'It's Caradoc. Morgan the smithy has seen him, talked to him. He seems to have lost his memory.' She looked at Morgan. 'Are you sure,' she asked, 'really sure, that it's Caradoc?'

'I'm sure, Miss Georgina. I knew your brother better than most. It's true he's changed – he's got a beard, his frame has filled out and his memory is gone – but there's no mistake. I was on my way to London but I came back to tell you the good news. Aren't you pleased, Miss?'

'Of course I am, but I'm afraid to believe it's true.'

'I must call your father at once,' Prudence said excitedly. 'George! Come quick! Caradoc's been found.'

George Jones hurried into the room and looked eagerly at Morgan. The hope in his eyes brought a lump to Georgina's throat. 'Is it true you've found my son?'

'It's true, sir,' Morgan said.

'Well, why isn't he with you now?' Georgina asked. She loved her brother but if he came home nothing would be the same. If his memory returned, he would try to come between her and Matt. But her dear brother was alive and well: that was the most important thing.

'He has matters to deal with before he comes home. In the meantime I've sent a message to his wife in London to ask her to come to Broadoaks as soon as she can.'

Georgina was about to speak but her father was grasping Morgan's arm. 'Surely this business you talk about can't be as important as coming home to his loved ones?' George asked, and Georgina saw that her father had become weak. The confident swagger that had come from knowing he was one of the richest men in the country had gone. All he cared about now was finding his son.

It was obvious how much he thought of Caradoc and how little he thought of her. But, still, she had Matt: he loved her and one day they would be together, in spite of anything her brother might do. She became aware that Morgan was speaking again.

'Your son is staying in a cottage a few miles from the river Wye,' Morgan said. 'He's looking quite well, sir, but he's not clear of anything about his past. I think what I told him came as a shock and he needed time to take it in.'

'You must go and fetch him, Georgina,' George said eagerly. 'Take one or two of the servants and you,' he turned to Morgan, 'you'll go too, won't you, please?'

Morgan nodded reluctantly. 'I can spare a few days, though I hoped I could go to London in time to bring Non home.'

'Good man.' George patted his arm. 'Good man.

You'll be well rewarded if you can bring my son back to me.' He sank into a chair. 'I'd come with you myself but I'd only slow you down. Go now,' he said to Georgina. 'Get ready! You must set out straight away. Prudence, you'll stay with me, won't you?'

'Of course I will, George. I want to see Caradoc as much as you do.'

Morgan nodded to Georgina. 'I'll go home and get some things together. I'll be ready in an hour. Will that suit you, Miss?'

'It will have to,' Georgina answered ungraciously. She flounced out of the room and stood in the hall. Her father had made her feel she was not important and she was hurt. Well, Caradoc wouldn't be able to handle any business affairs, not if he couldn't remember his own name. Papa would soon find that out.

She sighed. She wasn't looking forward to the journey but she'd make sure Matt was with her. As long as they were together, she could put up with anything.

Non stood in the kitchen and stared at the paper in her hand. She read and reread the words, unable to believe what she was seeing. She put her hand to her heart, which was beating so hard she could hardly breathe. 'Ruby!' she called. 'Ruby, come quick!'

Ruby hurried into the room, wiping her hands on her apron. 'What's all the shouting about?' She saw the letter in Non's hand and frowned. 'Not more bad news, is it?'

Non sat down suddenly. 'It's a letter from Morgan. He's seen Caradoc! Ruby, he's actually seen Caradoc! My husband is alive!'

'I don't understand,' Ruby said. 'If he's alive, why hasn't he come looking for you? Is he sick?'

'He was injured in the river. He can't remember anything about his past.' She began to sob, and Ruby hugged her.

'It's all right, chick, it's the best news ever.'

'He's alive, Ruby. He's alive! I can't believe it after all this time. I must go to him at once.'

'What about Albie? He's depending on you to speak for him. And there's your business – how can you just leave everything?' Ruby asked.

'It will all have to wait. Once I find Caradoc I'll bring him home to Treacle Lane and nurse him back to health – oh, Ruby, how wonderful! My darling Caradoc is alive!' She hugged the letter to her. 'Caradoc – my lovely boy is alive!'

Ruby caught her arms and danced her round the room. 'It's a miracle!' Her smile faded. 'Let's hope poor Jessie gets her own miracle and Albie is set free.'

'Oh, I'm sorry about Albie,' Non said, 'of course I am. I would have gone to court with Jessie to stand up for him, but I must go to my husband. You can see that, can't you?'

Ruby hesitated a moment. 'Aye, you must go, I suppose, but write a letter to the judge first. Say how good Albie is, how he saved you from a cunning thief. A letter is better than nothing.'

Non hurried up the stairs to her room, almost bursting with joy. She kissed the letter Morgan had sent her, folded it next to her breast, and then set about packing the clothes she would need for the journey. Caradoc was alive. Hadn't she always known it somewhere deep in her heart and soul? Soon, very soon, she would be in her husband's arms.

Jed Lambert watched from the hillside as the little retinue of people and horses wove along the banks of the river. Georgina Langland might think she had seen the last of him but she was mistaken. If he couldn't have her money he would ruin her life.

He knew she had killed her husband and he knew, too, that he couldn't prove it, so he would take the murdering gardener, who rode with her like a gentleman, and threaten to drown him in the river. Perhaps then she would pay him.

He followed at a safe distance, knowing the route the little party would take. It was a shame that Morgan the smithy was travelling with them: he was a strong man – he'd shown his fists to Jed more than once. Jed knew he wouldn't beat him in a straight fight, but perhaps there was another way. Hatred flooded into him. They would pay, all of them, for cheating Jed Lambert of what was rightfully his.

Georgina sulked in the saddle. She was tired of riding and frightened by the thought of seeing her brother again. How would he be? Out of his mind? Demented? A belligerent stranger who would want to take over the entire estate?

It was raining and the river was flowing fast. Georgina glanced to the bank, sloping away towards the torrent of water, and shuddered. Why had she come on this journey? She should have left it to Morgan to bring Caradoc home. But then Papa would have thought her uncaring and that would never do. She depended on him for her allowance: without him she would be penniless.

Suddenly the world seemed to turn on its head. There was a whooping and the sound of galloping hoofs. Startled, she looked behind to see Jed Lambert, hatless, his hair flying wildly around his face, riding straight towards her.

She screamed in terror as her horse reared, unseating her, and slid down the riverbank unable to stop herself. And then she was in the icy water of the Wye, gasping for breath, as her heavy skirts dragged her down.

The dark water closed over her head and she fought to rise to the surface. As she broke through the water she saw Matt swimming towards her but the flow was dragging him away. She made a mighty effort, reached out and their hands touched. He pulled her towards him, and together they struggled towards the bank. But the run of the river was too swift. 'We're going to die!' Georgina screamed. 'Matt, we're going to die!'

And then, wrapped in each other's arms, Georgina and her lover sank beneath the water.

CHAPTER THIRTY-NINE

Caradoc walked through the valley brooding on the mists of his past and on what the smithy had told him about his true identity. He had to get out of the cottage, away from Gwenllyn, who kept questioning him. He was so full of guilt that he didn't know what to say to her. He had a wife – so why couldn't he see her face, feel her touch, remember her scent? He had a son too, a father and a sister: why couldn't he remember them?

The silence of the day was broken abruptly by the sound of galloping hoofs and animals whinnying in distress, and then a woman screamed. Cries for help came from the river and, ignoring the pain in his leg, Caradoc began to run.

He stopped on the bank: horses were floundering in the rough swell, heads raised, eyes rolling in fright. And then he saw Jed Lambert, struggling to control his mount. The woman screamed again, thrashing in the water, and Jed's horse reared in fright, mane flying, eyes rolling.

Suddenly Jed was thrown from the saddle and landed with a splash in the water. He was being washed downstream, arms flailing, his face a mask of fear. His eyes met Caradoc's for a brief instant, and then the water sucked him under.

Caradoc plunged into the river, so cold it took his

breath away. As he swam towards the place where Jed had disappeared he saw a woman rise to the surface, water streaming from her hair. 'Matt!' she cried, to the man struggling at her side.

Caradoc took a deep breath and dived under the water but there was no sign of Jed. Gasping for air, he came to the surface but already he was tired, his damaged leg weakening as he dived again. But Jed was gone.

Caradoc heard the woman scream once more, and struck out towards her, straining every muscle to reach her side before she sank into the depths. The man surfaced beside her again and tried to drag her towards the bank, but it was an unequal struggle. If only Caradoc could reach her in time he could save her. But the river was powerful and Caradoc saw the couple cling to each other as slowly, moulded together, they disappeared beneath the foaming water.

A broken branch rushed towards him and crashed into his face. For a moment he was dazed, then felt blood run from his nose as he fought to keep afloat. Suddenly, in his mind's eye, he saw his father, and then his wife – his love, his Non – and she was holding their son in her arms.

Water filled his mouth and he coughed as the river washed over his head. He must not drown, not now that he knew his true identity. He struggled against the undertow but his strength was failing. Must he die just as his memory had returned? He fought his way back towards the surface and strong arms grasped him.

'Come on, man,' a voice said close to his ear. 'It's too late to save them. Let's get out of here before we all drown.'

'Morgan.' He saw the familiar face of the smithy and struggled against his grip. 'Is Non in the water?'

'No.'

'But Georgie, my sister, I must try to find her.'

'It's no use. She's gone, and Matt with her.'

Caradoc pulled away from Morgan's grip and dived beneath the rushing water. Weeds waved eerily in his face, and he could see no one. At last he surfaced.

'Come on! You're half drowned yourself – we've got to get out of here before we're all swept away!' Morgan shouted. Thankfully, Caradoc grasped the other man's shirt and together they made for the bank.

Caradoc lay there, tasting the river water in his mouth, knowing his sister had been lost to him at almost the same moment that he had found her again. Tears mingled with the water running from his hair. After a while he sat up and tried to put the pieces of his memory together. 'My poor sister, she must have come looking for me and now she's gone for ever.'

'Your sister did come looking for you,' Morgan said. 'We started off the trip with some servants but they were slowing our pace so we rode on ahead. We three, Miss Georgina, Matt and I, were coming to take you home. And then Jed Lambert rode up behind us, like the mad fool he is, upset the horses and drove us all into the river. It cost him his life.'

'Where's Non?' Caradoc asked. 'Where is my wife?'

'She's safe. I sent her a message and she's on her way here. There's nothing we can do just now but get into shelter and find ourselves some dry clothes.'

Caradoc felt a flare of joy. His wife, his Non, was coming for him. But Morgan was right. It was pointless to sit and look at the river: the Wye had claimed its victims and there was nothing he could do about it.

'We'll go to the cottage and get dry clothes, then you must ride home and ask my father to send out some of his men to search for my sister's body. But I don't think she'll be found. Her burial place will be the Wye.'

'She's with the man she cared for, if that's of any comfort,' Morgan said gently. 'I rode this far with them and I never saw a couple so in love.' He paused. 'Has your memory come back?'

Caradoc nodded. 'Yes. I know now that what you told me is true. I'm Caradoc Jones, my wife is Non and I love her with all my heart. When will she come, Morgan?'

'Very soon. She's looked for you for a long time. For a while she haunted the river, unable to leave it or her memories of you behind.'

Caradoc stood still for a moment, grieving for the sister he had found and lost again, then he began to walk towards the cottage. He had some explaining to do to Gwenllyn and it was not going to be easy.

Gwenllyn paced across the floor of the kitchen, stopping every now and then to look out of the window. Where was Caradoc? He should have been home long before now. He'd gone for a walk to clear his mind – at least, that was what he had told her – yet there was no sign that his memory had returned. As long as he remained in ignorance of his past she was safe.

Damn that smithy for trying to make Caradoc remember! He had a life, a woman back home, and he didn't know them. What hold could these people from his past have on him now? He loved her, she was sure of it. He had lived with her, made love to her, treated her as his wife. If fortune had been on her side she would have borne him a child by now, a son to follow in his footsteps.

She heard voices and ran to the window. He was coming towards the house and the smithy was with him. They were both dripping with water – there must have been some accident and her heart fluttered in fear. Then she saw the set of his shoulders and that his face had changed. He wasn't her man any more. Caradoc had remembered his past and he was coming to tell her he had to leave her and go back to his wife.

Non paused when the cottage came into view. There, inside, was the man she loved and would always love. She dismounted and felt in her pocket for Morgan's letter, then knocked on the door. It was opened at once by the woman Non had seen before, the woman who had lied to her.

'Come on,' Gwenllyn said dully. 'He's waiting for you.' Her face was tear-stained and her hands trembled. The angry words Non had been going to say melted away. She walked along the passage and into the kitchen – and there he was, the same but different, with a beard, long hair, and bronzed by working out-doors, but unmistakably her Caradoc.

He looked at her and held out his arms to her. She went into them, hardly daring to believe that he was alive and she had found him.

He kissed her, and it was as though he drew her heart out of her. 'Our son,' she said softly. 'Our son is dead.'

'Oh, my love, what happened?' Caradoc had tears in his eyes.

'It was a fever, and there was nothing to be done. I'm so sorry, my love.'

He put his cheek against hers and she knew he was crying. Over his shoulder she saw Gwenllyn's stricken look and drew gently away from him.

'I'm so sorry,' Gwenllyn sobbed. 'I knew I was doing wrong lying to you and keeping the truth from Caradoc, but I just couldn't let him go.'

'I know,' Non said softly. 'I understand.' Suddenly she knew what she had to do. 'I'm going to find a room in the nearest tavern,' she said gently. 'I'll leave you and Caradoc to say goodbye.'

'Thank you,' Gwenllyn said.

Morgan stepped forward. 'I'll come with you to the tavern, and in the morning I'll go home to Five Saints and tell your father-in-law all that's happened.'

Non gave Caradoc a lingering look and pressed her hand to his face. Then, calling on all her strength, she took a step towards the door. 'I'll see you soon, my lovely, but don't keep me waiting too long.'

Caradoc took her in his arms again and held her as if he would never let her go. They kissed, and she knew that all his love was for her. But she could be generous and let Gwenllyn part from him alone.

Later, as she waited in the bedroom at the Lamb and Flag, Non felt like a girl again, young and eager for love. She would never get over losing Rowan but she had found her husband, and for now they must rejoice in their reunion. She brushed her hair and rearranged her clothes for what seemed to be the hundredth time and then, at last, she heard his step on the stair. He entered the room and dropped his bag on to the floor. Then he took her in his arms, and she felt as if she could not breathe for joy. She held his face, loving him, then raised her lips to his.

In the morning, Non woke early. She propped herself on her elbow and looked at Caradoc's sleeping face. She was so lucky to have him back. Unable to resist, she pressed her lips to his. He woke at once and they made love, finding each other again. She clasped him to her, crying tears of happiness.

Then she remembered Albie, and as Caradoc turned

297

to her again, she shook her head. 'There's all the time in the world for making love, my darling,' she said softly, 'but now we have to get to London. I've a dear friend in trouble and he's going to need all the help I can give him.'

CHAPTER FORTY

'Do I look respectable enough to go to court?' Jessie gazed at her reflection in the mirror. Her bonnet was from one of the second-hand shops in Cutler Street and it curved becomingly close to her face. She couldn't afford fancy clothes but her coat, lent by Ruby, was smart and her newly mended boots were polished so that she could see her face in them.

'You look fresh, clean and, most important, honest. That's more than half the others in the courtroom will look.'

'I'm frightened out of my wits.' Jessie pressed her hands to her chest where her heart was fluttering like a caged bird. 'If only Non was here. She'd make the judge believe that Albie's a hero, not a villain.'

Ruby put her arms round Jessie's shoulders. 'At least you got her letter. The judge will take notice of it, you'll see. There's not many people can write a fine hand like Non.'

'But it would be better if she was here in person,' Jessie said. 'And then there's the business. Do you think Dan will be all right selling the milk on his own?'

'Stop worrying,' Ruby said. 'I remember something my mother said to me and very wise she was too.'

'Go on.'

' "Never trouble trouble till trouble troubles you."

That's what she said. Don't worry about something that may never happen.'

Jessie smiled in spite of herself. 'My man's going to be up before the judge, and the chief witness can't come and speak for him. How much more trouble do I need?'

'Jest try and be calm.' There was rap on the door and Ruby frowned. 'Whoever that is, send them away.'

Jessie walked slowly along the darkened passage, shoulders tense. 'Please, God, don't let anything else go wrong,' she murmured.

She opened the door a crack, then flung it wide. 'Non! You've come to speak up for my Albie.' She hugged her friend tightly, kissing her cheek over and over again, unable to believe she had come to London after all. She became aware of a tall figure standing behind Non and her mouth dropped open.

'Mr Jones, is it really you?' She was unable to move or say more until Ruby called out to ask who was there. Then she grasped Non's arm. 'It's a miracle, Ruby! Look who's here!'

She watched as Ruby hugged Non and nodded politely to Caradoc.

Non was radiant. 'I've found Caradoc. I've dreamed about it so often and this seems like yet another dream. But he's really here, alive and well.'

Jessie watched as Non sat at the kitchen table and took Caradoc's hands. 'He's been ill or he'd have come to me a long time ago. I'll explain it all to you later.'

Jessie looked at the clock. 'I must go now. You are coming to court with me to plead for Albie, aren't you?'

'Of course I am – that's why we rushed up to London.'

'I think the judge will believe you,' Jessie said.

300

'You're so well spoken and you look beautiful, like a bride on her wedding day.'

And, indeed, Non was glowing.

'Come on!' Jessie was impatient to be going. 'We'll be late for court.' She ushered them all out into the street. It was a dreary day, and she had hoped for fine weather that would put the judges in a good mood. She could hear the muffled sound of hoofs against the cobbles and a cab drew up, the horses tossing their heads. The door was flung open and Jessie looked inside. A voice with a soft Irish accent called to her: 'Jessie, I've come to fetch you to court. Climb aboard.'

Fred Dove got down from the cab and helped her in. 'There's room enough for everyone.'

Dan was already inside, his eyes wide with excitement. 'I'm coming with you, Jessie,' he said. 'I can tell you what's happening. I've been to court so many times with my dad.'

Jess squeezed in beside him, making room for Ruby. Caradoc sat opposite with Fred, and Non between them.

'Let's go, Fred,' Jessie said, and the horses were jerked into motion.

'I've heard dark tales,' Dan said gloomily, 'about the black dog.'

'What about the black dog?' Jessie asked, knowing she wasn't going to like the answer.

'The spirit of a black dog glides up and down outside the courts when there's going to be an execution,' Dan's eyes were wide, 'and while I was serving the milk one of the women said she'd seen it this morning.'

Jessie pressed her hand to her mouth in horror. 'Oh, Dan, don't say that – I couldn't bear it if anything happened to Albie.'

Fred took her hand. 'Nothing's going to happen to

Albie, not with all of us to speak up for him. As for the story about the black dog, it's just a foolish superstition.'

Jessie sat in unhappy silence for the rest of the journey. After what seemed an eternity, they arrived outside the court, where they met O'Flynn, the pick-pocket. Jessie looked up at the imposing building, trying to swallow her fear.

She was biting her fingernails as Caradoc led her to a seat in the crowded courtroom and sat down gratefully, her legs too weak to carry her any longer.

There was a case in progress, an old man who had been accused of stealing bread. After some questions his case was over and he retreated to a bench to await his fate.

Several others were tried and Jessie leaned against Dan to whisper, 'Why do the accused people have to sit down again without being sentenced?'

'It's all done in batches, Jessie. Gets it over quicker, then, see?'

Jessie stifled a cry as Albie was led into the court. He met her eyes and his face lit up as he smiled encouragingly at her.

Silence fell as the clerk read the charges of theft and violence against him. Jessie covered her mouth with her hands so that she wouldn't scream out that it was all lies.

A woman, the daughter of the man who had attacked Non, was called and she stared at Albie accusingly. 'My father was taken poorly and fell by accident against that lady sitting up there.' She pointed at Non. 'That man hit him so 'ard my father fell into a faint and later on he died. They should pay me some money for all my suffering.'

O'Flynn nudged Jessie and whispered urgently to her. 'But I saw him buying milk from you in Leman Street only yesterday!'

The woman put a grubby handkerchief to her eyes and there were murmurs of sympathy from the court. Jessie studied the crowd. The old man was probably in hiding now.

'Don't believe her.' Jessie couldn't keep quiet any longer. 'It's all lies – the man isn't dead, he bought milk from me yesterday!'

The woman glanced uneasily to the side and Jessie followed her gaze. That must be the man himself – she could see the guilty look on his face. He was the thief who had tried to rob Non. She got to her feet and pointed to him. 'He's there!' she said. 'He's no more dead than I am.'

A buzz of voices filled the court. People were gesturing, some rising to their feet, calling shame on the thief, who jumped up and ran from the court. His supposed daughter followed him, lifting her skirts so that she could put a safe distance between herself and the angry crowd.

Jessie saw the judge being handed a pair of white gloves and looked at Dan. 'What does it mean?'

'That there's no one put to death today. Albie's free, Jessie, he's free.'

Jessie pushed her way through the press of people towards him.

They stopped inches from each other. Albie looked thin and tired, and Jessie's heart melted with love for him. She held out her arms and he came to her. 'Jess, my beautiful Jess.' He fell on one knee, and the crowd gathered round, eager to see what would happen next. 'I got nothing to offer you, only my honest labour and my heart, but make me the happiest man in the world and say you'll be my wife.'

'I will, Albie – and I've got the shop I always wanted. I'm going to call it Halfpenny Field.' She touched his cheek. 'Now, get up from that dirty floor and give me a kiss.'

He got to his feet, smiled his sweet smile, and then Jessie was oblivious to the people who crowded round her cheering Albie on. His lips were on hers and she was safe in his arms. All her dreams had come true.